Dear President

thank you so much

Melissa for us. I present you a copy

of my first historical Western called

PETTICOAT

my pen name based off feminine first

as **Josephine Milton**

Joe M. Lawson

Cover art by Claudia Nagy-Trujillo

Cover typography and graphics by Reed Art & Imaging

ISBN: 978-0-359-27568-7

PublishNation LLC
www.publishnation.net

1

Maxwell Templeton stared at the young gunslinger who stood poised in the doorway. A cigar butt hung from Max's thick coarse lips. Long habit prevailing, he shifted the cigar from one side of his mouth to the other, always bringing a cockeyed grimace to his facial persona.

Years of smoking stogies yellowed his crooked teeth with layers of tobacco stains. Pulling the cigar stub from his mouth, Max rolled it between his calloused fingers and thumb. Even though it wasn't lit, he snuffed it out in a crystal ashtray on the hardwood desk in front of him as he stood. This lumbering man, rancher by trade, leaned forward upon his massive knuckles at the edge of his glass-covered desk. The tacit gunslinger stood still as a statue, staring back, one hand resting on the butt of a holstered revolver.

"I don't know," Big Max said, drawling out proof of his Texas upbringing. Putting his weight on a big fist he rubbed his wide chin across the back of his free, meaty hand. "You weren't quite what I expected. You're kinda young. No experience, yet, either. Are you sure you can handle the job?"

The gun fighter's weight shifted from one boot to the other. "As far as experience goes, everyone has to start from the beginning some time. I can handle it."

Templeton pointed to the slinger's small pistol resting in its custom fitted holster.

"That pop gun you're packing. Are you sure it's big enough to even stop a rabbit? Looks pretty small from where I stand."

"So? This isn't a big forty-four. No big deal," the gun fighter said, thumbing the hammer for drama's sake. "I'm no strapping six-footer. One should carry what one can handle. This here's big enough for me. Besides, the size of the bullet isn't everything. Where one puts it is what's important. No one else in the business is faster or more accurate than yours truly." This last statement was uttered as a matter of fact without a trace of braggadocio. "Right now I'm for hire. Take me for who I am, or tell me to hit the road."

Templeton settled his massive frame into the creaky wooden chair behind him. "So you are, for hire, that is. Your price is pretty high. For one just starting out you ought to reconsider. Maybe that's why you're still available. No one can afford your price."

"You can more than afford it," the young fast gun said. "As far as being available you're the first person looking for a hired gun that I've approached. If you don't accept my services there will be someone who will. Besides, you won't find another as good as me. Once your dangerous enemy is eliminated you'll think me cheap."

The gun-for-hire rested against the doorjamb with arms folded.

Maxwell picked up the cigar stub, rolling it between his fore finger and thumb, his movements deliberate. With bushy eyebrows furrowed in reflection he drummed his fingers of one hand upon his desktop. His stubby fingernails kept blunt from ranch work fell short of clicking on the glass cover. Instead, the thick tips of his rough fingers thumped a hoof beat rhythm.

"Still, a thousand big ones is a lot of cash. What about five hundred? Plus, I'll pay you a hundred of it in advance."

"This is a high risk business, I assure you. My expenses need to be met if the job is to be done right. Besides, a lifetime guarantee comes with the job. Plus, I don't take a retainer. If he wins you won't owe me. You won't even have the expense of a funeral. My plan is I intend to come back to collect for services rendered." Words laced with certainty gave off a confidence needed to get the job at the price desired.

Templeton shifted in his chair causing it to squeak an objection to his weight. Without taking his eyes from his guest he replaced the short stub with a fresh smoke from an ornate box on the desktop while offering one to his hopeful.

"No, thanks. Cigars don't fit my image."

"So they don't, I suppose." He set the cigar box on the corner of his desk. The gunslinger waited until Templeton had lit his second cigar, and then queried in an evocative tone, "Ever heard of Amos Kincaid?"

The big rancher snorted between puffs. For a moment the rising smoke shrouded his pudgy nose and laughing eyes in a thick gray cloud. "Sure! Who hasn't? When he was around, Amos Kincaid was regarded as the most hated, feared yet liked, and respected gunman in Colorado, New Mexico, and Texas. He your hero?"

"In a way. I'm going to take over where he left off."

"That's a pretty tall order, kid. Just to go out the same way? Seems such a waste for someone like you. Like all gunmen Amos Kincaid started pushing up lilies before his time. I heard he was bushwhacked. Don't recall who gunned him down. Often wonder where he's pushing up lilies." Max's last words sounded brooding.

"He's not," the young gun fighter countered. The piece of news caused Templeton to raise an eyebrow in surprise. "Nobody shot him down. He started that rumor himself. He wants everyone to think he's dead. That way he could retire in peace without worrying about someone always after him, either for revenge, to prove who's faster, or just hoping to get a name by ambushing him."

Maxwell leaned forward in his chair his expression serious. His question, slow and decisive, carried caution in an egg basket. "How do you know that?"

"Comes as a natural consequence of growing up with him. You see, Amos John Kincaid is my father," the gunslinger announced with a firm finality like a blackjack player tossing in the winning card. "He's the reason I know you're looking for a hired gun. Pa taught me every trick he knows. My draw is just as fast. my shot is just as straight."

Max Templeton jerked the cigar from his mouth in deliberation.

"Your father, eh. So you're Amos Kincaid's youngster. You mean to tell me that he put that—that pop gun in your hands then sent you out alone?" Again he pointed a meaty finger at the small weapon nestled in its holster.

The *pop gun* received an affectionate pat from its owner. "You still can't handle the fact that this is no forty-four. This gun was custom built by one of the best just for me. The bullets are of my own design. This baby has twice the range and penetration of a forty-four. It's also dead accurate. That allows for plenty of advantages for me.

"As far as sending me out by myself he had no choice. I'm just as stubborn as Pa, even more so. He dissuaded my two older brothers of a different grit from following in his footsteps. Not me. What worked for him will work even better for me. Pa figured that if I were that determined he'd better at least teach me the business. So here I am."

"What made you so determined to become a hired gun? This is a man's game."

"Most people mistake me for younger than my age. I'm twenty-two."

"That's not what I meant."

"Oh! You mean because I'm a woman. What do you care as long as the job gets done? If this is a man's game it's because men have been the only players until now. Besides, I know all the tricks of the trade, plus a few of my own."

Defiant, she stood erect with her arms akimbo, fists on hips, and her boots planted a short space apart. Her musical voice rang with a determination that commanded respect. Blue-gray eyes blazing above her slender, upturned nose mirrored her unyielding mettle.

"I've no doubt that you do," he agreed. Stuffing the cigar back into his big mouth with his arms resting on the arms of his chair Templeton leaned back, eyeing her. Dressed in a dark blue shirt, crisp jeans, and brilliant black boots, she was pretty. The more he gazed at her the more he realized how good-looking she was.

Max guessed her to stand five feet, four inches tall. The phantom freckles that adorned her cheeks reminded him of the time when, as a boy, he splattered India ink on his mother's kitchen wall. Try as he might to get the spots out they remained permanent shadows. In her case her freckles highlighted her beauty. Her looks could well be one of her tricks. She had hips that packed a six-gun better than any man ever—

"Are you through giving me the first degree, or would you like me to undress too?" she touted, glaring at his wandering eyes. Her own two eyes seemed to pierce right through him as effective as an arrow.

Max was unruffled by her curt question. He cast his gaze back to meet hers. Trying to humor her he said, "That's not a bad idea, though I doubt that you meant it."

Her expression remained as staid as stone. Would a smile show pretty white teeth inside that refined mouth? Did she ever smile? She just didn't look like a gun fighter. He would have enjoyed being at least twenty years younger right now.

4

"Let's keep this as strict business. You want Adrian Delgrin dead," she went on. "I can get close where a man can't. The fee is one thousand dollars, or I go elsewhere. You've agreed to one month for me to do the job. Any other questions, Mr. Templeton?"

"Yes, Miss Kincaid. Did Amos send you to me for this job?"

"He did. You're the only man alive that already knew about Pa's retirement. When you wired him a telegram asking for recommendations for a hired gun he offered the opportunity to me. Pa figured that an old friend of his would be an excellent person for me to approach for my first job. After all I come with the best credentials."

Templeton gazed off into a corner of his ranch house office as he harked back to former times. "Amos and I rode and worked together when we were much younger and wilder. Later, he did a lot of jobs for me, but I didn't know he was such a family man. Never talked much about it. But then, Amos wasn't a big talker about a lot of things. One of the best cowpunchers anyone could ever ride with. He's also the fastest gun I ever knew." His gaze returned to her. "You must look a lot like your mother."

"So I've been told."

"Amos Kincaid has always had an eye for beauty."

She nodded with grace, her auburn ponytail flipping around to caress her heart-shaped face. "Thank you, Mr. Templeton. Pa said you were a smooth talker with women. That's why he never let Ma meet you. Pa was afraid she might go for a wealthy rancher over a gun fighter whose future was always on the line. He didn't have anything to worry about. Ma loves Pa too much to leave him. Now that Pa is retired in relative safety they're both quite happy."

Max Templeton chuckled. "A way with women he says. Is that why I've lived on this ranch alone for almost twenty years?" He sighed. "No, Miss Kincaid, I suppose not. I never did seem to attract but one gal of promise, and she didn't last a year. Of course, as my holdings grew so did women's attentions to my money as well. They would have married me because of loving Max Templeton's ranch, not because of loving Max Templeton. None of them were worth pursuing. Having met you, if I had met the likes of your ma, though; well, I might have tried again."

"You're flattering," she accused, her eyes warming to his words. Her rosy cheeks lifted with the upturn of her slender lips.

"I'm trying to be," he smiled. His wrinkled, jovial face took on more humor in response. "At my age I can afford to be. You have a first name?"

"Dora," she smiled back. She did have pretty white teeth. "You do have a way with words, or perhaps it's your style. Maybe you'll yet find a worthy woman. Anyway, if you hire me, when this job is done you can call me by my trade name, Petticoat."

"Petticoat? Okay, Dora Kincaid, alias Petticoat, you've got the job. You're right. A woman can get close to Delgrin where a man can't. Plus, you can call me Max."

Dora stuck out her hand to shake his. "All right, Max. Pa says to always seal any agreement with a firm handshake."

Maxwell Templeton wasn't accustomed to shaking a woman's hand. Rising from his chair he met her halfway across the room. His beefy maw, thick and callused by the toil of long years, swallowed her slender fingers in its grasp. Surprising to him she had a firm grip, another mark of determination, he thought. She showed a fine balance between her parents, beauty from her mother, bravery from her father. She being a woman, a mere child on his first impression, was why he'd delayed in giving her the job at first.

The handshake had been too brief. When was the last time he had held a woman's soft, smooth hand? He couldn't remember. He had to imagine the feeling. His rough fingers could have been grasping a corncob and not have felt the difference.

"I suspect you'll be back for payment well before the month is past," he mused in confidence, "if you're anything like your father."

She turned toward the door. Calling over her shoulder Dora said, "I'll be back soon. Pa taught me to do a job well and quick."

2

The late-morning stagecoach rolled into Lamar, a small farm town lying along the Arkansas River in Colorado. After the coach lumbered by, the hot, dry dust of the road settled back into its tracks. The native Bush Morning Glories filled the warming air with their natural fragrance. Their large, purple bugle blossoms offered a welcome splash of color among the green grasses. A gentle breeze carried their perfumes wafting across the western prairie to the delight of all willing recipients.

Barefoot children browned by the June sun played tag in the morning rays. Strolling along the wooden plank sidewalks moved a score or so of citizens. Some were shop owners opening their doors for daily business, others their potential customers. The day dawned cool and clear, but was warming up fast.

Drawing up in front of the single hotel in town the dusty coach creaked to a halt. The old, lanky driver swung to the ground to open the coach door nearest the building. Grinning a rictus that exposed several missing teeth he offered his weathered hand to his sole passenger. Several passers-by stopped to gawk at the beautiful young lady stepping from the coach. From a prim sun hat balanced atop her hairdo fashioned to perfection to her delicate lace-up shoes that matched her royal blue gown she portrayed cultural refinement and wealth. Her dainty step to the ground spoke of elegance.

"Thank you, kind sir," she cooed with a graceful nod.

"My pleasure, ma'am. "Tain't ever' day I git a passenger purdy as you. In fact, I've never had one as purdy as you that I can recall."

Several pairs of observing eyes blinked their tacit agreement. The women stared in envy while the men ogled in wishful thinking.

She smiled in modesty. "You're too kind."

The lithe, young woman floated up the steps. As she glided her graceful form through the doorway of the hotel her petticoat flowed around, whispering soft, swishing sounds. Like a faithful puppy the driver, with her bags in hand, followed her into the lobby of the modest hotel bedecked in the traditional trappings of the west.

The hotel lobby appeared tidy with simple wooden furniture. Chairs and couches were covered with comfortable looking cushions. As the lady glided toward the counter her many rustling pleats caught the clerk's attention. Glancing up from his work his eyes panned past full hips, a svelte waist, an ample bosom, and a slender neck, until they rested upon a beautiful visage. Two sultry blue-gray eyes smiled as willing as her perfect mouth at him. At once his mundane expression broke into a radiant make-the-customer-welcome grin. Straightening up to his full stature he nodded an obsequious bow.

"Welcome, madam, to our humble establishment," he recited as if quoting from an invisible script. "We trust that your stay in Lamar will be a pleasant one." To the driver the clerk directed, "Arvis, leave her bags by the counter."

Old Arvis sat her luggage in the designated spot. With much reluctance and head nodding, not wanting to depart from the scenery too quick, he backed out of the hotel.

"I'd like a room with bath please," she said as pleasant as a clear June morning.

"You may have the best in the house if you wish. If you will just sign our registry."

He spun the big registry book around while offering her a dipped pen. In the habit of his profession he read her name upside-down as she wrote it.

"Dora Kinley," he read. "Miss, I presume?"

"Yes."

He smiled a pleasant response. "Will you be here long?"

"Several days I should expect. Perhaps a week. Shall I pay you in advance?"

"No that's quite all right, Miss Kinley. We can settle at the time of your departure."

The clerk struck a bell button on the counter. In just a moment a bonny, young girl of about fifteen appeared from a rear entry. Her countenance appeared melancholy.

"Missy, show Miss Kinley to room 3-B," he ordered, holding out a key to the lass.

"Yes, sir." Taking the key the girl called Missy retrieved Miss Kinley's baggage. "This way, please," she uttered in a disinterested voice.

As she followed the petite lass up the stairs Dora could see that the girl's small shoes were being worn far beyond their normal life span. Frayed threads and patches betrayed her plain dress, though clean, yet faded from countless washing.

Dora glanced over her shoulder. The desk clerk who was staring after her, smiled and turned back to the books that he had been poring over when she first entered the hotel. A nice looking man with dark wavy hair and average build he made a good choice for a hotel clerk.

As she continued after her young vassal a few facts that she'd researched came to mind. Adrian Delgrin owned the hotel. The clerk, the manager in all likeliness, complete with waistcoat and tie was much better dressed than this poor colleen. The image that Dora had painted in her mind so far of Adrian Delgrin's character was abominable. This delicate, young damsel seemed to occupy a prominent place in the picture. Was this Cinderella whom Dora thought she could be?

Unlocking the door with the key the maiden led the way into the room. She set Dora's luggage at the foot of the bed. Handing Dora the key she said, "Here you are, ma'am. We hope you enjoy your stay. Is there anything else for you?" This greeting all sounded rehearsed. The ennui in her voice was more obvious than warts on a toad.

Dora Kincaid gazed into those young, blue eyes, the dominant feature on Missy's dainty face. They were clear yet very sad. Missy was very pretty with a soft, soprano voice. She fit the portrait too well. Dora had to find out. She had to ask her some key questions, but with tact. Gaining the girl's confidence became the momentary priority.

"I would like a bath now. Would you prepare it please?"

"Yes, ma'am." Missy's expression exposed her real feeling, *If I have to!*

The girl walked to the tub. Above one end on the wall were two valves attached to the end of metal piping which disappeared through the ceiling. By opening the valves water was allowed to flow into the tub. Fitted in a hole in the bottom a chained plug kept it in. Dora watched in rapt interest.

"Interesting," Dora commented, taking the opportunity to converse. "I've seen modern plumbing in the large hotels in the big cities, but never in a small town. My understanding is that it's very expensive to have. How can one afford it here?"

Dora already knew some of the story, but wanted to hear it from the girl.

"My daddy invented and built this one," the girl replied, sounding pleased to talk about her father's handiwork. "It's very simple. The holding tanks are on the roof. One of them is built so that the sun warms the water quite a lot. You just open these valves for hot or cold water. The drain takes the water outside."

"Simple, eh. How does your father get the water to the tanks on the roof?"

"He built a hydraulic ram and a small water wheel to power it in the Arkansas River just out back. When the tanks are full there's a float that shuts the ram off to the hot water tank until the water level drops. The tank of cold water has an overflow back to the river. This is so the water stays fresh and cool by constant cycling."

Dora had heard of hydraulic rams to lift water to great heights from using some sort of plentiful water flow such as a river or a falls. The ram had been invented some fifty or sixty years ago. They were still popular where falling water existed in enough quantity to force water higher than the source.

"Your father must be very smart. Is that him we saw down at the counter?"

Fierce hatred flashed through the girl's eyes. "No! No! He's a—"

Turning away to hide the fire in her stare she checked her emotional outburst. Looking down at the filling tub to hide the moisture filling her eyes she murmured, "Mr. Delles is my boss. My father is dead."

"Oh! I see. I'm sorry."

"You don't have to be," Missy said in an apologetic tone. She gave a furtive glance around to the still open door. "You—you didn't know him."

What is she afraid of? Dora wondered. "No, I didn't know him. Yet I am sorry. I'm sorry for you. Pretty, young ladies should always have their fathers."

Missy cracked a nervous smile on her diminutive lips. The ice was cracking.

"What about your mother? She's alive, isn't she?"

The younger female betrayed her poignant feelings with a forlorn look. "She works as a cook and housekeeper for Adrian Delgrin."

Dora now understood for certain who this hapless maid was. In researching what she could discover about Delgrin a horrible tale had been told her. The cattle baron kept like a prisoner a beautiful woman on his ranch. Rumor was that she was a sex toy that Delgrin exploited for his conceited lusts.

Delgrin was a truculent autocrat letting nothing or no one get in his way for what he wanted, including the woman's husband. While not proven he was considered to be the reason for the husband's demise. This lass was of a truth the woman's daughter about whom Dora had learned. Here was a wealth of information on the man that she was hired to kill. She would have to tap this source.

"I've heard of him," Dora ventured, choosing her words with caution. "I understand that he's not too popular around here."

A look of extreme disgust flushed the maiden's face. "He's an awful man!" she whispered, her voice laced with bitterness.

Dora was treading on very sensitive ground. She had to set the right rapport to coax the information that she wanted from her young friend. This girl needed her friendship. Confident that she held a winning hand she tossed in an ace.

"Well, then I don't like him either!" Dora declared with finality and a quick nod.

Missy gazed at Dora Kincaid with a questioning stare. Was this someone ready to agree without being afraid to say so? This woman didn't know her. Was Dora that quick to take her word about Adrian? With the tub half full the girl shut off the water. Dora sensed her bemusement and considered her next move to win the girl's trust.

"Your father didn't build his plumbing system for Adrian Delgrin, did he?"

"No, he built it for Farius, Adrian's father. Farius was a good man, but he's dead now, and Adrian owns the hotel."

"That's too bad. Sometimes life throws us trials we don't want."

"Your bath is ready, Miss Kinley," the girl announced in a sweeter voice. Her face mellowed into a slight smile. Dora wondered when was the last time the youth had even turned up the corners of her pretty little mouth.

"Please call me Dora. May I ask what's your name?"

"Lillian. My mother calls me Lilly."

"What a pretty name, Lillian. I think it fits you very well."

"Thank you. You're very pretty, too," the young teen returned. Lillian smiled again just a bit broader.

"Thank you," Dora responded with gracious reserve. She took Lillian's hand in her own two. This young woman was pleading for a real friend. Wistful hope lighted her face. Dora went on. "I consider myself a good judge of character. I can see that you are a very good person. When you say that Adrian Delgrin is an awful man I know you're right. You've confirmed the bad things I've heard about him."

At that moment Lillian glanced toward the open door again, apprehension in her eyes. "I'd better go. Mr. Delles will be angry if I stay too long."

Dora furrowed her forehead, giving Lillian a questioning gaze. "Why should he get angry? Aren't you here to help the hotel's customers?"

"Yes, but I have to report in to Mr. Delles every few minutes. He thinks that I will run away. I would, but I'm afraid of what Mr. Delgrin might do to my mother if I did. They keep me here to threaten my mother. We tried to run away once—" she stopped short. Eyeing the door in trepidation she continued, a notch above a whisper, "—so I'm brought here every day to work. With Mr. Delgrin owning this hotel Mr. Delles is just one of his men."

"You're saying that your mother is being held like a prisoner. They keep you apart to discourage you from running away again?"

"Yes. I seldom see my mother except at dinner. Afterward we get locked into our rooms at night. Mr. Delles told me that if I ever ran away from here my mother would be killed."

3

Lillian's nervousness about the open door was beginning to affect Dora. She stole to the door and opened it wider to peek out. The hall was empty. Closing the door in silence and locking it she glided to the window to check the fire escape. The morning sun was the only occupant.

"No one's around to hear us. You can relax now," she told her new friend in a normal tone of voice.

Uttering a soft sigh Lillian appeared somewhat relieved by relaxing her shoulders.

"Look, mmm, may I call you Lilly?"

"Please do."

"Lilly, I haven't had lunch yet. Have you?"

"No. I—don't often eat lunch."

Poor child! She must not get to. "Fine. You'll be my guest for lunch after I've taken my bath. Riding in a stage is dusty."

Worry again filled Lilly's face. "Mr. Delles won't let me. I can't go anywhere without him or one of Mr. Delgrin's other men along."

"Don't fret, Lilly," Dora assured her with a gentle squeeze on her shoulder. "I'll take care of Mr. Delles. How much of this town does Delgrin own?"

"I don't know. A lot of it I think."

"Does the doctor in this town work for him, too?"

"Doc Hyatt? No, he's all right. He's an old friend of my family. He hates Mr. Delgrin. Mama said that Doc Hyatt told her once that Mr. Delgrin would like to kill him, except that doctors are hard to come by out here. Doctor Hyatt won't bend to Delgrin, but he has to be careful what he says about him."

"I see. Are any other of Delgrin's men working in the hotel?"

"No. There's just Mr. Delles and me."

Dora dug a silver dollar from her handbag and placed it in Lilly's hand. "Take this. It's a tip. You deserve it."

In awe, her eyes as large around as the coin, Lilly examined the dollar, turning it over several times in her dainty fingers. After several moments of ogling the bright coin she held it back out to her benefactor. "Thank you anyway, but I can't keep it. Mr. Delles takes all of my tips."

Dora scowled. "He does, does he? Here, I'll give you a dime. You can give that to dear Mr. Delles."

"He'll still find the silver dollar. The little room that I stay in downstairs has nothing but an old ladder-back chair. It doesn't even have a cushion. I have no place to hide the coin."

"Stick it in your shoe."

Tears welled in the girl's eyes. "He—he makes me take off all of my clothes each day before we leave. Then he—he—" Lilly broke into soft sobs and buried her face in her hands. Dora put her arms around the girl's small shoulders to offer her solace.

"If that worthless pile of donkey dung tried to make me take my clothes off," Dora menaced through clenched teeth, "you'd be calling him Humpty Dumpty. Your good friend Doc Hyatt wouldn't be able to put him back together."

"Mr. Delgrin told him to," she sobbed, dampening Dora's dress.

Miss "Kinley" could see that this whole affair was causing a terrible, emotional trauma on the poor child. She decided not to press the subject any more. Reaching into the bosom of her dress she produced a white lacy handkerchief and handed it to Lilly.

"There now. Dry your eyes with this. You can't let Mr. Delles see you crying. That would invoke questions you don't need."

Lilly took the offered hanky with thanks and blotted her eyes.

"I'll keep the silver dollar for you," Dora continued. "Take the dime for Delles. You go on downstairs to your usual routine. If that bum wants to know why you took so long tell him I had you wash my back before dismissing you. When I come down you call me ma'am. No names. Mr. Delles isn't to see we've become friends. Is that clear?"

Lilly nodded. Constraining her emotions and throwing her chin out she answered in a calmer voice, "Yes, Dora, I understand."

"Good girl! Here, wash your face before you go. That will help remove the teary evidence. Remember, you've got a friend now."

Wetting a washcloth in the warm tub of water Dora wrung it out and handed it to Lilly. Lilly wiped her face clean as instructed and returned the cloth to her benefactor. Satisfied with their talk Dora let her new friend out of the room to return to her post.

After Lillian had left, a more pressing matter weighed on Dora's mind than taking a bath, which she did in record time. Doctor Hyatt would of a certainty be on her call list today. The town's sole doctor would no doubt know more about its citizens than just about anyone else would. She was going to find out more about this scoundrel and child molester Delgrin, and why Lilly and her mother were literal prisoners.

Having redressed she freshened up her makeup. This was part of her master ruse. Put on with deft application the cosmetics created a paradox. The maquillage gave the illusion that she was older, while its presence suggested that she was a woman who used it to try to appear younger. With her head topped by a more mature hairstyle and her speech more formal the casual observer would be convinced that she was at least pushing thirty. Her elaborate dress put the finishing touch to her masquerade.

Dora locked her room and hurried on cat's paws down the hall toward the top of the stairs. From here she could survey the lobby area without immediate detection. Neither Lilly nor Mr. Delles were visible in the lobby below. Tiptoeing down the stairs she listened and looked for a clue that would reveal their whereabouts. She had just a few steps to go when she heard a muffled voice coming from behind the curtains of a side room from where Lilly had appeared earlier. No one else was apparent in the lobby.

The voice, low and garbled, was that of Mr. Delles. *Lilly must be giving audience, unwilling or not, to him,* she thought. A lecture? A scolding? Dora would have liked to eavesdrop, but here proved just the opportunity to put her plan into action.

First, she began humming rather loud. Next, she almost clomped down the last few steps to insure attracting their attention. On the last step she let out a loud gasp, tromped hard several times, then sat down on the steps to wait.

By the time Mr. Delles had managed to react to the ruckus and show up from behind the curtain he found a very wide eyed looking Miss Kinley sitting at the bottom of the steps. Wasting no time He dashed to her aid.

"Miss Kinley! What happened? Are you all right?" The alarm in his face mirrored that in his voice.

"I—I think so," she stammered in meekness. "Goodness, I don't know how I lost my footing. This is so embarrassing!"

"Here, let me help you to your feet." He extended a hand.

Dora took his offered hand with ladylike grace.

"Thank you. I—oh!" Catching herself on the banister as she stood she feigned pain in her right ankle while expressing an unmistakable grimace of anguish.

"Oh, dear! You're hurt!" Mr. Delles exclaimed with real worry.

"I think I may have twisted my ankle," she frowned. Dora tried to take a step, only to collapse onto Mr. Delles's arm. The hotel manager proved more than willing to offer his support. "Would you help me to the couch please?"

With noted pleasure he slipped his arm around her waist to help her hobble to the lobby divan. Once she was seated, as a teaser she rubbed a trim ankle. Mr. Delles ogled her action like a brand new groom on his wedding night.

"Can I help?" he offered, looking eager to do the massaging. Dora noticed that he had even leaned forward, his hands held out ready to take over the massaging.

"My ankle feels rather numb now," she told him, ignoring his offer. "I'm afraid I'd better get to the doctor. Would you help me, please?"

"It would be my pleasure!"

Delles reached out once again to help Miss Kinley to her feet.

"Oh, dear!" she exclaimed at once, taking on a perplexed facade. "Who will look after the hotel while you're gone?"

Baffled by this sudden realization he glanced around at the curtain across Lilly's little cubbyhole.

"That is a problem," he admitted, disappointment betraying his voice. "I'm the only one on duty at the desk at the moment."

"I don't suppose you could leave the little girl in your place could you?" Dora interjected. "She's just a bellhop. She's much too young to handle a job as important as yours I'm sure."

"Yes, I suppose you're right," he agreed with reluctance. "I couldn't leave her alone in charge. She wouldn't know what to do."

Sighing in resignation Miss Kinley patted him on the arm. "Well, I just can't see any way around it, Mr.—"

"Uh, Delles."

"—Mr. Delles. I would have appreciated your help, but you have your business to tend to. I suppose all I really need is someone to lean on. I can take the girl to help."

"The girl? Oh no, Miss Kinley, I couldn't do that."

"Why not?" Dora responded in mock surprise, knowing he'd protest.

"Well, ah, I don't know if she's, ah, strong enough."

"How sweet of you to be concerned, Mr. Delles, but rest assured I'm not that helpless. The girl will just have to do. You can do without her for a time can't you? If you will call her please."

Turning her attention to tidying her rumpled petticoat this was to show him that the problem had been resolved. After a moment she glanced back up at him in expectation.

"Well, yes, you're right of course, Miss Kinley. There's just one thing I must insist on, however."

"Whatever I can do to help," she offered, wondering what his demand would be.

"Fine. You see, she's sort of in my custody, and so I'm, ah, responsible for her whereabouts. You must stay with her at all times. She might try to run away."

"Oh? Has she been in—trouble?"

Mr. Delles gave her a slight nod along with a you-know-how-it-is look. She responded with a knowing nod of her own.

"She did appear rather distant to her work. Don't you worry, Mr. Delles," she assured him. "I won't let her out of my sight. That's a promise." Using the arm of the divan for balance Dora rose on her "good" foot to wait for the girl's help.

Smiling with some satisfaction at Dora's assurance he called for Lilly. "Missy! Come here!" As an afterthought he added, "Please!"

Lilly marched into the lobby to where the adults stood waiting.

"Miss Kinley has had a slight accident," Delles expressed. "She needs your help to get to the doctor. You do what she says."

"Just stand beside me, child," Dora directed. "I'll lean on your shoulder just a little. I think I twisted my ankle."

17

"Yes, ma'am," Lilly responded as she had, toneless, when Dora first arrived. She was following Dora's instruction to the letter.

Using the girl for a crutch Dora limped across the lobby to the front door. As they passed through the entry she looked over her shoulder with a smile and a nod. Mr. Delles reflected the signal as he returned to the counter.

When the duo had walked a few dozen steps from the hotel Dora asked in a murmur, "How far is it to Doc Hyatt's office?"

"Down the next street toward the edge of town," Lilly murmured back. "It's about a ten minute walk from here."

When they turned the corner for the next street Dora took Lilly by the hand. "Let's hurry," she urged with a smile while shifting into a rapid stride. The wooden slats of the sidewalk creaked a rhythm under their faster gait.

"For a moment back there I thought that you really had hurt your ankle," Lilly confessed to her new friend. "I heard everything that you and Mr. Delles talked about."

"Then you know I promised to keep you in sight at all times."

"And I promise to stay in your sight, too."

Lilly grinned at her. Dora wondered how long it had been since this pretty young lady had brightened her face with a happy smile, or lightened her heart with a laugh.

"Why does Mr. Delles call you Missy instead of Lilly?" Dora queried.

"Because I hate it."

"That figures. That's why I called you child to pretend that I didn't know your real name. Did he give you a lecture on spending too much time with the guests?"

"Oh, sort of. I told him what you said to tell him. He said okay. Then he asked me what you talked about. I said I didn't know. You talked a lot but I wasn't listening. Then he started lecturing on why I should pay attention; that it was important to listen to what the guests tell me. It was then I heard you humming. Then Mr. Delles heard you. When we heard you fall down the stairs I was really scared at first, because I thought you really were hurt. But then I realized that you were only fooling. You sure fooled Mr. Delles!" Lilly sniggered at that thought.

"To fool a fool like Delles is easy. I'll see if I can fool Mr. Delgrin, too. We'll get you and your mother loose from that tyrant."

"That would be wonderful!" Lilly breathed. "What will you do?"

"Leave it to me," Dora assured her. "I've got a plan."

"Please be careful," Lilly warned. "He's a dangerous man."

Their brisk pace soon brought them to the office door of Dr. Peter Hyatt. As they approached the portal Dora took up her hobble again, leaning on Lilly's shoulder as she did in the hotel.

"Just in case there's a hostile face inside," she told the girl, "we'd better put on a show again. We don't know friend from foe."

Lilly nodded in understanding.

Pushing the door open they stepped inside. Except for a few simple chairs and a table with a kerosene lamp the waiting room was unoccupied. As they closed the door behind them an inner one swung open in response to reveal a tall, slender man with chiseled features and graying at the temples. Upon catching sight of Dora's young companion his face brightened. In delighted surprise a grin spread at once across his clean, shaven face.

"Lilly! What a pleasant surprise! I haven't seen you since you had the fever this past spring. How's your mother? Are you still working at the hotel?"

"She's okay," Lilly responded to his guarded queries. "Dr. Hyatt, this is Miss Kinley. She's my friend. She got me out of the hotel by spraining her ankle."

"Well, that's a funny way to make a friend, Lilly." He turned to Dora. "Now, Miss Kinley, if you'll come into the office I'll examine your ankle."

"My ankle is all right, Doctor. I faked an accident to have an excuse to get Lilly away from the hotel. She tells me that you are an old friend of the family. I want to know why this poor girl is kept like a prisoner in that hotel."

Cautious concern furrowed the doctor's brow, which Dora expected. "What is your interest in Lilly's welfare?" he queried.

"I came here to do a possible business venture on behalf of my father," she explained. "Mr. Adrian Delgrin is the man with whom I am to deal.

"My father keeps strict standards of business. As is our policy we always check the honesty and integrity of potential clients before we

19

solidify any business deals. We don't want a poor reputation to reflect on our business. From the contacts that I've made so far I've found that Mr. Delgrin has proven to be of a very questionable character.

"Our normal policy when discovering such reprehensible character is to cease all business endeavors without delay. However, I've never heard of the likes of Delgrin. When the story arose that he kept a woman a virtual slave in his house who would've believed that? Since meeting Lilly, though, I'm convinced that the tale is true. Why is this? Why hasn't the law done something for them? What can I do?"

Doctor Hyatt rubbed his narrow chin in deep thought. After a moment he said, "To be frank I don't know what you can do that I haven't tried, but it's noble of you to offer. Come back into my private office. I'll tell you the story behind Lillian James."

4

The trio seated themselves in comfortable chairs before Doctor Hyatt related his unsavory tale.

"What I am about to tell you, Miss Kinley," he began, "you should keep in the strictest confidence. This isn't an ironclad secret, but for your own sake my advice is that you tell no one what you'll have learned here today. A silent tongue attracts no undue attention. I'm going to tell you what you're up against.

"Lillian's father, Arnold James, was an honest, hard working man, as honest as old Abe. He brought his new bride out here before Lilly was born. I delivered her. So you see, I've known the family for more than fifteen years.

"At that time old Farius Delgrin was still alive. He had lost his wife and two children to yellow fever a couple of years before that, but he still had two teenage sons, Adrian and Horatio. Farius never remarried.

"Perhaps the loss of his mother made him worse, but Adrian was ruthless and power hungry from the start. When he was a boy I could see that he was manipulative, wanting everyone around him to bend to his whims. The only person who could keep him halfway in line was Farius himself. To do that he had to often threaten to disinherit his scoundrel son and leave everything to Horatio.

"Up front Adrian appeared to give in to his father's demands. In reality he just became more devious. By using the promise of his father's wealth, which he was plotting to get for himself, he began to attract a lot of shady characters. With them he concocted all sorts of underhanded deals. Some of these characters he managed to get hired onto his father's ranch without his father's knowledge of their covert connection.

"When Farius got wind of what Adrian was up to trying to steal the ranch he kicked his son off the ranch, telling him not to return. Adrian swore his revenge.

"What I'm not sure of is if Farius knew that many of his men were loyal to Adrian. Farius was a very trusting soul and may have thought that with Adrian banished from the ranch all of his men would turn their loyalty to him. Whatever the truth, I feel that he didn't know their connection to his son. Adrian could have told them to come looking for work when more hands were needed, but make no mention of their friendship with him in case his father wouldn't hire them."

Dr. Hyatt paused for a moment, leaning forward in his chair and lowering his voice as an emphasis before continuing with his story.

"Two days after Adrian's expulsion Horatio was found dead in the alley behind the saloon. His head had been beaten in and he was reeking with the smell of liquor. Adrian had disappeared also. No one had seen hide or hair of him since that morning.

"Somebody started the story that Horatio had gotten drunk, had gotten into a brawl outside the back of the saloon, and wound up getting his head smashed because of it. No witnesses came forth as to who did it. Yet, Farius never believed that rumor. He knew that Adrian was behind Horatio's death, and he swore that he would avenge Horatio."

"Could there have been any truth to the story?" Dora queried.

"Not in a 'coon's age. Horatio very seldom frequented the saloon. When he did he was always with his father. He was never known to get drunk. Also, Horatio was easy going like his mother. Adrian had more of his father's drive and business savvy. Farius was rather concerned about leaving the entire ranch to Horatio. If Adrian had been as good as his brother they could have run the ranch together after Farius retired and been successful. If Adrian wasn't so villainous they could have worked together.

"As it was, Farius was an honest if shrewd cattle baron. I think he was hoping that he could teach Horatio some business smarts to go with his son's honesty. Adrian changed those plans. The night Horatio was found bludgeoned to death in the alley Farius didn't even know where he had gone. Farius told me that he just disappeared off the ranch, his whereabouts unknown until he was found outside the saloon.

"I suspect that Slim Shelley, Adrian's foreman was behind Horatio's disappearance. Shelley was working for Farius as a hired hand, but he was in cahoots with Adrian. Unknown to Farius, Shelley was also plotting the elder Delgrin's murder. Slim set up a trap for

Adrian to ambush his father. To lure Farius into ambush Shelley told him that he thought he knew where Adrian was hiding out on his own ranch. The plot was to get old man Delgrin to where Adrian was waiting for him. Adrian shot his father off the back of his horse."

"How did you find this out?" Dora questioned.

"One of Farius's men, his foreman survived the ambush long enough to get to me before he died of his wounds. He was left for dead which is why he managed to climb on his horse and ride. I did what I could for him, but he was pretty shot up. He told me the story you just heard. The mortician and you two are now the only ones who know."

"Why didn't you report this to the sheriff?"

"The sheriff was in on the plot. He and Slim picked the 'posse' that was supposed to bring Adrian in for questioning. Except for Farius and his few trusted hands all of them were working for Adrian. When Adrian bushwhacked his father his men opened fire on his father's men. As I said, the foreman was the only one to survive long enough to expose the truth before he died."

"Couldn't you have called in a U. S. marshal?"

"That occurred to me. As soon as the undertaker had come to take care of the man's remains I hurried over to the telegraph station to wire Denver for a U. S. marshal to be sent here. Not too long after that Sheriff Hilliard showed up at my door asking why I had sent the message. I told him that Slade Jenkins—that was Farius's foreman, had ridden in here all shot up. Before he died he'd manage to mumble something about 'posse' and 'ambush'. Wiring for some help seemed to be the proper action to take. Hilliard was miffed that I had wired without notifying him. To appease him I told him that I knew he was out with the 'posse'. Not knowing if he were one of the casualties too, I decided to send for help. Since the sheriff knew about the telegram I was glad that I hadn't put in any details about Slade's witness of the ambush. If Hilliard knew the real reason for the telegram yours truly would be buried on boot hill also.

"At least that's the story that Hilliard got. His story was some renegade Indians had ambushed them, but that everything was under control. Then he told me in so many words to stick to my doctoring and let him take care of the law. When the law is on the side of evil there is no law. No response ever came from that telegram. I'm sure it was never sent. The telegraph operator doesn't have my trust any more. Telegrams are supposed to be confidential. If I ever send another I'm going somewhere else."

"There haven't been reports of Indian problems in years," Dora reflected. "When did all this happen?"

"Two years ago."

"Wasn't Adrian Delgrin ever brought to trial for either count?"

"No. Hilliard said there was no proof that Horatio was killed any other way than in a drunken fight, although no 'witnesses' could ever be found to verify it. Since Indians were blamed for the death of Farius and the others in the ambush Adrian was 'innocent' of any foul play. No one was ever arrested, Indians or otherwise. No charges were ever brought. To my knowledge no investigation was ever made.

"Adrian was free to take over his father's ranch. From that point on he began to run just about everything around here. Most everybody in these parts owed Farius a lot. He helped many of them get their start. Now Adrian uses these debts to coerce people into submission. For those who don't obey he destroys them, one way or another. Even the few of us who owe him nothing toe the line. I'm sure he wouldn't hesitate to do the same to you if you crossed him."

This was a chapter of Delgrin's nefarious life of which Dora had only previous inklings. From Maxwell Templeton she had gleaned a few sketchy rumors with which he was acquainted. He had hired her because of the threat that Adrian Delgrin posed on his own life. In an effort to gain possession of the Templeton ranch Delgrin had attempted to kill Max, who has no heirs. With the facts that Doctor Hyatt had supplied, the more detailed account made the picture much clearer. She had tapped the right reservoir.

"I suppose that all the 'survivors' of the posse testified to the Indian ambush," she mused, "making your one man witness, via a dead man, hard to substantiate. Too bad you don't have a second witness."

Doctor Hyatt ran his long, slender fingers through his thin, dark hair. His deep-set eyes, full of sorrow, betrayed his inability to expose the truth to the world.

"Miss Kinley, I've kept this knowledge to myself for the past two years," he told her with a weary voice. "Maybe you shouldn't have been told this now, but when you proved to be a willing ear with a common interest, well—"

"I'm glad you did," she interjected. "Knowing these matters may make my job that much easier. Where do Lilly and her mother fit into this incubus?"

"Arnold James was somewhat of an inventor and an innovator. When he told Farius that he could put running water in the hotel the elder Delgrin hired him to do it. Farius was one who believed in the progress of industry. Impressed with Arnold's work he hired him on as a permanent hand. Using part of the wages he was earning, Lilly's father bought from Farius a choice piece of ground to farm. Besides being industrious James was very clever, always inventing some little gadget to do a job better. Some of these he built for me.

"Before Arnold James finished his own little house on his farm he and his family lived on the Delgrin ranch in the main house. Jill James is an excellent cook and a beautiful woman. Lilly looks a lot like her mother. After Farius's wife died Jill took over all the cooking for the ranch. Somewhere during this time Adrian tried to woo her. His father ordered him to leave her alone or else. Fearing expulsion he did. Yet, he already had it in his mind that he would have her some day, any way he could.

"After James built his house and paid off his debt to his benefactor he took his family out to their new home. They were living there when Farius was murdered. Less than a month later while they were here in town running some errands their house burned to the ground. One can only guess what or who caused the fire. Arnold had a barn under construction. This became their temporary quarters until he could rebuild his house. Adrian offered to loan Arnold the money to rebuild. He refused the loan, saying that he wouldn't obligate himself to someone by being in debt again.

"If not Delgrin, fate itself went against the James. One day when his wheat crop was almost grown the worst hailstorm anyone can recall in these parts blew in, destroying his crop and demolishing his barn. Again Adrian offered to help, but James wouldn't take it. He had dug a root cellar, so they moved into it for the time being.

"Adrian told him he had all the hands he needed right then. Arnold went to work around town to earn money to put his small farm back together. This didn't last long. Although he was a hard worker he lost his job after only a few days. No one else would hire him, thanks to Adrian I would imagine. With nowhere else to turn he tried to sell what was left of his farm and leave. There were no takers.

"At last Adrian talked him into taking his job back on the ranch again. Jill could be the cook if she wanted it back. She didn't want to go back, but Arnold convinced her that their stay would be a short one. As quick as they could they would save up what they made and rebuild the house and barn. Much of the barn wood was still salvageable. With it he could start building another house on his free time. As soon as they could they would be back on their farm. He could still plant winter wheat for harvest in spring.

"As expected, Adrian's true motives for hiring James weren't honorable. I doubt that Adrian ever did anything that was. No sooner had the family moved back onto the ranch Adrian was flirting with Jill again. Hoping that their stay wouldn't last long she resisted his advances with all the discretion she could."

"She never told Arnold what Adrian was doing?" Dora queried.

"Jill was afraid to, afraid of what Adrian and his thugs might do to Arnold if she did tell him. She was also worried about Lilly."

Doctor Hyatt retrieved a cup of water from a pitcher on his desk before continuing with his tale. He offered some to his guests. Dora declined while Lilly gulped down a cup of his offering. Dora reckoned that the girl didn't get much water during the day.

"At first Adrian was subtle, telling her that she deserved more than what Arnold was giving her. Next, he offered her the ranch and everything else she could want if she would leave Arnold. As tactful as she could she kept telling him no. When she kept resisting his advances he tried to force himself on her. She beat him off and told him never to come near her again. In a fit of rage he threatened to kill her husband if she didn't succumb to his wishes. Plus, if she said anything to Arnold about what had happened that morning he would kill her husband on the spot. Jill fled from the house to get away from Adrian. If it weren't for her family she'd have run away.

"That very afternoon Arnold James and his horse were found lying at the bottom of a deep ravine. When he was brought in to me he was a pitiful sight. From my point of view a man in his condition couldn't last very long. To find him even still alive was a big surprise. He was in a coma. I did everything in my power to save him."

Doctor Hyatt's dark, recessed eyes took on a distant stare. His bushy eyebrows shadowed his eyes even more. He added with feeling, "He was a strong man with a fierce, tremendous will to live." As if to reinforce his declaration Hyatt's square jaw clenched tight when he pursed his small mouth. Leaning back in his chair his gaze penetrated the ceiling. Dora let him have his moment.

His attention returned to his audience. "At my suggestion Jill had a quiet funeral. Since she had little a few of us his friends paid for it. Only a handful of people viewed the closed coffin. Jill was devastated, but she had no time to mourn. After Arnold was gone Adrian wasted no time to start using Lilly to get his way with her mother. If she didn't cooperate Lilly would be the one to suffer."

"She's a prisoner in his house," Dora pondered.

"They both are. I tried to help them escape once. The plan was to meet them with my buckboard about a mile from Delgrin's ranch. At that time there was a U. S. marshal in La Junta. My intention was to take them there to tell their story to him. They would also have been safe there under his protective custody.

"As luck would have it the weather was dark and stormy that night when Jill and Lilly slipped away. The ground was muddy and slick, making their progress slow. Too soon Adrian discovered that they were missing. With their footprints in the mud showing the way he caught up to them before they could reach me."

With a forlorn look on his ruddy face Doctor Hyatt glanced over at his young friend who was now fighting to hold back the tears. Bowing her head she bit her lip. Dora could sense her visceral feelings that hung in the air like fog. Their capture must have been horrible. Reliving that night for her must have been wretched.

"Lilly, if you'd rather you can leave the room while the doctor finishes his story," she offered, wanting to save her young friend the grief.

"No, that's all right," she replied in a strained voice, her eyes growing moist. "I'd rather stay here with you."

The medical man took a deep breath before continuing his story. "When Delgrin got them back to the house he had Jill tied to a chair. In vengeful anger he tore off Lilly's clothes, and—raped her in front of her mother. He threatened to kill them both if they ever tried running away again. After that he started locking them in at night."

Lillian started sobbing into her dainty hands. Putting her arm around the girl Dora pulled her tearful face to her shoulder. Doctor Hyatt's thin frame slumped in his chair, as if exhausted from bearing a huge, heavy burden. His narrow chin softened as his thin mouth parted with a muted sigh. Moments passed while sorrowful sentience subsided.

"Adrian never knew you were trying to help them escape?" Dora pressed when the emotional fog had thinned out.

"No," the Doctor affirmed. "There's no doubt that he would have eliminated me right away if he knew of my involvement, even with me being the only doctor in town. When Jill and Lilly didn't reach me well after the appointed time I feared that they had been apprehended. Not until a couple of days later did the knowledge of what happened that night reach my ears. A friend overheard some of Delgrin's men bragging about the foul deed in the saloon.

"That was the first time in my life that the desire to kill a man ever tempted me to break my oath. As a doctor I'm sworn to save men's lives not take them."

"Delgrin is no man. He's a pedophile and less than an animal," she stated. "I'm going to get Lilly and her mother away from that demon."

"What can you do?" Hyatt queried, his brow mirroring his doubt.

"What you couldn't. I'm a woman, something that Adrian Delgrin has a weakness for in his own demented way."

"You have a point. Maybe you can do something. Jill lives in constant fear for her daughter's life. To be frank peace hasn't been my partner either. This old man doesn't take orders from that wicked scoundrel, but he does keep a low profile taking on the appearance of one quite ignorant for his own health. Besides, if he were dead he'd be no help at all to Jill and Lilly. Adrian is a dangerous man. He won't hesitate to kill for what he wants. Please be careful."

"I intend to be. He's to meet me this afternoon. He received a telegram from me telling him that I'd be here today on business." She cradled Lilly's delicate face in her hands and gazed into those big, blue eyes. "If my attention to Mr. Delgrin grows to be too cozy, Dear, don't think evil of me. This young woman has an idea to take care of Adrian Delgrin and get you out of his clutches. He needs to turn his attention toward me and away from your mother."

"I understand, Dora. I hope you can for me and mother."

"Doctor Hyatt, please accept this money from me in behalf of our girl. Get her a fine dress with some new shoes. Whatever is left I entrust to your care for Lilly and her mother once they are out of the clutches of Delgrin."

She held out a five dollar bill. Hesitating he glanced at Lilly before taking it. Lilly just contributed a coy smile before looking away. Dora pressed the money into his hand.

"Call me Pete," he invited.

She smiled. "My friends know me as Dora." She glanced at the grandfather clock in the corner. "Now my friend, tell me what, in your professional judgment, is to be done for my ankle? How long before it can be walked on normally? Also, tell me where the best place is in town to take this young lady to lunch."

5

Dora Kincaid had lessened her limp from her initial masquerade when they walked into the hotel lobby a little before noon. Upon seeing her enter, Mr. Delles was as quick to reach her side as a dog to tree a cat.

"Ah, Miss Kinley, you seem to be walking much easier," he consoled, an eager gleam in his brown eyes.

"Yes, thank you, Mr. Delles. Your Doctor Hyatt has magic hands. He said that I should be all right in just a day or two. He's under the impression that I just pinched a nerve. There isn't any swelling. My ankle just feels a little sore still ."

"Did you have any trouble?" he asked in a lowered voice, bobbing a discreet nod toward Lilly who was staring at the floor in pretended boredom.

"My goodness, no. We got along just fine. But then I did bribe her a little. On the way back I treated her to lunch. That was the least that I could do for her help."

"That's fine. That's fine. I'm very glad to hear that your ankle isn't serious. Mr. Delgrin has been concerned, too. He'll be happy to hear about this."

"Oh? You know Mr. Delgrin?" she asked in mock innocence.

"Yes, he owns the hotel. While you were out he stopped by to see if you'd arrived. Of course, he was concerned for your welfare."

"Of course. That's very thoughtful of him. Did he tell you that he's to meet me here this afternoon?"

"Yes. He said that he would be back in an hour. I'll tell him you've returned."

"Splendid! I'm looking forward to his visit."

Still standing nearby, Lilly had remained silent. Dora turned to her and patted her on the head. "Thank you for your help, Lucy."

Her junior companion picked up on the cue. "Lilly, ma'am," she corrected in annoyance as if having done so several times before.

"Oh, yes, Lilly." Dora gave her a wink that Mr. Delles couldn't see. As she had been directed during lunch Lilly kept a poker face.

"One more time, child. If you will help me up the stairs to my room I shan't bore you any more."

"Yes, ma'am," Lilly replied, sounding reluctant.

Continuing their parts, together the two females ascended the staircase. At her door Dora dismissed her young charge.

"Good work," she whispered to Lilly. "Mr. Delles should believe that you don't like me too well. I could tell by the look on his face when we started up the stairs. After all, I'm doing business with your archenemy. Now it's time to get ready to meet our 'illustrious' Adrian Delgrin. See you later."

"Okay, Dora," Lillian replied with a radiant smile. "Thank you for everything." She left while Dora slipped into her room.

In just over an hour Dora Kincaid was responding to a knock on her door. She opened it in mock anticipation. "Yes?"

"Miss Kinley?" a small, wiry man announced. Dora half expected someone else to step into view, and introduce himself as the man she had been hired to kill. Had he sent a messenger, or was this the notorious tyrant of Lamar?

"Yes?" she repeated in expectancy.

"I'm Adrian Delgrin."

Dora hoped that she switched the spark of surprise into a look of delight before Mr. Delgrin had noticed. This man in her doorway did not at all fit the mental image that she had envisioned of a cruel tyrant. The real Adrian Delgrin, less than an inch taller than her, reminded her more of a quiet, little, smile-for-the-customer teller in a bank than a ruthless, cunning murderer controlling half a town and the land around it. Even Delles better fit the part. In retrospect she considered that Napoleon had been no giant either.

"Mr. Delgrin, come in, please!" she offered on a bright note.

Nodding, he strolled in and took a chair. From his jacket he pulled a big cigar, struck a match on his boot, and drew on the brown tube in his mouth. In a moment the end glowed red.

"Mind if I smoke?" he asked between puffs.

"Be my guest. I've always loved the smell of a good cigar," she lied. He smiled, as if satisfied with her approval. If he had any, her visitor appeared to be incapable of showing his manners first. She resisted the urge to wrinkle her nose in disgust. "Won't you have a seat?" she said, avoiding adding sarcasm to her offer.

"I got your wire." His brief comment came from the corner of his mouth. With the big cigar jammed into his cheek, which made his head look even smaller, he looked her over with leering eyes.

Dora returned the *admiration*. She figured him to be in his early thirties. His leering smile behind that cigar betrayed the secrets of his thoughts. She could see why Jill and Lilly feared him so. While he was handsome enough, his lack of manners, and his egotistical approach would make him repulsive to any woman but the basest of harlots. Their interest in him would be more monetary than physical.

"I suppose you are here to conduct business, Mr. Delgrin?" she posed, playing the part of a professional woman.

"Call me Adrian. No need to be formal."

"No, I suppose not. You may call me Dora."

"Dora. Nice name. Pretty name for a pretty face. Delles said that you were a good looking gal. He understated your appearance."

"Why, thank you, Adrian," she replied in a coy voice. The blackguard didn't mince words. "You flatter me. Now, shall we get on with the details of my company's proposal? Did you understand our earlier correspondence?"

Delgrin spit out a piece of cigar before responding with a question. "I gather your firm is in the crude oil business?"

"That's right. Are you familiar with crude oil?"

"Not much. I'm a cattleman myself. However, I hear that Texas has dug a few holes looking for it. Rumor has it that it looks like black, sticky molasses, and smells ten times worse."

"That's a fair comparison," she agreed. "We at Dan Kinley and Company like to call it black gold."

The word "gold" sparked a flicker of interest in Delgrin's shrewd eyes. "Black gold? Why? Is this oil all that valuable?"

"Yes, and growing more so every day. In five years a man who has five producing oil wells pumping today would amass a king's ransom."

"How much?" He was sitting on the edge of his chair now.

"Of course, this is an educated guess, but I would say about two million dollars."

Withdrawing the cigar from his mouth in deliberation, Delgrin rubbed the side of his jaw with his knuckles. Unlike Max Templeton, his hands weren't rough and callused. "With just five wells, huh?"

"That's right." She let these two words sink in.

"Just how do you go about finding this oil?"

Dora had sat on the edge of the bed right after her guest had made himself at home. Pulling up a second chair to face him she sat on its edge and leaned toward him with her hands clasped in a dramatic display of what she was about to say was more exciting than breaking a wild mustang.

"We use specialists in the field, geologists, who study the terrain to determine where the oil lies. And," she added, lowering her voice in enthusiastic emphasis, "we know that oil exists in this area. We have one successful test hole right now, not far from your ranch. Conditions look right for others to pay off, too."

"A test hole?" he echoed, his voice as low. "Around here? Where is it?" The lack of this knowledge appeared to agitate him.

"It's on the property of a Mr. Maxwell Templeton."

"Templeton!" he snorted. "I should have guessed."

"Ah, you know Mr. Templeton."

"We're, ah, old acquaintances, you might say."

"Oh, good! Since you know each other would you like to go see the test hole we've drilled on his ranch for yourself?" She already knew the answer to that.

"I said old, not close. We have a special agreement. He stays off my place; I stay off his. Otherwise we'd shoot each other."

Dora put her hand to her cheek in mock alarm. "Oh, my!" she exclaimed. "We wouldn't want that to happen."

Delgrin waved his hand in a gesture of impatience. "I don't need to see any test hole. What you've told me so far interests me. What sort of proposal do you have to offer?"

"You have the land. We have the know-how and the equipment. First, we determine the best places for drilling wells. When a well comes in, that is, starts producing oil, we put a pump on it. The wells will never interfere with your cattle operation.

"We use a lease contract on each well which allows us to operate it as long as it produces. Once it's dry, which may be fifty or sixty years from now, we close it off and cancel the lease." The next statement Dora stressed with added emphasis. "Our lease agreement would pay you twenty percent of the net profits on each well."

Delgrin's eyes narrowed in response to this statement. "Twenty percent? And all I have to do is sign an agreement saying you can drill a hole on my ranch?"

"That's right! You see, you own the rights to the oil under your land. We are willing to buy that oil from you. We know that oil is profitable enough for both of us. Without it, or the right to drill for it, we wouldn't be in business. So, we make our offer attractive enough to interest land owners."

"What if I decided to drill my own wells and keep all of the profits from the oil?"

Dora shrugged her shoulders in nonchalance. She'd figured that he might counter with such a question. "You could do that. However, you would have to locate the equipment and the men to run it. There are very few drilling crews around. This is still a young enterprise. Then you would have to hire a geologist to determine where to drill. Oil doesn't always show up where a geologist thinks it should be. Dry holes are expensive and time-consuming. So are equipment breakdowns, should they occur. You'd be out there every day worrying about your drill striking on every hole. Oil or not, you'd have payroll to meet. Your profits, if any, could turn out to be less than our offer. With us you lose nothing. We take the risks. You see oil is a tricky business. Like you said, you're a cattleman. Leave the oil drilling to experts."

"I see," he pondered some more. "You have a point. Okay, let's say I bought your proposition. How long before you start drilling?"

"First, I make a tour of your property. If the conditions look right our geologist comes in to perform a thorough study of the terrain. Once he pinpoints any area our drilling team sinks a test hole. If it taps oil we drill as many wells as it takes to pump the oil out. We then pump it to the railroad into tank cars and ship it to the refinery. My part should take about a week. If our findings are favorable we should have a drilling crew here within a month."

"You'll be here for a week?"

"If you accept our offer," she reminded him. "I'm here ready to look for oil when you are."

"Drilling for oil sounds like the wells are quite deep. You're bound to hit water you know. What do you about the water?"

"We're prepared for that. When we hit water we drill through it until we hit bottom on the aquifer. At that time we send a casing down to seal if off from the well. That way we get what we're after. No water, just oil."

Delgrin stood and sauntered to the door. "I brought the wagon in to town today to pick up some supplies. It's loaded and ready to go. We can start the tour this afternoon."

"Then you accept our offer."

"In the face of such beauty, I can't refuse."

Dora rubbed the butt of her gun which was hidden under the folds of her dress. She had a hunch that her custom pistol was going to come in handy soon. Grabbing her handbag she preceded him out the door. Adrian hadn't forgotten all of his manners.

Dora gimped for several steps on her "favored" ankle before Adrian noticed.

"Oh, yes," he recalled, "I understand that you had a little accident on the stairs this morning."

"Yes. Doctor Hyatt said that I pinched a nerve. My ankle is just a little sore, now. Thank you for your concern."

The wagon was parked just outside the hotel. Delgrin helped his passenger into the seat before heading out of town. They were beyond the outskirts before Dora brought up a conversation again. As she did she laid her hand on his forearm. He noticed.

"May I suggest that you not mention this oil well business to anyone else at this time."

"Why?"

"Suppose we found oil near your property line. Part of that oil may lie under your neighbor's property. If he were to find out that you had hit oil nearby he could drill and hit the same reserve of oil. This happened to us in Oklahoma. Our man told his neighbor about his well, which had hit just the boundary line of the reserve. His neighbor had us drill several wells on his side of their property line. His wells pumped all the oil away from the first well leaving it dry. In time that would have happened anyway, but the neighbor's wells sped up the process by many years. We still got the oil, but the first man was out his profit."

Delgrin laughed. "The fool! He gave it away! Don't worry. My only neighbor is Templeton. The only thing he'd get out of me is a spot on boot hill. I'd say nothing that might get back to him."

6

The trip out to the Delgrin ranch seemed like a short half-hour to Dora. The country was open, rolling range thick with prairie grass and sagebrush. Small, thick stands of piñons and junipers carpeted the shallow valleys here and there while an occasional piñon dotted the tan hills. On the distant western horizon green and brown peaks of the magnificent Rockies cut the skyline like jagged teeth. Remnants of late spring snows glistened on the higher peaks above timberline.

In all other directions the endless range evanesced into the horizon.

As they crossed over a slight rise several buildings came into view in the shallow, wide valley beyond them. Nestled in a grove of trees the ranch house, a two-story affair, boasted a mixture of river rock and wood as its veneer. Rare in the west a number of large windows adorned the walls of the house. As they drew closer she could see that the building structure appeared to combine both native and imported materials in excellent craftsmanship of construction. Non-spared expense to erect the lavish residence showed throughout. Against the backdrop of the plains it was almost too elaborate.

Beyond the dwelling about fifty yards away stood the ornate barn. An impressive structure as well its appearance of construction resembled that of the house with the same mixture of river rock and wood veneer. Surrounding the building stood a number of staunch corrals. Eyewitness confirmed that Farius Delgrin had not skimped on cost or quality. Even Max's place, while fancy enough for the western plains, took a distant second place.

To the right of the barn sat two cabins built to the same high caliber of construction. Dora could guess their purpose. The larger one would be the bunkhouse for the ranch hands while the other cabin served as the tack room for their equipment.

To complete the idyllic scene several large cottonwood trees along with a few ponderosa pines offered leafy shade from the summer sun on the house. Beyond the barnyard, stands of silver-leaf

Russian olive, hackberry, elm, gambel oak, piñon pine and locust trees, and lilac and nanking cherry bushes grew as a windbreak against the harsh winter winds. The pungent smell of sagebrush wafted across their path. If one didn't know that Farius and his wife had built this ranch one could give Adrian wrongful credit for its construction.

Delgrin pulled out his watch when they stopped in front of the house. "It's a quarter to two o'clock. We have time to see the front acreage. We'll take the buckboard today. Tomorrow, horses will do much better. Think you'll be up to it?"

"I think so. My ankle hurts only a little now."

"Good. Let's go in and freshen up before we start. You can meet some of the household."

He helped her to the ground. At the door stood a tall, slender man of about thirty, waiting for their entry. While he was dressed for ranch work, his clothes appeared crisp and near new.

"Slim," Delgrin instructed, "hitch a fresh team to the buckboard. Then unload the wagon."

"Okay, Boss," the man called Slim acknowledged. Slim climbed into the loaded wagon and drove it around to the barn. Dora figured that this was Slim Shelley, about whom Pete Hyatt told her. Something seemed to be familiar about him. Was it his Texas drawl? Or his hard facial features? Dora didn't think that they'd ever met. Otherwise he might have reacted to seeing her. What caused the recognition on her part eluded her for now. She decided not to let it show.

Adrian held the door open for his guest. Sometime from his past some earlier training of manners and courtesy must have been emerging. He was acting more the gentleman's part. *How long would this last?* Dora wondered. "Thank you," she expressed.

"Come in and meet my cook," he said, "the best in this country."

Dora followed her host through the spacious house. Elegant exotic furnishings lavished the living room. A potpourri of imported crystal and silver decorated shelves like a museum showplace.

In the dining room stood a heavy, ornate, hand carved, oak table with eight matching chairs. Behind the glass doors of a Victorian cabinet fine China sparkled. Tapestries adorned windows and cushions alike. Heavy, woven rugs completed the extravagant interior.

The kitchen proved to be just as meticulous as what she had seen so far. Dora could imagine that the rest of the rooms were similar in detail and tidiness. Whatever the cook's present station in this household Jill James kept it spotless and precise to the detail. Every bit of the decor Dora credited to Farius Delgrin's, or his wife's, tastes. She doubted that Adrian ever lifted a finger to keep the house this clean, or to choose its decor. He ignored it now.

When a woman appeared in a doorway of what Dora reasoned to be the entrance to the pantry she knew that this had to be Jill James. Lillian James mirrored a near perfect replica of her mother. As she'd heard, Jill was a beautiful woman. Although her personal grooming was just as meticulous, which Delgrin may have insisted upon, her lovely persona couldn't hide the unmistakable sadness in her eyes.

"Jill, we have a guest. This is Miss Dora Kinley. We have some business to transact this afternoon. Set a place for dinner for her tonight. Then prepare the guestroom for her. She'll be staying with us for a while."

"Oh, no, Adrian! I couldn't trouble you like this."

His last announcement surprised Dora. She feigned to decline in modesty knowing that her objection would be overruled. Being in the same house with Jill and Lilly proved to be more to her liking. She would have an easier time collaborating with them about her plan.

"I insist, Dora. There's no point in you making an extra one hour round trip when we have plenty of room here."

"Well, I suppose, if I'm not an inconvenience," she acquiesced. "But what about my luggage? It's all back at the hotel."

"I'll send one of the boys in a wagon to get it. So you see? It's all solved."

"Not quite. I still owe for the bath if not the room."

"It's on the house, my dear. Any other objections?"

"Oh, I'm not objecting, just making sure everything is solved as you said. In fact, I'm sure this will make my job that much easier. Thank you for the offer."

Jill had remained silent during this discussion. She offered nothing more than a cold stare for Dora. The tinge of hostility that flashed through her eyes reflected to Dora the woman's instant hatred for her presence being there. Jill would harbor distrust for anyone who entertained Delgrin as a friend. When that friend is female threatening her and Lilly's fragile domain just tacit malice and contempt could exist for such a rival.

Had the moment been opportune Dora would have been tempted to try to win her confidence in the real mission that she came to perform. Until that time she would continue to play her role through the final act if necessary. Jill's misguided bitterness would have to suffice unless Lilly would have a chance to talk to her mother later about Dora. With them being always watched or locked apart the opportunity for such a meeting seemed slim at best.

"Shall we get started?" Adrian suggested.

"By all means," Dora consented. "I'm happy to meet you, Jill. I'd love to see the rest of the house when we return."

Jill's eyes narrowed. No utterance came from her lips. She merely nodded and returned through the doorway from where she had first entered. Dora could only feel for her misplaced malice.

Adrian made the offer. "After we get back from our first tour I'll show you around the place before dinner."

As they went out they found the buckboard standing ready with a fresh team of horses. Slim was directing two other hands in unloading the wagon. Adrian and Dora climbed aboard the buckboard to head for the open range. As they drove away she wondered what feature of Slim caught her remembrance. His shifty eyes? His humped nose? That cleft chin? Not that she had ever met him before she was certain.

"How much land do you have here?" Dora asked, putting the daunting lack of recognition of Slim aside.

"As far as the eye can see," he replied, sweeping his hand in front of him. Then, being more specific, "About a million acres. A lot of ground for a man to run alone."

"Alone? You must have a lot of men under your employ."

"Hired help may give a man some company, but a lonely man needs a good woman to make his home and keep him warm at night."

"You seem to have a very good housekeeper," Dora ventured, "and she's pretty. Haven't you considered marrying her?"

"Jill won't consider any man since her husband was killed. Besides, she keeps herself strapped down to the housework all the time. I don't like it, but she won't slow down and I can't let her go. One can't find a cook and housekeeper like her at all easy. Nope. Too different, though, her and me."

Scanning the landscape in marked exploration was Dora showing just partial awareness of Delgrin's conversation. Sure of where this was going she allowed several moments to pass before answering.

"Yes, it's nice to have a cook," she remarked in a casual tone. "That's one talent I haven't mastered well."

"You don't need to."

This last remark she chose to ignore making comment to, instead changing the subject. "Adrian, head for that rise over there," she directed, pointing to the spot she meant. "That will give us a good look at the surrounding terrain." Against his premature and bumptious advances she'd act hard to get to entice his efforts.

Adrian complied, driving the rig to the place that Dora chose. Using the vantage point of the higher ground Dora climbed down from the buckboard. She walked around studying the horizon on all sides with intensity. The conditions and timing had to be right, but not for oil as Delgrin supposed.

To the west of their present location the terrain grew more rugged. The hills were cut by steep washes too rough for the buckboard to travel she was sure. Out there they would ride tomorrow. Out there would be the perfect spot. Out there was the place Delgrin would breathe his last.

"Out there," she told him, waving her hand. "Your best location is out there I'd say. Tomorrow we'll have to survey out there."

Delgrin left the buckboard to join her. He peered to the west. "So you think there's oil over there?" he queried.

"That shows the most promise," she explained. "There are good possibilities all around here. Even where we're standing has its merits. I've just begun looking, though. Tomorrow we'll ride over there."

Removing his hat, revealing thick, sandy hair, Delgrin stared with interest toward tomorrow's intended destination. The evil gleam in his eyes gave away the greed in his mind. Here was promised more wealth, more power for him. Avarice was written all over his face. No woman who had any morals could be happy with this kind of man. He wanted only for himself, stopping at nothing to get it.

"How can you tell there's oil out there?" he posed after a moment of silence while staring at the horizon in ignorance.

"It's hard to explain," she told him. "You have to look for certain features that give you some clue to what's deep below the surface. Unless you're a geologist you'd find the topic boring."

"Nothing you could say would bore me, Dora."

Dora smiled, more to herself. This seducer of women and rapist of little girls wasted no time in trying his crude tricks on her. Going better than she'd hoped she'd play up to him to his utter downfall.

"Shall we continue," she suggested, returning to the buckboard. "I'm fascinated by all this open range."

"You like being out here?" he asked when they were under way again.

"I love the outdoors. When I was little I always played on the large boulders near our home. That's one reason why I enjoy doing what I do. The open spaces refresh me."

"Me, too," he agreed. "You and I have a lot in common. Someone like you is just whom I need to share all this with."

He put his arm around her shoulders. Dora withstood the urge to smash in his teeth. Instead, she acted with reserve, using just enough resistance to pique his desire to try harder. She would pander his pitiful ego for now.

"You're very generous, Adrian, but we hardly know each other. I don't feel ready to settle down." She added in emphasis, "At least not just yet. With the right man I might have a change of heart."

Smiling his leering, repulsive smile Delgrin went back to using two hands on the reins. Dora busied herself by primping her hair and smoothing her dress as if nervous and unsure of what else to do. She would make Adrian think of her as a blushing maiden untrained in the world of men. He'd be in for a surprise soon enough.

"I'd like you to stay here awhile and get to know the ranch," Delgrin offered. "The place just may grow on you."

"But, Adrian, I have a job," she protested with a little resistance. "Father doesn't have a son to follow in his footsteps, just me. And if I quit, well, Father would be disappointed." How true that was!

"Dora, a beautiful woman like you shouldn't need to work," he reasoned. "Your father would just need to understand that. But whatever you decide about staying for some time the choice is yours. In the meantime will you consider this your home when you're not traveling?"

"Well, I'd have to give this some thought," she contemplated aloud. "This is all so sudden. I do appreciate your offer, but I must have some time to think about it."

"Of course," he nodded his understanding at her pretended bewilderment. "Take your time. Meanwhile, I'll just enjoy your company for the coming week."

Dora could have laughed with sarcasm, wondering if Delgrin had heaped as much delusion upon Jill James as what he was using at this moment. How foolish he would feel when he discovered that he was the one being deceived! How dead this malefactor was going to be! She was enjoying this job more and more.

"Let's look around some more," she suggested, changing the subject again. "There's a lot of ground here to check out."

Delgrin drove the buckboard slow revealing his obvious enjoyment of the ride with his new-found "hopeful." Dora kept her attention on the landscape to tease him. On occasion she would point out a part of the terrain as a possible spot for oil.

"The conditions are fair," she would say, "but we'll start with the best spot first."

By late afternoon Delgrin had decided to quit the survey for the day. He aimed the team and carriage toward the house. By the time they returned Jill had dinner almost prepared and the table set. Mr. Delles was sitting in the kitchen watching her. That meant that Lilly was in the house somewhere.

"Mr. Delles," Dora greeted with a nod. "Good afternoon."

"Ah, Miss Kinley," he acknowledged. "So nice to see you again. I brought your luggage here. The night clerk gave me the message that you would be staying here at the house."

Night clerk! Delgrin had already planned on having her luggage brought out to the ranch. She gave Delgrin a suspicious glance which the rancher missed.

"Thank you, Mr. Delles. That was considerate of you. If you will show me where it is I'll change for dinner."

"I set it in your room. Follow me."

42

Delles led the way through the house upstairs to where he had left Dora's baggage in an immaculate bedroom. Once they were there she took the opportunity to ask about Lilly. "Where's the girl?" she asked in disinterest. "Does she live here, too?"

He pointed at the far door down the hall.

"We have to lock her in," he told her. "We can't trust her; she's tried to run away."

Shaking her head in pretended bemusement Dora reflected with solemnity, "I can't understand a child like that. Where in the world would she run to? She sounds like she has no appreciation for such a nice home."

Dora stepped into her bedroom. She waved good-bye to Delles. "If you will excuse me I'll put on something more comfortable for dinner. I shan't be too long."

As she shut the door behind the retreating man she leaped into action. Popping open one of her bags she took out a ring of keys. In quick fashion she stepped out of her dress exposing another outfit of more casual attire. Without a sound she cracked open the door. The hallway was devoid of human occupancy. She could still hear Mr. Delles's receding footsteps on the last few stairs. When they had faded into silence she stole to the top of the landing. He had moved out of sight. Whirling around, Dora slipped down the hall to Lilly's room.

A quick examination of the lock revealed it to be of a conventional make. Selecting a suitable key Dora unlocked the door and entered the room. Young Lillian who was sitting on the edge of the bed brightened in surprise when she saw her new friend.

"Dora, how did you get in?" she whispered, her eyes opened as wide as saucers.

Slipping the key off the ring Dora handed it to Lilly.

"Here, put this in a safe place," Dora instructed in hushed tones. "You're going to find a use for it very soon. I wanted you to know I'm here. Tonight, when everyone else is in bed we'll get together.

"Right now I'd better get back before I'm missed. See you at dinner. Lock the door when I leave and don't leave the key in the keyhole."

Lilly nodded her acknowledgment. Making a quick check of the hall again Dora backed out of the room and returned to her own. She secreted the ring of keys once again into her bag before returning to the kitchen on the first floor.

7

Delgrin was waiting for her in the dining room. He beckoned with a wave of his hand for her to take a seat beside him.

"How long before dinner?" she inquired, standing before him.

"Fifteen minutes."

"Enough time for you to show me around the grounds."

"My pleasure," he submitted with a smile, rising to accompany her.

With her arm around his they left the house through the kitchen door. Jill had turned her back to them as they exited the room, but not before Dora had caught her icy stare. Adrian missed her glare.

They strolled across the yard to the massive barn. Within the spotless stalls sleek horses nodded and neighed their greetings to their owner. For the first time since Dora had met him Delgrin was showing a genuine interest and affection on his face for something living besides himself. His mouth spread into a wide grin.

"These are my beauties," he announced with pride. In loving caress she stroked the silky mane and neck of a big chestnut mare in the first stall. "These are the real workers on my ranch. An operation like this couldn't exist without such magnificent animals."

Dora tickled the horse's muzzle to show it affection. The mare neighed nodding her pleasure. "Which is your favorite?" Dora asked.

"None of them. I favor them all. Every horse is different. You have to treat each one for what it is, but always with a gentle hand. Treat a horse right and it'll always treat you the same."

Funny how that works with most people! "Are you going to pick out a horse for me to ride tomorrow?"

He shrugged. "I could. How good can you ride?"

"I grew up on a horse."

He smiled his cocky smile. "I'll give you Spirit. He's the big bay stud in the last stall. He'll give you all the ride you want."

Dora walked over to the last stall to look in on Spirit. He was a big quarter horse looking capable of doing what his name implied. The man knew his horses well. Smiling within at the choice of the ride Adrian had made she held her hand out to him. He came over to allow her to scratch his nose.

"Hello, big fellow," she cooed. "Let's get to know each other before we team up tomorrow morning."

Spirit nodded his agreement with a nicker. Adrian showed his visual delight that Dora and Spirit had straightaway hit it off. After a moment of stroking his mane and coddling his nose Dora glanced over at her host.

"I'd like to give him a workout," she decided. Looking around the rest of the barn she went on, "Shall we continue?"

From the barn they strolled through the corral area to the tack room. Here more than a score of saddle racks hung from the walls. Most of the saddles and tack were missing from their resting places. The room was just as well kept as everything else she had seen. Dora wondered if the cleanliness of the ancillary buildings were Jill's charge, or if Adrian held his men responsible for it.

Delgrin led her to the bunkhouse next door where only a few of the bunks showed signs of recent use.

"I haven't seen very many hands around," she commented as they walked in.

"Most of them are out on drive," Delgrin informed her, although she knew that from Max as many of his men were also out on drive. "We started moving some of the cattle to market last week. With the railroad getting closer we can move 'em faster than we used to. But the business is getting too crowded. That's one reason why I like your oil proposal."

Templeton had his timing figured right. Hire a gunslinger to get rid of Delgrin while most of his men are gone. Dora liked the plan that way, too. Her job would be that much easier. More and more she was beginning to enjoy her part in this ploy.

"With a few good oil wells you could give up cattle ranching altogether if you wanted," she agreed with emphasis to fuel the fire.

They strolled back to the main house where they found the few remaining members of the ranch gathering around the table for dinner.

Lilly remembered her instructions well keeping a poker face at Dora's appearance. Jill avoided looking at her "competition" at all while all of the men greeted her in eager friendliness. Dora turned on the charm for their benefit.

"Boys, you've heard me talk about Miss Kinley coming here on business," Delgrin began. "Now you've met her. She's going to be staying with us for a while, so mind your manners. She's a real lady."

Delgrin's last statement seemed to infer that Jill wasn't a "real lady." What other treatment might she be receiving in this household?

Questions began to come at Dora from all sides as to the who, what, and why of her visit. With brevity she responded to the questions while avoiding any mention of oil. When Slim asked her point blank if she had intentions of staying at the ranch for very long her answer was vague.

"That remains to be seen."

Delgrin's face went hopeful at it.

At this remark, Jill, who had said nothing during the course of the questioning, slammed her fork on the table and hurried to the kitchen. None of the men, not even Delgrin, showed signs of noticing her hasty departure. Had she remembered something that she was cooking, or did Dora's remark cause her retreat? Jill's slamming the fork caused her to think the latter. Dora was quite aware of the antipathy that Jill already harbored for her. What bothered her was why the hostility existed so strong in Lilly's mother. Why did her sudden presence provoke Jill to such hatred? Jealousy was out of the question. She hoped to meet with Mrs. James alone soon.

For the rest of the dinner Jill did not reenter the room to resume her meal. Dora managed to cast a questioning glance toward Lilly who shrugged her shoulders in bewilderment about her mother's actions. The younger James made no move to follow her mother from the room. That the two of them would not be left alone together for long, Dora was certain. If Lilly did leave, someone, the obvious choice Delles, would follow her to keep an eye on her whereabouts.

After dinner the party, except for Jill, Lilly, and Mr. Delles, moved into the living room to more comfortable conditions. Delles appeared alone several moments later from the stairway. That was the sign that Lilly had been locked away in her room again.

Dora could only guess at Jill's disappearance. She may have been locked away, too, but Dora doubted that. Dishes would have to be cleaned up after dinner. Also, Jill seemed to have the run of the house. As long as Lilly was under physical restraint her mother wouldn't try running away again.

In a few minutes Slim and the other two hands with him excused themselves from the room to return to their duties. For part of the evening Dora engaged in light conversation with the two remaining men. About an hour later after subtle innuendos from Delgrin Delles went out to the kitchen leaving Adrian and Dora alone.

As soon as they were by themselves Delgrin started on her again, moving closer to sit by her side.

"Have you given much thought to my offer?" he asked.

"I really haven't had time to. Perhaps in the next few days after I've been around here for a while I might have an answer to your question. By then we'll get to know each other a little better." She patted his cheek with affection. "I want you to know that I think you're very sweet, Adrian. That much I can say now."

He responded with his repulsive smile. His evil leer must have developed from years of unconscious habit, she reasoned. She wasn't getting used to it, either. When his face wasn't distorted that way he was quite good looking. In an effort to change the subject from her she threw a new line of questions at him.

"How did you acquire such a ranch?"

Delgrin settled back into his seat. He extracted a cigar from his coat pocket to toy with it. "Lived here all my life. Ma, and the rest of the kids, except Horatio my brother, died from the fever a long time ago. Pa got killed by a bunch of renegade Indians in an ambush two years ago. The ranch was left to me."

"What happened to Horatio?"

"He was found out behind the saloon in town one night with his head bashed in. Guess he got into a fight after getting drunk and lost for keeps."

"That's a terrible thing to happen," she sympathized. "I'm very sorry to hear that. You have my condolences."

There was not even an eyelash flicker of emotion in Delgrin's disinterested remarks. Not only was he cold and ruthless in his conceited pursuits, but he was a bad actor as well. Maybe he didn't realize that he could be read like the bold headlines of a newspaper. Maybe he didn't care. The habit of ruling a town and many of its inhabitants may have made him care less if not careless.

"Now all this nice big ranch is mine alone to share with someone like you," he was saying. That leering smile was betraying his face once again. Even more so, shadowed by the late hour it was creepy.

Dora could see that only one thing was going to stop his advances at this moment. The grandfather clock struck eight. She mustered a yawn, smothering it with polite pats from the tips of her fingers.

"Please excuse me," she apologized. "This has been a very busy day. I've just realized that the hour is growing late. We should get some rest for an early start tomorrow. Don't you agree?"

A look of disappointment almost hostile flashed across his face before he resumed his usual smile. He put the cigar back into his coat pocket. "As you wish, my dear," he conceded. "I'll see you to your room."

At her door Dora bid her host a good night. In a flash she slipped inside to shut him out. Putting her ear to the keyhole she listened to his receding footsteps on the stairs. All at once they stopped. Muted tones of a woman's voice seeped through the keyhole. They were answered by Delgrin's voice. Dora strained to hear what they were saying. Too muffled were the words they exchanged.

The voices stopped. Two sets of footsteps were now ascending the staircase. They walked by her room to a further point down the hall. The footsteps shuffled, hesitated, shuffled again. The click of a latch was followed by silence.

Jill James must have met Delgrin on the stairs and went on to Jill's room for some purpose, Dora mused. Cautious she opened her door to peer out. Finding the hallway empty she crept like a cougar down the corridor to the first doorway beyond her own. Circumspect of her immediate surroundings she put her ear to the keyhole of this door. No sound issued from within. Peeking through the keyhole she saw a darkening room caused by the oncoming twilight.

She was about to step to the door across the hall when the creaking of the stairs caught her attention. On cat's paws she bolted back into her room and swung the door shut, twisting the doorknob to keep the latch from snapping with a click into position. Dropping to the keyhole she peered through it.

Dora was none too soon. The new footsteps sounded at the top of the landing. From across the hall the first door swished open and then shut with a dull thud. She reasoned that the dark figure that

48

passed her door must have been Delles who had just gone into his room. Being the hotel manager he could be residing in the house instead of in the bunkhouse with the cowhands. With Lilly under his charge he could keep closer vigilance by being on the same floor as she.

There were six rooms on the second floor of Delgrin's mansion. Delles was in the first while Lilly was in the last on the same side of the hall as Dora's room. Jill was in one of the two remaining rooms to be checked. She wondered, *Does Delgrin also have a room on the second floor?*

Dora wanted to find Jill's room to listen in at the door. She had a hunch that Jill and Adrian's impromptu meeting on the staircase was about her. With Delles in his room the risk of getting caught eavesdropping was far greater. She deliberated for a moment before deciding to try again. Locating Jill's room seemed paramount.

As she was about to open her door again intuition told her to wait for another moment. During that moment Delles swung open his. Closing the door behind him with a thump he went back down the stairs. Dora acted at once. Before his footsteps finished their descent she had reached the next door down the hall. Again silence and shadows prevailed. The last door was across from Lilly's room. This had to be Jill's room.

Crouched down by the keyhole Dora listened. Delgrin's sour tones reached her ears. She had caught only part of his statement.

"—much good to me much longer. You've been good company, but your heart's never been in it when we've made love. This is the first time you've ever made the first move. Are you jealous?"

Definite sarcasm rang in his voice. Dora cocked her eye to the keyhole. On the edge of the bed sat Jill James, her dress pulled open to expose her bosom. Delgrin was not in Dora's line of vision. Jill was straining to maintain a poker expression. Her eyes red with hate betrayed her real loathing.

"I have an interest in my daughter's welfare," Jill answered in a monotone. "You know I've nothing to be jealous about."

"I'll give you a choice. If you can prove you'll get passionate when I want you I'll keep both of you around."

Delgrin moved into view. Sitting next to her he put his arms around her and began to kiss and caress her on the neck. She sat as

49

rigid as a rock her face reflecting unfeigned disgust. In response he shoved her down against the bed. Standing over her he taunted, "You'll never change. Soon I won't need you any more. When Dora says yes, I'll have a real lover. I'll turn you over to Delles and the rest of the boys. Until then I'll continue to take what I want."

He threw himself down on top of her. Jill struggled without hope against him. That was the last that Dora saw and heard. What she had witnessed was repulsive enough. Before she was compelled to barge in and blow Adrian Delgrin away in Jill's room she had to get away.

This was not the time. Tomorrow was. She hurried back to her room.

Echoing in her mind were his words to keep both of them around. Did he mean Jill and Lilly? Or Jill and Dora? In either case he intended to have a wife *and* a mistress under the same roof. To harass Jill Delgrin was using Dora against her. Now she knew why Jill had looked so hateful toward her. Killing scum like Adrian Delgrin was going to be a pleasure. Tomorrow seemed an eternity away.

After about fifteen minutes she heard Jill's door swing open, then shut. A key rattled the lock into place. Heavy steps like those from a man's boots passed through the hall and down the staircase. To her relief he didn't stop at her door. After what she had just witnessed she wasn't ready for his company again tonight.

A plan had been forming in Dora's mind. She would need to gain Jill's confidence if she were going to help her and Lilly get out of this house. How long this might take she could only guess. Jill's first impression of her was already off on the wrong foot. To a great extent the success of her plan rested upon Jill's acceptance of it.

Once again the staircase groaned under someone's weight. Dora strained to hear the tread of boots upon the steps. Only an occasional creaking stair betrayed the person's presence. Whoever was ascending the stairs appeared to be furtive in his actions. Peering through her own keyhole Dora saw a dim shadow flicker by. Darkness was beginning to prevail outside. Although there was a window at each end of the hallway the day was growing even dimmer with the approaching twilight. Whoever had passed by her door had been too close to it in the encroaching gloaming to be more than a shadow. Silent stealth continued to be the mystery man's passage along the hall.

A faint click filtered through the keyhole to her ear. She figured that someone had just unlocked another door. Opening her own on silent hinges she again peeked around the jamb. The door to Jill James's bedroom was just swinging shut. The lock clicked once more. Whoever went into her room locked the door from the inside.

On tiptoe Dora hurried down the hall once more to see if she could discover the identity of this new party. This time she found the keyhole blocked. The key had been left in the lock.

Dora pursed her lips together in disgust. With the key in the lock any conversation that may have been taking place was also being muffled. Disappointed she returned to her room to wait out this new visitor's call. Patience wasn't one of her best virtues.

It must be Delles, she mused. Since Delgrin had just left Jill little reason existed for him to be returning so soon. After all he had just taken what he wanted. Also, she saw no reason why Delgrin would've been furtive in his own house, trying to sneak up the steps and along the hall.

She allowed that Slim or one of the other hands still on the ranch could be the second occupant in Jill's room. This could explain the furtive advance. Even so she deduced that Delles was the most logical choice. Since he lived in the house with his bedroom on the same floor his presence shouldn't raise any accusing questions.

The second part of this puzzle was why had he gone to Jill's room? Why the stealth since his room was on the same floor? Was Jill open game to any who wanted to force his will onto her? Perhaps Delles was taking "privileges" not being granted to him. Dora had the feeling that a lot of questions needed answers this night.

A scant five minutes had elapsed when she heard a door latch click again. Dora had been keeping vigil outside her own door. When she saw Jill's door start to open she dashed back inside and closed hers. Retreating to her keyhole again she watched and waited. A few seconds passed before she heard the latch click once more. No rattle of a key in the lock followed. Shoe leather scuffed along the hardwood floor. Outside her door a shadow paused.

Standing up Dora backed away from the door. The knob began a slow rotation. She felt certain that she was about to face the mysterious person who had just stolen up to Jill's room.

When the door swung open Dora was startled at the identity of the intruder. Fire blazed in Jill James's eyes as she leveled the lethal end of a big forty-four right at Dora!

8

With the way Dora carried her own hidden revolver under her clothes she could have whipped out her pistol and shot the revolver out of Jill's grip. Making such a move would create a ruckus that would bring unwanted attention. Delgrin and whoever else within earshot would be up in seconds after the shot was fired. He, or they, would find Jill with a stung hand and a forty-four revolver lying on the floor at her feet. Even though Dora would have her own gun back out of sight both women would be left in an awkward position to explain.

The younger woman would have to start talking fast if she were to convince Mrs. James that she didn't want to use that gun. Only as a last resort would Dora draw on her.

"Mrs. James! What is this?" she implored, allowing alarm in her voice.

"I want you to scream, Miss Kinley," Jill hissed through her teeth. "I want you to scream just before I shoot you, so that Delgrin will come running up here. Then I'm going to blow that piece of scum wide open!"

"I understand your hatred of Delgrin, but why me?"

A puzzled frown swept across Jill's pretty face. "How did you know I loathe that— thing less than a man that owns this ranch?"

Dora sat upon the edge of the bed in a disarming fashion.

"Your daughter, Lilly, and Doctor Hyatt have told me a lot about you. I know you're kept a prisoner in this house. To help you escape is what brought me here."

"You came to help me escape?" Jill almost scoffed, but not sounding quite as hateful as she did when she'd entered Dora's room. "The way Delgrin has been drooling over you and you've been taking it in, my only escape would be in a pine box."

Dora beckoned to the desperate woman. "Come in and close the door. Please. We need to talk."

Hesitating at first, Jill obliged, keeping her weapon trained on Dora. A slight trembling of her hand revealed her anger was fading.

"My purpose here is to conduct some business," Dora continued. "Part of that business is to get you and Lilly out of here to safety. If I seem too amicable with Delgrin, that's because I can see no other way to gain his attention and allow you to escape. To tell you the truth he's quite repulsive to me."

The barrel of Jill's gun dropped a little. "Why else did you come here? Not just for Lilly and me."

"We women have to stick together in this untamed country. When I found out about you and your situation I made some changes in my original plans. All of Mr. Delgrin's intentions will be frustrated in this business matter."

"I don't want him frustrated," Jill growled. "I want him dead."

"That may be true," Dora concurred. "You just don't look like a killer to me. Even if you could shoot Delgrin what about the others still on the ranch? How are you going to escape from them? If you did manage to escape, Sheriff Hilliard would hunt you down. He couldn't chance you revealing his connection with Delgrin and the murders of Farius and Horatio. You know that, don't you?"

From the look on Jill's face Dora knew that the flood of facts she sprung on her caught the hapless housekeeper by surprise. The gun barrel drooped even lower. As Jill stood there contemplating the situation a soft tap came at the door. Startled at the sound Jill stiffened in alarm. Grave concern flashed across her face.

"Dora?" spoke a quiet voice. "Dora, this is Lilly."

Before Jill could react to her daughter's voice Dora replied in kind, "Come in, Lilly."

Jill made a quick attempt to conceal the big pistol from her daughter's sight. As the younger James entered Dora's room her mother stuffed the revolver between the folds of her dress. Lilly was startled when she saw her mother standing there.

"Mama!" she murmured in surprise. "What are you doing here? How did you get out of your room? I thought I heard you get locked in."

"I might ask you the same question, my child," Jill countered, pulling parental privilege. "You act as if you already know Miss Kinley quite well since you called to her by her first name. I might also ask how you two met without me knowing."

Dora beckoned toward her latest visitor. "Come in and shut the door. Our voices may carry to undesirable ears."

Lilly obeyed. As quiet as a thief she closed the door behind her.

"Since we are all here together," Dora went on, "we can make our plans as to how to get the two of you out of here."

"Where did you get to know my daughter?" Jill queried, her initial hatred gone. "I've never seen you here on the ranch before."

"At the hotel. By faking a sprained ankle I was able to get Lilly away from Mr. Delles long enough to talk to her. We had a long chat with Doctor Hyatt. Mr. Delles was easy to fool."

"Mr. Delles was a fool," Jill muttered in response. "So, Lilly, how did you get out of your locked room?"

"Just before dinner Dora came into my room. She had unlocked my door with a key she had. She gave it to me so that I could get out to come see her tonight."

Lilly's mother cocked a questioning eye at Dora.

"A skeleton key," she explained. "This is a rather common type of lock on these doors. I happen to have a skeleton key that fits."

Dora changed the subject. "Jill, you just said, 'Mr. Delles *was* a fool'. What do you mean, was?"

Jill's face faded to an ashen gray. "I—I killed him tonight in my room. I've never killed anyone before. When you came here though I feared that Lilly's life was in jeopardy. I already hated you for Delgrin's sake. So I talked Delles into coming to my room. I told him that Delgrin would get rid of Lilly and me because of you. I offered him anything I could give him if he would save us."

Jill James trembled in terror. She sought the support of a chair resting in the corner of the room before she continued. "His lust for me was no secret. Delgrin would have killed him if he dared try touching me any other time. Instead, he gave Delles free rein with Lilly to keep his lustful wickedness appeased.

"You don't know how much I hated that man for what he's done to her, a mere child. This time I was offering myself to him. Under the circumstances he figured I was desperate and had no choice. As I think about it I guess I was. When he came upstairs to my room I killed him." Having made her confession she sagged in her chair.

So Jill wasn't fair game. That's why Delles had been so furtive, Dora reasoned. "How did you kill him? I heard no shot."

"I told him that my natural modesty kept me from undressing in front of him. When he turned his back I picked up a big skillet that was hidden under my pillow and hit him on the head. I was just going to knock him out and get his key, but I must have hit him much harder than I thought."

"Are you sure he's dead?" Dora pressed.

"I think so. He was bleeding all over from where I hit him. On impulse I took his gun and came down here thinking to attract Delgrin up here to shoot him. My thinking wasn't very clear forgetting the other hands still on the ranch. Now I'm scared. I hated Delles, but I didn't mean to kill him. What am I going to do?"

"You mean, what are we going to do," Dora corrected her. "We're in this together, remember." She stood up and walked to the door. "You two stay here. I'm going to go check on Mr. Delles to see if he is dead. I shouldn't be gone very long."

"Dora," Jill called to her. "I'm sorry I misjudged you."

Dora smiled in understanding at her momentary adversary. "That's okay. Under the circumstances who can blame you?"

"But I could have shot you."

If only she knew! "You wouldn't have. That's not your nature."

Dora slipped down the hall post haste to Jill's room. Upon entering she found Delles sprawled face down across the foot of the bed. His head and arm drooped over the end. The back of his head was drenched with drying blood. The wound was no longer bleeding, a sign that his heart had stopped. Making a careful check she found no pulse or breath in the man. Despite her petite stature, but powered by hate Jill had wielded a lethal skillet which lay on the bed next to the body. Within the minute she was back in her own room again.

"Delles won't be leaving your room under his own power, nor ever molesting Lilly again," she reported to the anxious pair. "Don't let his ill-timed departure from mortality weigh you down. You've done us all a service. Now we're going to have to cover his disappearance until I can get Delgrin away from the house tomorrow. Mrs. James, where is Adrian's room?"

"His is the master bedroom on the main floor."

"Good. Lilly, what time do you leave for the hotel?"

"Just before seven. We're supposed to be there by seven thirty."

"How do you get there?"

"By horseback. I always get them ready. Mr. Delles never helped."

"All right." Dora turned to Jill. "Mrs. James, who lets you out of your room in the morning, and what time?"

"Delles did, about five thirty, before he'd let Lilly out."

"What time do you serve breakfast?"

"Six o'clock," she replied. "I feed the help first, then my daughter, Mr. Delles, and Adrian come in to breakfast at six thirty. How are we going to explain for Delles's absence at breakfast?"

Pondering how to handle the change in Jill's routine Dora tapped her cheek with a finger. "I'm going to have to divert Adrian from the house just about that time. Lilly, you put the horses out front in the morning. Then eat a quick breakfast and ride for Doc Hyatt's place. Tell him what's happened. Whatever you do stay with him. He's the one person in town that you know you can trust."

Dora directed her next instructions to the older woman. "Mrs. James, make sure there are still two sets of dirty dishes on the table when Adrian and I return. Adrian should think that Delles and Lilly will have eaten and gone on their way. After we've had breakfast and left on our ride take the other horse out front and ride to Doc Hyatt's, too. Take Delles's gun with you."

"What about you?" Mrs. James queried.

"My job will be to keep Mr. Delgrin occupied with a ride to some remote part of the ranch. You'll be long gone before he ever finds out. Once you're at Doc Hyatt's we'll figure out where to get you out of the territory. Now," she concluded, "we'd best get some rest. Mrs. James, I suggest you stay in Lilly's room tonight. Delles has taken your bed. I don't think you'd enjoy a dead man's company."

Jill shuddered. "Sleeping with a dead Delles rather than a live one is preferable, but sleeping with Lilly is the better choice." With an inconspicuous gesture she left the revolver on the dresser near her chair. "Dora, I'll leave this in your keeping for the night. Come, my daughter," she beckoned, with the other hand on Lilly's shoulder. "Let us leave this good lady to her rest. Oh, and Dora, please call me Jill."

After they departed for their room Dora took little time preparing for bed. In a few minutes she was in a deep slumber.

9

Dora was up and dressed when she heard Jill James's light rap on her door. She opened it to see a happy face.

"I just wanted to be sure you were awakened on time," Jill explained with a smile. "I can see you're way ahead of me. Did you sleep well?"

"Like a baby. How about you two?"

"The best sleep we've had in years."

"I'll be down in just a bit. Remember to look like you still hate my presence when Delgrin is around us."

"That's right," Jill agreed. "He'd get suspicious if he saw a sudden friendship between us."

After the older woman went downstairs to tend to her usual chores Dora picked up the gun that Jill had left on the dresser the previous night and returned to Jill's room. She put the weapon back into its holster on Delles's body. If someone should discover Delles too soon she didn't want the gun to show up in the wrong place.

Searching through his coat pocket she found his wallet full of small bills. She extracted these and counted fifty-two dollars. Replacing the wallet she left Jill's room and went to Lilly's where she found the smiling teenager getting ready to leave.

"I have something for you," Dora announced, handing the wad of bills to the girl. "Plus, I still have your silver dollar."

Staring at the roll of money Lilly's eyes went wider than the silver dollar she saw the day before. "Oh, no, I couldn't—" she started to protest.

"Yes, you can. That's a small contribution from our dear Mr. Delles. He has no need of it now, and this won't even begin to repay what he's done to you. At the least it will help you and your mother." She pressed the money into Lilly's hand. "Hide this on you some place," she instructed. "Don't stop to talk to anyone except Doc Hyatt. You may want the doctor to put this money in a safe place for now. If you can, pick a fast horse to ride. Just don't take Spirit. He's to be my ride today. Don't push your ride too hard going to town.

That way, if anyone starts chasing you your horse won't be too tired to outrun your pursuer. Is that clear?"

"Yes, Dora, I understand. Thank you. Thank you again."

"You're welcome. Be careful and keep your eyes open."

Dora went downstairs where she found Slim and the other two men, the balance of the hands not out on the drive, just finishing up breakfast. She smiled a cordial greeting before she returned to the parlor to await the arrival of Adrian Delgrin.

Her wait was short. Delgrin appeared in the doorway only moments later his usual repulsive smile distorting his otherwise handsome features.

"Are you ready for a good, hearty breakfast before our ride, my dear?" he asked in his usual "charming" way.

"I haven't been awake very long," she answered. "I need to take a little walk before sitting down to eat. Shall we go out and tend to the horses? We could go ahead and have them saddled up and ready to go as soon as we've eaten. By then my appetite will be ready."

Dora Kincaid could have always sat down to a nice big breakfast before starting the day. Getting Delgrin away from the house right at that moment was more important than the rumbling of her stomach. He nodded assent his smile telling her that he was pleased with her suggestion.

"As you wish," he agreed. "If you'd like I'll have Mrs. James hold ours until seven. Everyone else will be done and gone. Then we can dine alone."

Delgrin's desire to have Dora to himself worked right in with her plans. She agreed at once to his suggestion to his perceptible pleasure. After Jill had received these instructions the couple strolled out to the barn. Glancing around, Dora caught a glimpse of Lilly leading two mounts around the corner of the house.

To while away the time was simple enough. Adrian was easily wrapped up in his attention to his animals during the next half-hour.

She made Spirit a big part of their conversation asking questions about his lineage, his age, which was four years, and his manner. Adrian answered all of them with the aplomb of a man who knows his horses.

"You two have really hit it off," he observed. "I made a good pick for you."

"Yes, you did," Dora admitted without hesitation.

"He could become yours, you know," he implyed.

The time had slipped away before they realized. Mrs. James had to yell for them to come to breakfast before it grew cold.

"I do believe I'm ready for it now," Dora concurred, glad to go eat.

When they returned to the dining room they found Jill removing two sets of dishes from the table. Dora gave her an inquiring look about Lilly with a quick glance to the ceiling towards the girl's room to which Jill gave a slight nod. *So far, so good.*

"Delles and Lilly gone?" Delgrin half asked, half stated.

"Yes," Jill replied over her shoulder as she disappeared through the kitchen door.

After a filling breakfast Dora excused herself for the bathroom. Delgrin then followed suit. With him so occupied she took the opportunity to tell Jill that she had returned Delles's gun to his holster, the reason why, and not to forget to take it. Jill acknowledged.

As soon as Delgrin was back the two of them left for their morning ride. Dora could only hope that Jill would get out all right. After she had disposed of Adrian Delgrin she wouldn't be able to return to the ranch until later to retrieve her bags. His men would wonder where he was. Instead she would be riding across country back to Doc Hyatt's place to make sure this mother and daughter were safe.

High clouds kept the day's heat at bay. For almost an hour they rode over rolling plain. Here and there were small herds of cattle grazing on prairie grasses. They even spotted two herds of deer and one of pronghorns. When they had topped a high ridge that dropped at a sharp grade to the valley floor several hundred feet down slope Dora reined in her mount. She slipped from her saddle. This was as good a spot as any, far enough from the house, and long enough to have given Jill James time to make her escape.

"This shows real promise, Adrian," she called, making a sweep of her arm toward the valley. "Along this ridge line and down through this valley looks like the right type of terrain for drilling." While he would think oil, she meant bullet.

Adrian dismounted to join her. "This had to be far enough away from the house. Been nice if it could have been a little closer in. Handier to get to that way."

"Ah, but one must go to where the oil is to find it," she sighed. "This country is quiet and peaceful out here. There's a certain beauty in the prairie. I think I shall like working at this place."

"I like being out here with you."

He put an arm around her shoulders. Her first instinct was to punch him in the gut with her elbow. Instead she forced herself to remain relaxed. Now was the time to offer the bait.

"I've been thinking about your offer to call this a second home," she contemplated aloud. She added in haste as a teaser to pique his desire, "Just the same this isn't definite, yet. After being here for the rest of the week I should have an answer to your offer. I'd like to get to know you better."

Now she was pandering to him. If she had this lustful lecherous character half figured he would jump right out of the water for this next lure. Dora gazed into his eyes with an alluring "what are you going to do about it" look.

Delgrin swallowed the bait, the sinker, the line, and even the rod. His arm dropped to her waist. "Now is as good a time as any to start getting better acquainted, Dora, darling. Don't you agree?"

She allowed him to turn her by the shoulders until she faced him. This fish turning out to be of the sucker family was now inspecting the prized lure she had cast in front of him. Time to wiggle it a little.

"I'm not too versed on such matters," she cooed through puckering lips. "I was brought up with such a sheltered life."

That brought the sucker in even closer. "Let me take care of those matters for you," he offered. "I can give you everything you could ever want. You won't ever have to work again."

In response, part of the lure quivered into an enticing, moist, red curvature, exposing fine white pearls within. The sucker swam straight for the hook.

And got it! Dora's left hook sent him staggering backward a good ten feet before he sprawled flat on his back. Gun fighting wasn't her only ability. Other talents her father had taught her included keeping in shape and using her fists. Knowing how to properly pack a punch she could have beaten the hell out of him. While the idea was

61

tempting just a beating was far too good for him. She began to taunt him as he lay groveling in surprise on the ground.

"You despicable pig!" she hissed in arrogance. "I'd rather kiss a cactus over you!" She towered over him in defiance goading him.

As he managed to stagger to his feet anger and confusion mingled in his expression. He clasped his jaw also seeking for some understanding. "Now, Dora, maybe I was—"

"Don't Dora me, you scum," she growled. Now that she had smashed his pitiful ego she was going to trample it into the dirt. "Maxwell was right about you, you child molester! I have news for you, you big jerk. Jill and Lilly are both gone. You'll never see them again!"

A minatory scowl crossed his face. As she suspected he had a short temper with a shorter fuse. "You've got a deal with Templeton? Lady, you just said the wrong thing!" He started to reach for the weapon at his side.

"Touch it and you're dead, buster! Kincaid's the name!"

Startled by her statement he became aware of the pistol she was packing on her own hip her hand poised above it. His jaw dropped. Stark reality shut it again. His mouth curled into a vicious snarl. "So, Templeton hires a gun slinging woman does he? To hide behind her petticoat? I always knew he was a scoundrel and a sneak. You must be related to Amos—"

All of a sudden he went for his gun. Dora's own weapon became an instant blur exploding into life. BLAM! Delgrin was knocked back from the direct hit. Becoming useless his gun dropped to the ground next to its lifeless owner. Her bullet had shattered his wicked heart.

I warned him. Got a debt to settle now. She smiled to herself holstering her gun. For her first kill she felt a satisfying justice.

Templeton had demanded proof of a finished job. Bringing back Delgrin's pistol was the proof he wanted. Since the grip had been hand crafted for Farius who had been Max's friend Templeton would recognize it. Dora knelt to pick it up.

CRACK! The sting of hot lead seared her shoulder an instant before she heard the rifle report. Following her instincts she pitched herself over the ridge onto the steeper slope of the hill.

From somewhere behind her the shot had come. The terrain in this area was rocky and rolling providing an ample number of hiding places for a bushwhacker. Not knowing where the ambush came from, and with only her shorter-range pistol against a rifle she stayed below the edge of the ridge. Lying on her stomach she faced the crest of the ridge with her gun held in both hands ahead of her.

She watched and waited.

Moments later the clip of distant hoof beats reached her ears. Dora crawled to the top of the ridge in time to watch the sniper riding over the top of the next knoll. He was too far away for Dora to make a good shot, or for him to be recognized. Even his horse showed no distinguishable marks. From this distance she guessed that his mount might be a chestnut or bay.

Hot, wet pain began to stiffen her shoulder. Ripping her left sleeve open she examined the wound as best she could. Across the back corner of her shoulder was a shallow lesion. The injury appeared to be superficial. Had she not knelt down just before the bullet struck her the shot could have been lethal.

Ripping strips from her petticoat she bandaged the wound as well as she could with one hand. For the second time she went after Delgrin's pistol sticking it into her gun belt under her dress. Retrieving her horse which had wandered a few yards away Dora spurred off in the direction that the sniper had taken.

When she reached the knoll that the ambushing stranger had ridden from he was no longer in sight. She discovered his horse's tracks near the crest. Dora followed his trail which led in the general direction of the Delgrin ranch house. At the bottom on the other side of the knoll however, the tracks turned into a shallow wash heading toward open prairie. Their spacing told her that he was riding fast.

She followed a short distance to assure herself of the direction the man had taken. The tracks continued due west out of the wash when the course of his trail turned to the south. After crossing several more rises and washes in pursuit she was convinced that he was heading for open country. Out of sight he had too much of a lead to catch.

The pain of her shoulder was beginning to make her dizzy. In her condition further pursuit at this quick pace was unwise. Dora studied the hoof prints for a clue. The shoes were well worn, but showed no distinguishing marks. She was about to turn her mount back toward the ranch when the glint of the mid-morning sun on an object a short distance up the trail caught her eye. She rode up to investigate. There in the dust lay a freshly thrown horseshoe.

Before heading back toward the ranch house she studied the tracks ahead. Here was a little bit of luck. If she could find the horse that had thrown a right rear shoe she just might find the bushwhacker. She had a score to settle with this scoundrel.

Dora pressed her steed toward the late Delgrin's home as fast as her injured shoulder and the rising heat of the day would allow. Whoever this would-be assassin had been was baffling. At first she had suspected that one of Delgrin's hands had followed from afar and was taking revenge after she had shot his boss. If so he would have ridden up to check on Delgrin, not just ride away toward open prairie.

The next logical reasoning was that he was one of Templeton's men who had been sent out to dispose of her so that he wouldn't have to pay her fee. According to her father's account of his old ranch buddy that was out of character for him. Still a man could change. Her father hadn't seen Templeton for a few years.

For a man to follow them unnoticed through this country could have been done easy enough. Neither she nor Delgrin would have been expecting to be followed. Once they had stopped the bushwhacker just had to sneak close enough for a good shot. With Dora and Delgrin being engaged in a showdown the ambushing dog could have moved in quite close without being detected. Since Templeton's spread bordered Delgrin's the sniper would have ridden back to there if he were Max's man. He had headed for open country after the shooting however, instead of toward Templeton's ranch. Besides Templeton no one knew of her real purpose with Delgrin. This made Max the prime suspect, but the bushwhacker's direction of departure didn't support that thesis.

Although her shoulder still throbbed from the wound the bandage had stopped the bleeding. Feigning half-consciousness she slumped over her horse's neck as she rode up to the Delgrin house.

"Help!" she cried in anguish. "Help, somebody! I've been shot!"

10

Slim rushed out of the barn in response to her call. "Josh! Git out here quick!" he shouted as he ran to her aid. A second man dashed from the barn. Together they helped Dora down from her horse and into the house. Shock filled their faces when they saw her bloody bandage.

"You've been hurt, ma'am! What happened?" Slim demanded.

"Ambush!" she moaned, gasping the news. "Mr. Delgrin—hurt bad—maybe dead—I'm afraid. I'm lucky—to be alive."

"Where is he?"

"An hour's ride—south. On a high ridge—like a plateau. There's a valley below—lots of trees in it."

"I know the place. I'll take Morey with me out there to git 'im. Josh, you ride into town and git Doc Hyatt. Tell 'im we got Miss Kinley here with a gunshot wound. She looks hurt bad."

"Okay, Slim!" Josh bolted out the door.

Just then Jill James appeared at the kitchen doorway. Dora was surprised, but managed to hide her reaction to seeing the woman still present in the house. "Mrs. James," Dora groaned.

"Mrs. James," Slim commanded, "help me git Miss Kinley to a bed. Watch after her till the doc comes."

They helped Dora to Delgrin's room since his was the only bedroom on the first floor. Slim left Jill to tend to Dora's care while he carried on with his task. As soon as he had left the house Dora was off the bed to watch from the bedroom window. Jill hurried closer to offer her a helping hand.

"Are you strong enough to get up?" Jill asked, her question laced with concern.

"Except for a sore, stiff shoulder I'm fine," Dora assured her. "The damage isn't as bad as one might imagine. The act was to get rid of the men. Tell me why are you still here? What happened?"

Jill James's face filled with worry. "Not long after you left I was preparing to take the second horse that Lilly had left out front. Then Josh came into the house through the front door. He was trying to figure out why there was an extra horse standing out front saddled and ready to ride.

"I had to think quick. I told him that perhaps the animal had something wrong with it, and there had been no time to put it away and get another one before Delles and Lilly had to leave. It seemed like a weak reason at the time, but I convinced Josh that they must have ridden double on to town.

"Just to be sure Josh wanted to check to see if Delles was in his room. He took me up there with him. Of course Josh didn't find Delles in his room. He didn't find Lilly in hers either so that he conceded that my assumption was right.

"Josh took the horse and put it away. Since then someone has always been around. I haven't been able to get out to the barn to get another ride ready."

"Are Slim, Josh, and Morey the only ones left to run the ranch?" Dora queried.

Jill nodded. "The rest of the hands are still out on drive. Where are the three of them going?"

Dora had been watching the three men through the bedroom window as they saddled up and rode away on their extempore missions. Slim and Morey had become mere specks on the horizon before she turned to Mrs. James.

"Now they're all gone," Dora said. "Riding hard Slim and Morey will be there and back in less than an hour. They're going after Adrian's body. As far as Josh's errand to fetch Hyatt I'd like us to catch the good doctor before he gets out of town. Let's get ourselves out of here while we have time. Start packing. I'm going to hitch up a team and wagon. Get your stuff together as quick as you can."

"That shouldn't take long. We don't have much."

The two women went in opposite directions, Jill upstairs to pack, and Dora outside to the barn. The pain in her shoulder hampered the movement of her left arm, but she managed to get the team and wagon ready. Placing Spirit's saddle and tack in the back of the wagon she hitched him as one of the team. When she returned to the house she found Jill in Lilly's room. In haphazard fashion Jill was stuffing her daughter's few belongings into a small satchel all the while looking quite pale.

"Are you all right?" Dora asked.

"I—haven't packed my things yet," Jill stammered. "I tried to. Even though I hated the man his dead body on my bedroom floor—I'm sorry, it's just—"

Dora patted Jill's shoulder to offer solace. "I'll bring your things in here."

She caught Jill's grateful smile as she hurried into the room across the hall. With nimbleness she stepped around the body which had since slid off the bed. Dora checked the few dresser drawers for their meager contents. Stacking these on the bed she grabbed Delles's weapon from its holster to lay the revolver on top of the clothes. A good weapon could come in handy. Dora carried the stack of clothes into Lilly's room to place them upon the bed. Jill was just opening a second satchel. She started to stuff in her clothes.

"If you're done with this bag I'll take it down with me," Dora volunteered, grasping the grips. Jill nodded assent.

Dora carried the satchel out back where the wagon stood waiting. Next she brought her own two pieces of luggage down. On the third trip she found Jill ready to go. Her color and composure had returned. They wasted no time stashing the last piece of luggage and putting their rig on the road. They'd made it in twenty minutes.

"I never want to see this place again," Jill muttered as they drove away. "Are you sure Delgrin is dead?"

He's dead, shot through the heart," Dora assured her. "That should make you more than happy. You're out of his clutches now."

"Of Adrian's, yes, but not of Slim's. I won't rest easy until Lilly and I are far away from here. Lilly and I aren't safe yet. Slim will be out to get us for sure."

"Slim? Why Slim?"

"To protect his own hide. He wants the ranch, but he has a price on his head, and I know it. Do you think he'd let me stand in his way of getting the ranch? I could put a noose around his neck. With his neck and the ranch at stake he'll be out to get me."

Recollections began to click into place in Dora's brain. Jill's last statement had reminded her of something she knew about Slim, but had forgotten. She realized that what Jill had just said was true. Even more imperative She had to get Jill and Lilly away, far away, from there. Slim was more dangerous to them than Sheriff Hilliard.

As they reached the crest of the road where Dora had first seen the ranch buildings the day before they could see the trail ahead of them stretch into the horizon. In the distance she guessed about a mile away a cloud of dust was being raised. Someone was coming in their direction at a fair clip. Dora turned the team around.

"They may be coming to the ranch," she reasoned. "Until we know if they're friend or foe we'd better take refuge back at the house. There's no cover on this ridge."

She urged the horses back along the road at a quicker gait than they had been going. Leaving the team and wagon behind the house the women hastened through the dwelling to a front window where they could watch the approaching road to the ranch.

After a few minutes another wagon appeared on the crest followed by a single horseman. As the approaching party took the fork to the ranch off the main road they drew close enough for the women to recognize them.

"It's Doctor Hyatt!" Jill exclaimed. "He's got Lilly with him. That's Josh riding behind."

"Josh hasn't had time to reach town and get back with Doctor Hyatt already," Dora mused. "He must have met them on the road. That means that Hyatt and Lilly were on the way here."

"Why would they come here?" Jill posed.

"To get you. Remember, you were to show up not long after Lilly. You didn't. Now they're looking for you. We may be able to use this change of affairs to our advantage. When they get here send the doctor on in. I'll be back in Adrian's room waiting."

Peter Hyatt found his waiting patient in good spirits in spite of the wound. He tended to the injury in a deft and professional manner replacing her soaked piece of cloth with a clean bandage.

"Well, Miss Kinley, you did an admirable job of doctoring your own wound considering what you had to work with," the doctor told her as he was finishing up. "Just be gentle with your shoulder. I do say you've recovered well. Josh had you half dead."

"I bounce back fast." Having been sitting on the edge of the bed she got to her feet. "I should like to return to town. Can you give Jill, Lilly, and me a ride there in your wagon?"

"I was coming to get Jill, and you now, but what about Josh? As sure as sugar he'll object to Jill and Lilly leaving."

"I'll take care of him. You'll find another wagon sitting out back with all of our luggage in it. Take Lilly with you to help you carry it to your wagon. Also, loosen the big bay stud from the harness and tie him to the back of your wagon. His saddle and tack are in the wagon. Grab it too, please. I'm supposed to be too weak to do it."

Nodding agreement Peter Hyatt opened the bedroom door for Dora. As she entered the living room where the two James and Josh were waiting she resumed the role of a semi-helpless woman. Dora went straight to Jill while Pete and Lilly hurried outside.

"Mrs. James, Doctor Hyatt tells me that I should have a personal attendant to help me until I'm healed again. If you're interested I'm offering you the job. That includes your daughter. She should come along."

Josh butted in. "Uh, wait a minute, Miss Kinley, she can't."

"Oh? Why not?" Dora pressed. "Mrs. James is more than capable of stating her own decisions. With Mr. Delgrin gone she may not wish to stay here." She turned to Jill again. "Would you like the job?"

"I'd be delighted to take it," Jill accepted.

Josh fidgeted with his hands rubbing his rough, weathered face, trying to determine what to do. "Ah, are you planning to leave soon?"

"Right away," Dora asserted. "I'm sure the local sheriff will need a statement from me so that he can take proper action. Doctor Hyatt will be driving us into town."

"But Doc Hyatt should wait here until Slim and Morey bring Mr. Delgrin in," Josh objected, seeking for a way to detain the party. "He'll sure need a doctor's attention—"

Sounding sympathetic Dora cut him off. "You don't need a doctor for Mr. Delgrin you need an undertaker. Mr. Delgrin was shot square in the heart. You can rest assured that your former boss is quite dead. I came close enough to death myself. Now I need to see the sheriff. Time is of the essence to track that bushwhacker down. The later the time gets the harder to catch that man."

Dora turned her attention once again to Jill. They engaged in conversation about Jill's help for Dora, ignoring a flustered Josh.

Before long Pete Hyatt re-entered the house through the front door.

"Shall we go, Doctor?" Dora asked.

"I'm ready," he said. Showing chivalry he pulled the door open for the women. They paraded out leaving a fretful looking Josh undecided what to do standing in the house alone.

Soon the foursome was leaving the ranch behind. No one spoke until they reached the junction of the main road.

"What happened out here today?" Pete inquired once they had turned onto the main road to town. "Josh said you were ambushed."

"Adrian and I were about an hour's ride south of here. Someone must have tailed us," Dora related. "We had stopped on a ridge, made ourselves perfect targets when the bushwhacker made his move. I don't know who he was or why he shot me. Reason told me to lie still and play dead until he rode away. He was too far away for me to see who he was. I tried to follow his trail, but he got away."

"Maybe he didn't want any witnesses," Hyatt interjected. "You were lucky his aim was off."

Dora frowned. She knew that Hyatt's hypothesis was incorrect. If the bushwhacker were just after Delgrin with his job already done by her he could have just stayed out of sight until she had ridden away. For some unknown reason she had also been the target right along with Delgrin she was sure. That reason she would have to discover.

"You must have been on your way to the ranch," she ventured, changing the subject. "To find what happened to Jill?"

"Yes. When Jill didn't show up in a reasonable time we decided to come looking. We met Josh on the road. After he told me about you he wanted to know why I had Lilly with me. I told him that she was suffering from lentigines and would have to be quarantined. Josh didn't get too close after that."

"What are lentigines?" Dora quizzed.

"Freckles."

Dora laughed. "Maybe she caught them from me."

Everyone chuckled which helped to ease the sobering conditions.

They rode on in silence for some time, Jill and Lilly riding in the back to allow Dora the comfort of the seat because of her injury.

About half way to town the road cut down the side of a gorge, then across a wash. While they were in the wash all at once three riders galloped up from around a bend. They were Slim, Josh, and

Morey. They had been riding fast for their lathered horses were breathing hard. The trio blocked the roadway. Hyatt reined in.

Mother and daughter sat in rigid fear in the back while Peter Hyatt appeared perturbed at the trio's actions.

"If you gentlemen will be kind enough to move," he said in a gruff voice, "I'm transporting my patient back to town."

"Sure, Doc," Slim retorted, "just as soon as we git what we come after. Mrs. James, you and your daughter are goin' back to the ranch with us. There are some things, uh, of Mr. Delgrin's that you need to clear up."

Dora offered an alternative. "I'm sure you can handle it, Slim. Mrs. James is now working for me as my nurse. Doctor Hyatt suggested that I have one. Mrs. James was free to take the job."

Slim tipped his hat. "Miss Kinley, I understand your need. But, you see Mrs. James isn't free to go just yet. She was in debt to Mr. Delgrin. Being in charge of his ranch now I have to collect that debt."

"You said that Mrs. James *was* in debt to Mr. Delgrin who is now dead is he not?" Dora countered. "Where is he now?"

"Yeah, he's dead. We hauled his body back to the ranch."

"Then his death frees Mrs. James of any debt she may have owed him, unless you have some contractual proof that you or anyone else have the right to collect such a debt," she reasoned.

"I don't know about any contractual—whatever, but Mrs. James owes the debt and I'm gonna collect it," Slim insisted.

"Well, I'm not up to debating the issue at this time. Tell me what her debt is and I'll pay it right now." Dora opened her handbag.

"You don't seem to understand, Miss Kinley. Jill James's debt can't be paid with money. She and her daughter must return to the ranch right now."

"Really, Slim, this is getting silly," Dora sighed in impatience. "You make it sound as if Mrs. James and Lilly were slaves. Slavery was abolished in this country years ago. I'll be in the hotel for a few days. You can come see me there to settle this. You gentlemen need to clear the roadway. Please proceed, Doctor."

Pete lifted the reins in response. Slim reached out and grabbed the harness of the nearest horse. The other two men stood their ground.

"Mrs. James and Lilly are going back with us," Slim demanded in a stern voice. "This is none of your concern, Miss Kinley. If you give us any more trouble we'll take all of you back."

None of the men had pulled his gun since the wagon party appeared to be unarmed. As a gesture of enforcement of Slim's threat Josh and Morey rested their hands on the butts of their revolvers.

Dora Kincaid stood up in the wagon her revolver now very visible on her hip. The surprise on the men's faces betrayed their reaction to the strange contrast in front of them.

"You'd better plan on using those guns," she growled, "because you're not taking Jill and Lilly from this wagon. Unhand that horse, Slim Cramer. The only thing you'll get is a noose around your neck."

Shock, fear, and hate blazed in Cramer's eyes all at once. Someone had recognized him in his true identity. Josh and Morey sat frozen to their saddles. With his eyes riveted to Dora's pistol Cramer finally found his tongue.

"Take her, boys!" he barked.

11

A revolver roared in response. BLAM! BLAM! Morey's weapon never left his holster. Josh's had barely cleared his. BLAM! BLAM!

Slim's shot had been an instant too slow. The bullet splintered the wood at the rear edge of the wagon. Before the gunfire quit echoing around the gorge three men lay dead on the ground. Each had a bullet through what was left of his wicked heart.

Hyatt gazed in wonder at the three corpses lying on the ground in front of their team and wagon. Jill and Lilly peered over the back edge of the seat. Their eyes bulged frog-eyed with amazement.

"What happened?" Lilly said, gasping in astonishment.

"That's mighty straight shooting, Dora," the doctor managed. "I haven't seen anyone out shoot three gunmen before. Come to think of it I haven't ever seen a female pack a gun like that, much less outdraw and shoot down someone in a fight. No one's been known to shoot like that since Amos Kincaid was around."

"He was my father." She holstered her gun, which vanished within the folds of her dress once more. "My real name is Dora Kincaid."

"Like father, like daughter," he mused aloud. "Dora Kinley is Dora Kincaid." He pointed at Slim's corpse. "You called him Slim Cramer. Cramer was a notorious fast gun from Texas until a couple of years ago when he disappeared. He had a price on his head for killing a U. S. Marshal in Amarillo. You out shot Slim Cramer *after* you out shot two other men."

Dora climbed down from the wagon. "I recognized Cramer from my father's collection of wanted posters, but I couldn't recall at first who he was. The tip off came when Jill told me that he was a threat to her and Lilly. I realized, then, that he was dangerous.

"When he grabbed your horse's harness I knew that gave me an advantage. To get to his gun he had to let go to sit up straight.

"Also, masquerading under an alias while working for Delgrin he may have been out of practice."

She checked the hoof prints being left by the three rider-less horses. None of them was missing a shoe.

"You forgot advantage number three," Pete was saying.

"Which is?"

"Besides using an alias yourself to hide your last name as Slim was you're a beautiful woman. How many men could be that committed to gun you down?"

Dora reached her opposite hand across to her wounded shoulder in emphasis. "At least one other besides Cramer."

"Are you sure?" Pete countered. "His aim was off."

"Maybe not. I moved just when he shot at me. Some men will shoot anyone."

Jill threw in a request. "From what we have just witnessed here I'd like to know who gunned down Adrian Delgrin. I was under the impression that the sniper who shot you, killed him."

Dora pulled out her revolver to dump the empty shells into her hand. She handed them to Jill, afterward putting fresh rounds into the chamber in their place. With a puzzled countenance Jill stared at the casings given her. She looked askance at Dora.

"These are the shells I have fired today," Dora informed her. "I didn't get a shot off at the sniper. Count them."

"Four!" Jill answered in satisfaction. "May you go down in the annals of history as the avenging angel."

"Thank you, Jill. I don't know about angel, but I like the title. Pete, we have three bodies to haul in. There's a big reward to collect on at least Slim. Let's load them up."

By the time Pete had gotten down to help her Dora had already tossed one of the dead men across his saddle. She took care of the second man while he loaded up the last. They lashed the bodies down with the men's own lariats, then strung their horses onto the rear of the wagon. She rounded up their dropped pistols and placed them in the back of the wagon.

"You're a rather remarkable woman," Pete told her when they were under way again. "You threw those two men across their saddles like a couple of blankets. And you with an injured shoulder. Remind me never to pick a fight with you."

She laughed at his remark. "Papa taught me how to take care of myself. When one knows how, throwing a dead man across a saddle isn't too difficult even with a sore shoulder. Pa was a thorough teacher. I keep in shape, too. Working out is good for the morale."

"What are you going to do now, Dora?" Lilly asked.

"When we get to town Pete can make arrangements to collect the reward on Cramer, then deliver these three to the undertaker if he will. You and your mother can stay with me at the hotel."

Pete Hyatt protested. "Staying at the hotel now isn't safe. I won't agree to that for the safety of all of you. Delgrin still has other loyal followers around there. No one in town knows that he's dead yet. They won't until we report it, although people are going to wonder when we haul in these three. I'll have Barclay the undertaker take a trustworthy deputy out to pick up Delgrin's and Delles's remains. Lilly told me about the skillet incident.

"With Delles not at the hotel someone I'm sure is wondering what has happened to him. Going back to the hotel is not a good idea. You'll all be much safer staying at my place."

"For the safety of Jill and Lilly I'm glad you offered," Dora answered for the three of them. "We accept."

Upon reaching town Pete parked his wagon by his house. Since his house lay on the outskirts of town just a few citizens noticed the unusual procession arrive at the Hyatt residence and office. He ushered the three women inside.

"Make yourselves at home. I'm going to load those three bodies into the wagon and cover them up. Old Barclay the undertaker doesn't give hoots about Delgrin or any of his men, but I don't want everyone else around town knowing about them just yet."

"I'll give you a hand," Dora offered. "Jill, Lilly, shall we get our baggage off the wagon to make room for the bodies?"

While the two of them were transferring the bodies to the wagon to be hauled to the undertakers Dora made a request. "You're going to need the means to pay for the burial of these three. I suggest that you sell their horses and tack to raise the money. Any that's left over can be given to the James. When you take them to the livery to sell them take my horse and tack to sell, too, please. Give that money to the James as well. That's just a small contribution from Adrian Delgrin. Do what you think best with these firearms."

"Okay, Dora," Pete complied, laying the guns in the wagon.

"One more thing," she added. "Do you know how Sheriff Hilliard spends his evenings?"

"He plays poker down at the saloon almost every night," Pete informed her. "Why do you want to know?"

"Remember, I have a report to make to the sheriff. I think that tonight would be the best time to make it," she said, a mysterious gleam in her eye. "Meanwhile, would you take me to the telegraph office? I'm going to wire Denver about Slim Cramer. We need official identification on him to collect the reward. Hilliard isn't to know."

"But the operator can't be trusted," Hyatt reminded her.

"Don't worry," she assured him. "I'll take care of that."

Doc Hyatt dropped her off at the telegraph station while he drove on to take care of his several errands. "I may be rather late," he told her before driving away. "I have something important to do. Help yourself to my pantry for dinner for you and the James. Don't wait for me. Good luck in there."

Dora went in to deliver her message to the operator. While he sent it she stood there waiting. After listening to the first several dozen dots and dashes she stepped behind the counter and pressed the barrel of her gun against the nape of his neck. He froze at the feel of hard steel.

"Mister, I can read code," she growled. "I didn't tell you to send the latest weather report to La Junta. You key the right message you've been given, or I'm going to separate your ears from the rest of you. The quick way!"

"Y-yes, Ma'am!"

With the forceful persuasion of cold steel against his neck the second time he sent the message she'd given him. She'd requested an immediate answer to the 'gram so she found a comfortable spot to wait and keep the operator under her surveillance. While she waited no one else came into the office.

Fifteen minutes later the clicker came to life. Dora watched as the operator copied the message down. She swept it up from in front of him and pushed it into her pocket.

"Acknowledge it," she ordered. "Then shut your key down."

The operator complied, signaling all that his key was going off.

"Now you're going to close a little early today. There are a few people in town that aren't to know about this answer just yet. Since you can't be trusted you're going to spend the night here."

Dora locked the front door and raised the CLOSED sign. Then she tied him with bandage from the doctor to his chair. After she gagged him she reversed her pistol and struck him with the handle on the back of his head in just the right place. He slumped into unconsciousness.

"There. That will keep you out for several hours. When you come to you won't even have a headache."

The time was almost five o'clock in the afternoon, just minutes before the normal closing time. Dora left by the back door, locking it behind her with the key left in the lock. She hurried back to Doctor Hyatt's house where Lilly and Jill were happy to see her. Visual relief adorned both their faces.

"I'm glad you're back. This whole affair has me feeling rather on edge right now," Jill confessed. "Your and Pete's welfare concern me. There aren't any other two people in the world that I'd rather have on our side right now. I'd hate to see any harm come to either of you."

"Pete said that he might be late for dinner. He had something important to do," Dora reported. "He didn't say what, but he did say to go ahead and fix dinner. Jill, why don't you see what you can find in the kitchen to whip up? I could enjoy a good meal of yours again."

"This will be the first meal in a long time that I'm going to enjoy making," the elder James replied in satisfaction.

Jill went to work in the kitchen. Finding a bedroom Dora set about changing her outfit. Lilly had followed and watched her. Dora removed her damaged dress to reveal blue jeans and a dark shirt. From her luggage she took a leather Stetson of black.

On the corner dresser was a small mirror which she used to help herself wipe off all her makeup. She brushed her hair down and back into a long ponytail. Pulling on the Stetson and a pair of boots Dora looked herself over. The change took about ten minutes. Dora Kinley was now Dora Kincaid.

Lilly, who had been watching her in total fascination, at last spoke. "Dora, you're just full of surprises."

"That's what keeps life interesting," Dora responded as she finished up the transformation.

When they sat down for dinner Jill stared at her in amazement.

"Why, you look ten years younger!" she exclaimed. "You hardly look like the same woman. You could pass for your own younger sister."

Taking the comment as a future idea Amos Kincaid's offspring winked her eye. "That's what I intended. That way the bad guys are kept guessing who I really am."

The doctor had not yet returned by the time dinner was over. While waiting the three companions sat around making meaningful conversation. Dora led it keeping her two new female friends busy answering questions about what they were going to do next. She knew this preoccupation would ease the tension they still experienced while giving her something constructive to do until dark.

Dusk was settling in before they heard the good doctor's wagon draw up outside. He was not alone. Peering out a window the trio watched as he helped a second, shadowy figure out of the wagon's bed. The second shadow limped along with the aid of a cane as if he were an old man. Aided by the good doctor the newcomer hobbled toward the house.

Dora opened the door to let them in. Not until the pair had entered the lighted room could she see the man's features. A fine looking man he wasn't old, in his mid thirties she reckoned, but she didn't recognize him. Jill and Lilly's gasps of astonishment showed her that they knew the stranger. Both of her female companions looked as if they had seen a ghost. For all purposes they could have.

The newcomer gazed at Jill and Lilly James with blue, amorous eyes for eternal seconds before he spoke in deep, gentle tones. "Jill darling. Lilly." He limped toward them at a quicker hobble.

Jill stood petrified. "Oh!" she gasped. "You—can't be! But you are—Arnold!"

12

Doctor Hyatt's nod of affirmation was all Jill needed to rush into Arnold's arms with an instant deluge of tears. This sudden emotional reunion of her parents prompted Lilly to join in.

"Papa!" She exclaimed as she clasped his waist in a tight embrace.

"Arnold! Arnold!" Jill kept repeating, her tears cascading down her cheeks onto his massive shoulder. "You're alive! You're alive!"

With tenderness Dora viewed this happy reunion. She slipped to Pete's side to question him about Arnold James who was supposed to be dead. "How is it that Arnold James has come back from the dead, Pete? Is this a miracle of modern medicine?"

"Actually, Dora, he's more than that. He's the miracle of a tenacious will. I've been waiting for this moment when I could see this couple reunited free from the clutches of that demon, Adrian Delgrin. I wanted you to be here too, because without you we wouldn't be witnessing this scene tonight."

"Thanks, Pete. What's Arnold's story?"

He patted her forearm in a gesture of patience. "As soon as this little reunion has settled down I'll tell you all."

While she waited Dora sized up Arnold James. Several inches shorter than the doctor he was a large-framed man with powerful arms and shoulders. The strength of his hands revealed that he wasn't afraid of work. Thick blond hair covered his crown. His handsome features portrayed determined yet gentle character. Somehow he had lived through the fall in the ravine, and that's the story that Dora was curious to hear about now. Jill and Lilly would want to know, too.

After an indeterminate period of time Dora guessed to be at least fifteen minutes Jill James managed to gain some composure. "Oh, Pete!" she exclaimed. "Why didn't you tell me that Arnold was still alive? Why did you hide him from me?"

Peter Hyatt shooed the James family over to a comfortable looking couch. "If you want to know sit down and I'll tell you the whole story the last secret to get off an old man's mind."

With Arnold James surrounded on each side by his two females and Dora Kincaid sitting nearby, Doc Hyatt began his story.

"When Delgrin's men brought Arnold in at least they had the decency to lay him in a wagon instead of throwing him over a horse. As I've said he was in mighty bad shape. I couldn't expect him to live. He wasn't even conscious enough to talk or hear. But Arnold had an astounding will to live. He had his two females to live for.

"Arnold was with me for maybe an hour when Jill managed to get here. I let her in to see him and to talk to him in hopes that her presence would bring him around. He never showed any outward sign of recognition though. There was no giving Jill any hope that Arnold would pull through. Instead I pronounced him dead and sent her home.

"Something told me that as long as he was alive Adrian had to be kept from finding out. I was sure that Delgrin was responsible for the 'accident.' To help me hide Arnold I called in old man Barclay. Since he's the undertaker and he hated Delgrin as much as I did, his part made our plan successful. We faked Arnold's funeral. Through my coaxing Jill agreed to keep the coffin closed since Arnold looked pretty beat up. She had already taken his appearance rather hard when she saw him in that condition. Another concern of hers was Lilly's reaction if she saw her father in such a mess."

Jill nodded in remembrance. "She didn't need to go through that. She'd taken the news of his death hard enough."

"For the next month Barclay and I kept Arnold in one of Barclay's extra coffins. If he hadn't made it we'd have dug up his weighted coffin at night and buried him in secret. After all we'd already had his funeral. He couldn't talk to us, but we managed to get soups and other liquids down him. Then, on the thirty-fourth day after his fall when I went in to see Arnold he opened his eyes and called me by name. Josiah Barclay and I just about kissed each other. That's a figurative statement of course.

"We wouldn't let Arnold talk much for the first few days in order to conserve his strength. We wanted him to get stronger before he tried. A few days later he had improved enough so that we let him tell us what happened. He said that he had seen a cow lying injured in the ravine and was going down to check it out. His job was to look for strays. Since the ravine was too steep to ride a horse down in safety he started to dismount to climb down alone. Just as he swung out of his saddle someone shot his horse in the flank. The animal bolted throwing both of them over the edge. As they slid into the ravine his horse rolled over on top of him. That's the last thing he could remember until he woke up and saw Josiah and me.

"Arnold just knew that he was set up. He had every reason to suspect that Delgrin was behind it. He told us that he wasn't blind to Adrian's attention to Jill. We told him about the fake funeral and that even Jill didn't know that he was alive. He wanted to take revenge on Delgrin right then, but there was no way he was going to get up and walk yet. His right leg had been so messed up when he was brought in that I didn't know if he would ever walk again if he lived. In fact I was glad Arnold was comatose when I reset all the breaks in that leg. The pain might have killed him.

"Sheriff Hilliard couldn't be trusted to make an investigation. If we had tried to call in outside help we couldn't have come up with enough evidence to convict Delgrin of any wrongdoing. Arnold's horse took a bullet, not him. I'm sure if the animal had to be destroyed he was led somewhere out in some ravine to be left to scavengers.

"We did get Arnold to promise not to try anything foolish even when he was well enough to walk. There was too much chance that Delgrin would find out that he was still alive and set out a second time to make sure he killed him. Arnold had to stay hidden and work on getting himself stronger while I would try to get Jill and Lilly away from the ranch. As you see he still needs a cane for that leg.

"Jill, we didn't like to hide Arnold from you, but we were afraid for your and Lilly's safety and for Arnold's life."

Jill gave her man a hug around the neck. "You and Josiah Barclay would've been at risk, too. I've got Arnold back again and that's all that matters. Adrian Delgrin will never bother us again."

"Neither will Slim Cramer," Dora added.

"Thanks to Dora," Hyatt reminded them. "I told Arnold all about you, young lady. By the way, you're looking a lot younger tonight than you were earlier today."

"I've got a 'date' tonight. I've got to look the part."

"A date, huh? With whom?"

"I'll tell you about it when I get back. This is a blind date. I haven't met him yet. I won't be long." Dora stood up and moved to the door. "Lilly, you take good care of your parents now. They have a farm to tend to again. They'll need your help." She was out the door before anyone could answer.

The Lamar saloon was just a few blocks away. She peeked over the entry. Putrid cigar smoke shrouded the already dim lanterns. A few of the tables supported the bodies of passed-out drunks. Others felt the heat of heavy poker games. Several stood open and ready to service fresh clientele.

Through the swinging doors Dora entered the saloon without fanfare. By easing the doors shut behind her she kept them from swinging to a noisy stop. Everyone was too engaged in his own affair to notice her entry. She sauntered around the perimeter of the room while surveying the occupants. The near end of the bar curved around to meet the wall. In that corner the lighting was poorer. Dora glided as quiet as a specter until she reached the corner stool obscured in the shadow. If anyone did glance up, her clothes and her hair tucked under her hat, along with the dimness, would have shrouded her sex.

From this vantage point she again scanned the room. During her reconnaissance two cowboys entered the saloon. After calling out an order to the bartender for drinks they sat down at a table near the center. At the bar one of the drunks managed to gain his feet. He stumbled toward the doors. Bumping into a table surrounded by poker players the drunk almost tumbled into the lap of the closest man. Irritated, the man shoved the drunk away. "Watch it, you clumsy oaf!" the player growled.

"Don' get pusshhy," the drunk slurred, "or I'll—"

One of the other men half rose from his chair to turn toward the drunk enough that Dora caught the glint of the metal object pinned to his chest. He clamped a big hand on the drunk's shoulder to silence the inebriated man. The sight of the star stopped the drunk's diatribe.

"Stow it, Hector," the man barked, "or I'll run you in for being drunk and disorderly. Now go on home and sleep it off."

"Sure, ssheriff. I was just going to say, I'd report him to you, but you already saw it. That'th okay. Forget it. No harm done." The drunk staggered to and disappeared through the swinging doors.

Sheriff Hilliard had resumed his seat by that time. Because of the drunk's encounter Dora's search for her quarry was already culminated in success. Hilliard was sitting with his left shoulder toward her. The balding, paunchy lawman appeared to be in his late thirties. His pudgy nose, cheeks, and chin even had a minatory look. His persona alone may have intimidated many a malefactor.

Pete had been right. She'd found the man she was after sitting in the saloon tonight playing his usual game of cards. Knowing this date would be short she searched for an opening to play her own hand.

The bartender had gone to the table where the two new customers had parked themselves. He came back to the bar to fill more orders which brought him to her end of the bar. Dora was leaning against the wall her hat pulled down to her eyes. As he filled the glasses the bartender happened to spot her shadowy figure.

"Be with yuh in a moment," he muttered as he sauntered away with a tray full of drinks. She gave a slight nod to his broad, retreating back.

When he came back in no big hurry he asked in a disinterested tone, "What'll it be?"

"A message to the sheriff," she murmured.

Her female voice startled him. Leaning closer he peered at her through the shadows. She sat like a stone waiting for his reaction.

"Why, you're a girl! You old enough to be in here?"

He had raised his voice but no one noticed his exclamation or question.

Keeping her gun in her hand she laid it on the bar in front of him. "I can use this better than any man in here. Is this sufficient proof that I'm old enough, or would you like a demonstration?"

"Hey, kid, don't try to be funny. If you ain't careful I'll sic the sheriff on you. He's right over there at that table." He nodded his portly head in the sheriff's direction.

"What? Are you deaf? Go ahead. I said I had a message for him. He owes a debt to a friend of mine. I came here to collect it. With this." She hoisted the pistol in emphasis.

The bartender changed his tune. "Now miss, don't go getting yourself in trouble. Why don't you be a good little girl, put your toy gun away, and run on home?"

She looked him over. He had a beer belly that rolled way over his belt. A stubby beard came up short for hiding his fat neck.

"Look, Tubs," she retorted, "if you don't have the nerve to go tattle to the sheriff go lick the customers' boots. I'll get his attention some other way."

"Tubs" burned a smoldering crimson. Gritting his teeth in anger he reached his chubby fingers for her lapels. "Why, you little—"

"Good at catching toy bullets in your teeth?"

The menace in her voice and the business end of her gun an inch below his nose stopped his hasty move. "Blowing a hole in your big fat head would get his attention," she added in a low growl. "My 'toy gun' looks a little meaner at this angle doesn't it?"

"I'll go get him," the bartender volunteered in a sudden change of heart. Eyeing her pistol still aimed at his middle he waddled a hasty retreat to the other end of the bar. Dora kept the muzzle trained on his fat paunch until he had reached the sheriff's side.

As "Tubs" bent close to the sheriff's ear Hilliard averted his attention from the card game to the bartender. They exchanged words to which "Tubs" nodded pointing in Dora's direction several times as he spoke. A perturbed look on his scowling face Hilliard squinted into the dark corner where Dora had melted back into the shadows again.

Putting down a cigar and the hand of cards just dealt to him the sheriff rose to his feet to step over to the bar. Dora pushed the Stetson to the back of her head. She walked beyond the bend of the counter to where the lanterns illuminated the room brighter.

"That's far enough, Hilliard," she barked. "Did 'Tubs' give you the message that I'm here to collect a debt from you for a friend?"

The sound of a woman's voice in the saloon shut the buzz of all conversation off like a tomb door. All eyes still capable of seeing turned to discover a gun-packing female, her hand resting near her holstered weapon, calling a show down to the sheriff. A new buzz at a lower volume rippled through the crowd. Hilliard stopped dead in his tracks.

"Young lady, I don't appreciate your humor," he scolded. "If you've been drinking too much—"

"I never drink," she cut him off. "I came to give you what you gave Farius Delgrin, his foreman Slade Jenkins, and the rest of his men two years ago. Only difference is I'm challenging you to a fair fight, more than you deserve, you murderer."

Hilliard stiffened. In a slow yet deliberate move he laid his shooting hand on the edge of the bar. "What are you driving at?"

"Let's tell the whole town. You helped Adrian Delgrin kill his own father in that phony Indian ambush. Slade Jenkins was there, too, and so you shot him down. Only thing is you didn't kill him outright. He lived long enough to tell his story. You can consider me their avenging angel."

"You? Why you're a woman, and not much more than a child at that. Besides it *was* renegade Indians. Where's your witness?"

"Indians, Ha! And child? Adrian Delgrin would disagree with you if he could, but you see he's dead. God is my witness."

"Dead?" Hilliard's shocked response received a muffled chorus from around the room. The bartender backed out of range.

"He's lying at the undertaker's morgue compliments of yours truly. He didn't die though until I found out how you fit into the picture. You must be pretty wealthy by now fleecing your own neighbors while hiding behind that tin badge. When this town finds out the truth about their sheriff you'll be through. There is just one of two places you're going from this saloon, to jail or the grave."

"That's right," a man at the sheriff's table agreed. "I've always wondered how you got all your money to play cards almost every night. Certainly not out of a sheriff's salary. I've seen you lots of times entering the bank with Adrian Delgrin and leaving with a fistful of cash. You're a traitor to your own town, Hilliard."

Hilliard's hands shook in nervous irritation. "This is crazy talk," he growled. "Don't listen to her. We all know that the posse testified that renegade Indians attacked our party. She's lying!"

Dora's accusations had been part conjecture, but she had managed to strike the right chord.

"Am I? Who helped Adrian stage Horatio's death to make it look like he was beaten to death in a drunken brawl? Who led Farius into an ambush by his own son? Wasn't it you and Slim Shelley? Except you knew him as Slim Cramer the outlaw gun fighter from Texas. Cramer is now also lying dead in the undertaker's office along with Josh and Morey. They got in my way."

"You? Beat the likes of Cramer—." He realized too late what he was saying.

"That's right. I came here to avenge those wronged. A man's conscience preys on him if he lies. It slows his reflexes, clouds his thinking. If I'm lying you have nothing to fear. You can be the executioner and walk out of here the sheriff like you've always been. I'll just be another statistic on your files. But if *you're* lying—."

The man at his table egged him on. "Come on, Hilliard. Where's the big tough sheriff that's suppose to protect this town? Are you going to let some little gun-toting gal put the big sheriff down?"

Hilliard's right hand slipped from the bar to his side. "She's crazy!" he scoffed no conviction in his voice. Sweat broke out on his balding brow. He backed up toward his table. "I oughta run you in."

"For what? You phony!" she hissed. "Even now you're blowing your bluff, you pompous wind bag. You aren't man enough to take my gun. How did you like working for a man who'd rape a little girl in front of her mother? Or treat her mother as some sex toy whenever he wanted keeping them both prisoners in his house? Did you get in on that deal, too?"

All of the most sober eyes were staring at the sheriff waiting for his response. His own eyes failed in their attempt to hold back the glare of his opponent burning holes into his soul.

"Molesting a mere child!" the man at the table accused. He spat at the sheriff's feet. Hilliard went for his gun. One deafening roar exploded in the saloon. The other men at the table scrambled aside as the body, scattering cards, chips, and shot glasses, rolled across the table and onto the floor. Dora's bullet on the way to his evil heart had severed one tip of the star upon his vest.

"When you find yourself a new sheriff remember that Petticoat is the one who gave you the chance to find a good one."

She was gone from the saloon before anyone could collect his senses. Before anyone could have had a chance to seek her out her shadow had merged into the melting pot of night.

13

Just half an hour had passed by the time Dora had returned to Doctor Hyatt's home and office. The three James were still sitting on the living room couch. While Lilly had fallen asleep on her father's broad shoulder Arnold and Jill were still in the thralls of getting reacquainted. A plate of food half gone sat on Arnold's lap.

Dora hurried on through the room so as not to disturb this happy and long overdue reunion. Entering the kitchen she found the doctor sitting at his table, finishing the last of his dinner. He glanced up with a smile as she walked in.

"Welcome back," he greeted. "Your 'date' didn't take very long. I'm glad there was enough of Jill's good cooking left for Arnold and me to warm up and eat. How is Arnold doing on his dinner?"

"He's got half a plateful left. Right now he's more occupied with Jill than with eating, even if it is her cooking."

"That would be expected. Two years was a long time to keep those two apart. I'll have to go in there and encourage him to eat all his dinner to keep his strength growing. How was your 'date'?"

"Successful at least for me. Because of it you can expect at any moment now someone seeking your services. Sorry for interrupting your evening meal, Pete. Your time will be wasted on him. He's a customer for Josiah Barclay to tend to."

"Interruptions come with the territory. Who is it this time?"

"Sheriff Hilliard."

"I might have guessed. Just the same I can't condone any of this killing, Dora. I'm dedicated to preserving life not taking it. At least you don't pick on the salt of the earth. Considering those you've stood against I don't condemn it either."

"I take on those who are past feeling except for themselves," she said. "Weigh them against Cain and you'll see what I mean. Besides other evils they were wanton killers as evil as Cain. I gave them a sporting chance which is more than they deserved."

Pete went to the basin to wash up while Dora leaned on the edge of the table with her knuckles.

"I understand your position, Pete," she continued. "That's why I make sure I save you a lot of trouble patching these bums up."

He gave her a wry smile as he dried his hands. "Sometimes justice gets served in 'interesting' ways."

Just then someone banged on his front door. Pete laid his towel next to the washbasin.

"Sounds like I'm wanted all right," he said as he walked out of the kitchen. "Better stay here. I would imagine your appearance here would raise some eyebrows."

Dora listened from the kitchen doorway while the doctor answered the knock. "Who is it?"

"Doc, we got the sheriff out here," someone exclaimed. "We think he's dead, but you'd better look at him just in case."

"I'm entertaining guests right now," Pete answered. "Carry him next door to my office. I'll be right there."

After she heard the doctor exit through the adjoining door into his office she sat down at the table and waited. A good ten minutes passed before Peter Hyatt returned to the house alone. When he stepped back into the kitchen he tossed the sheriff's badge onto the table to land in front of her.

"A souvenir for you," he told her. "One of the points is gone so they'll need a new badge for the next sheriff. Seems the missing point was right where the bullet hole in his chest is."

"That point gave me a target to aim at," she replied.

"As if you needed one," he reflected. "By bringing him here they saved me a trip to the saloon. One doesn't have to be a doctor to see that he was dead. I told them to take his body over to old man Barclay. Josiah is going to love you for all this business.

"After I pronounced him dead they expected me to ask what happened. I sure got the story. Seems the 'prettiest little gun fighter' anyone has ever seen just showed up from nowhere, put the sheriff on trial, found him guilty, passed the sentence, and disappeared just as quick. According to accounts there wasn't anyone on his side.

"One of Hilliard's carriers said that you called yourself an avenging angel. He said that he'd love to meet that angel again, but not the same way as the sheriff. What made you so sure he was a party to all of Delgrin's crimes?"

"I wasn't, at least not for everything. His link with Delgrin had me certain that he was aware of what was going on with Jill and Lilly. He took part in the ambush of Farius and his men. Those in his 'posse' should be arrested. I also guessed right that he knew Shelley to be Cramer. Hilliard even gave himself away on that."

"Who would ever expect to see a woman as a hired gun," he confessed. "But then, times are changing. Who hired you to kill these men?"

"I was only hired to get Delgrin. I'm sure you know by whom."

"Maxwell Templeton. Delgrin was a threat to his life, too."

"Figured you would. Slim and his cronies got in the way as you saw. That was okay because Slim was a threat to Jill's life. She knew who he was. Hilliard was a traitor to his town and just as much a killer as Delgrin. He was also a threat to the James family."

"You mean to say that you shot Hilliard just for what he was? Not for money?"

She shifted her position on the chair. "If I hadn't thought that Delgrin was despicable enough to kill him I wouldn't have, not for any amount of money. That goes for Sheriff Hilliard, too. Sure I don't mind making a buck as much as anyone, but I only put prices on scoundrels lower than skunks. As I said they were past feeling."

"I'm glad you said that," Pete declared digging into his pocket. "This pleases me to give this to you. The boys gave me the pleasure of passing this on to you because you aren't expecting it. Here."

He handed her a wad of bills. Taking it with reluctance Dora gave him a questioning stare. "What is this?"

"Hilliard was having a real streak of luck for a change they told me. He had won every hand tonight till you showed up. This is what was on him plus what he had won that was on the table. Except for what I sent on to pay Barclay for Hilliard's burial this is yours. Bill Oates picked the money up after you shot Hilliard. Since he has no next of kin that we know of everyone in the party decided to give this to the little lady who did this town a great service. I told them that I had an idea where you could be found and would pass it on to you."

"This is considerate of you, Pete, and everyone else. You could have kept it for yourself and no one would have been the wiser."

"Not me. You earned it. Besides," he chuckled, "I've seen you shoot. If you found out—." He let his statement trail off.

She grinned. "Doc, you'd have to do much worse than that to put yourself on my enemy list. I do applaud your honesty." She fanned the wad of money with her thumb. "How much is here?"

"I don't know. I didn't ask. Why don't you count it?"

Dora sat up to the table to start sorting the bills out according to size. "Who is Bill Oates?" she queried as she counted.

"President of the bank. He always played cards with Hilliard every night that the sheriff played which was most of them."

"Lean face with thin, gray hair and wire-rimmed glasses?"

"That's him. Delgrin couldn't get him under his thumb, but Bill had to walk a straight trail. Bankers are easier to find than doctors are. He was secretly building up bank reserves enough to loan everyone in debt to Delgrin so that they could pay him off. That would have taken Bill several more years. Much of the money came from what he won from Hilliard every night. That's because he was working with a card-shark named Winkle. Hilliard was a compulsive gambler. Delgrin paid him enough to support his habit. They were just getting back what he helped take from the people. Tonight they were letting Hilliard win for a change. He was certain his luck had changed."

"Nope, he still lost. Losers never win in the end. Hilliard was a big-time loser." Dora shook her head in wonder. "There's over twelve hundred dollars here!" she exclaimed with a whistle.

"That's right decent pay for one bullet," Pete ventured.

She rolled off some bills and handed them to Pete. "Here's a couple of hundred for your services to the James. You deserve it."

"I won't argue," he said tucking them into a shirt pocket. "I don't want to get on your list by refusing it."

"You're already on my list, my list of friends." She stepped to the kitchen door. "Let's go see how your guests are doing."

The scene in the living room hadn't changed since she'd returned to the house. Their setting was a photographer's delight.

"You two can't sit there all night," Pete teased his guests. "What will the neighbors think? Come on, you can have my room tonight. Arnold, I'll take your plate. You can finish this later."

With a gentle touch on her arm Arnold woke his daughter from her sleep. Yawning and stretching, Lilly sat erect. Jill and Pete helped Arnold to his feet. Lilly grabbed his cane and handed it to her father.

"Thanks, Doc," Arnold said. "I owe you more than I can repay."

"You owe me nothing. Besides the various time savers you've made me since you've been up and around, your bill is settled."

Jill raised her eyebrows. "By whom?"

"By me," Dora interjected. "Call it an anniversary gift in honor of your reunion tonight. Come tomorrow when you collect half the reward on Slim Cramer you can start to rebuild your farm again."

"Half the reward?" Jill echoed.

"Tomorrow?" Pete echoed another part of Dora's statement. "How do you know you'll have the reward that soon?"

Dora raised her hands in protest. "One at a time. First, Jill, your earlier remark about Slim being a threat made me remember who Cramer was. When we met him and his cronies on the road I was ready for them. Otherwise Arnold might have been a widower, Lamar without a doctor, and my career cut short. So you deserve half the reward.

"Pete, to answer your question I requested and received an answer from the telegram that I sent to Denver for a U. S. Marshal. There's a marshal due to be in Lamar sometime tomorrow morning. He can identify Cramer's body and authorize the reward with a bank draft. As for Josh and Morley they picked the wrong side to be on."

"How did you get any straight answers from that telegraph operator?" Pete inquired. "You know he worked for Delgrin."

"I can read code," Dora told him. "One needs to know all one can in my business. That's something my father always taught me. With a little persuasion I made sure the operator sent just what I told him to send. Seems that he got all tied up in his work this evening and decided to take a little snooze while he was detained."

"So Hilliard never found out about your message, huh?"

"I reckon not. If the telegraph office is still closed in the morning someone will have to go through the back door and untie the operator. I left the key in the lock. With this marshal coming you can have him look into some of the affairs of this town. He can help clean up the rest of the rattlesnakes in Delgrin's lair."

Jill tried to stifle a yawn. Still using her father's shoulder as a pillow Lilly was drifting off to sleep standing next to him. Her sagging knees kept waking her.

"We can discuss our next plans tomorrow," Pete decided. "For now I suggest that we all get some sleep. Dora, you can have the extra room with Lilly. I'll take the couch."

14

After the marshal had arrived in town in the latter part of the morning he made positive identification of Slim Cramer's body. From the undertaker's he went to the bank to have a draft made for the thousand dollar reward for Slim's capture dead or alive. Dora cashed it, giving the promised half to Arnold and Jill.

"That's a lot of money," Jill said with bated breath. "I've never held so much in my hand all at one time before."

"That should go a long way toward rebuilding your farm," Dora suggested. "If I come this way again I think I know where I can always find a good meal and a night's rest. Deal?"

"Deal!" Arnold exclaimed, "I can't thank you enough for this."

"If you don't come stay with us when you're in the area I'll wonder what we've done wrong," Jill added.

"That goes for me, too," Pete interjected. "My door is always open to you, Dora. My cooking isn't as good, but I've got room."

"Thanks. It's friends like you I'll always remember." She hefted her two bags that had been stashed in a corner of Pete's living room. "The time has come for me to make my departure. I have another debt to collect. Lilly, take good care of your folks."

Lilly frowned. "I'm going to miss you, Dora. I wish you could stay. You've been the best friend a girl could ever have."

Dora dropped her bags and threw her arms around the girl. "I'm going to miss you too, Lilly. I have two older brothers but no sister. You've been just like a younger sister to me. Oh, I almost forgot." She reached into her pocket and extracted a coin. "Here's your silver dollar I've kept for you." She laid it in Lilly's palm.

Lilly pressed the coin to her bosom. "I'll keep this always to remember you by. Thank you, Dora, for everything."

"Thank you all for being the kind of people that makes this country great." Dora hefted her bags. "Pete, where's the stable?"

"Main Street. To your right, then three blocks." Then he added, "Take care of that shoulder."

"Thanks, I will." Having answered she was gone.

* * *

The stable keeper eyed the young, pretty woman dressed in jeans and a bright red shirt as she marched in lugging two satchels. She dropped them at the door.

"Will you please show me the horses you have for sale?" she requested. "I want one with excellent stamina and disposition."

He led her to a few stalls where several horses were being kept. In one of them she found Spirit as she reckoned she would. Bidding the keeper to get him out she looked him over as if she were examining him for the first time. Spirit neighed in recognition. The keeper took this response as an opportunity to push a sale.

"He likes you, ma'am," he encouraged. "He'd make an excellent rider for ya, plus he comes from good blood lines."

Either the man knew his horses well, or he was acquainted with Adrian Delgrin's steeds. Allowing that the man made his living with caring for and trading in horses Dora gave him credit for the former reason.

"Not gelded," she noted. "I prefer a stud to a gelding."

"Yes, ma'am. He's really spirited. He's faster than the wind, too. I can see you could handle him though."

"That's a good name for him, Spirit. How much for him?"

The keeper rubbed his whiskery chin as if in thought. "I've got to have a hundred dollars for him."

Leading Spirit to the tack rack Dora found the saddle and tack that she had used on him the day before. The quality of the equipment was top notch, a given for Farius Delgrin. Pointing to it she offered, "If you'll throw in this saddle and tack as part of the price I'll take him."

This time the man scratched his bald head in deliberation. At last he replied, "You drive a hard bargain, but okay. It's a deal."

Knowing what Pete had been paid for Spirit with tack she knew that the stable keeper was making a good profit from her "hard bargain." She handed him a crisp, new one-hundred-dollar bill, obtained a bill of sale, and watched as he saddled the horse for her. He strapped her bags securely to the back to keep them from bouncing.

"Thanks," she offered as she swung into the saddle. When he saw that Dora was packing a gun on her hip the keeper's face jaw-dropped in an expression of surprise. He hadn't noticed a firearm on her when she had first entered the stable.

"Say, are you the—"

"Could be," she called back, spurring her "new" mount away from the stable and out of town. When Dora had first come to see Max she was riding her old gelding. Once she became Dora Kinley she had sold him for her stage ticket to town. While she missed her old horse she knew that she needed to acquire a much younger one. Spirit fit the bill.

Pacing Spirit at a steady gallop she covered the miles in quick time. The stallion's gait was as smooth as butter, his stamina excellent. Not until she could see the buildings of the Templeton spread did she slow her steed to a walk.

The ranch left the impression in the air that it was abandoned. She knew that most of Templeton's hands were still out on the big cattle drive to the railroad, but they were due back any day. Still, there was an ominous feeling about the place. Hitching her horse to the post in front of the house she stepped onto the porch, extra wary of her surroundings. A loose slat creaked its complaint. She hadn't wanted a calling card.

Were hidden eyes watching from the windows? She rapped on the door. A muffled echo off the low hills around the ranch returned the sole answer. Borrowing caution she pushed the unlocked door open.

A circumspect scan of the living room reassured her that the room was occupied by nothing but its furniture. Dora stole across the room and down the hall to the door that led to Templeton's study where she had stood making an agreement with Max less than a dozen days before. She tapped on the portal.

The only response was a sinister silence. What foreboding evil waited behind his door? Her intuition told her that something foul was afoot. It also told her to continue her quest.

Standing off to one side Dora shoved the door ajar. She peered around the corner. Behind his desk sat Templeton. Clutched in his hand was a big forty-four aimed at the spot where she would have been standing in making a normal entrance. He lowered the barrel in recognition.

"Dora Kincaid, you're a sight to behold!" he exclaimed

"This is a strange way to greet your visitors," she replied. He had had his chance. If Templeton had been the one behind the ambush on her he had just missed his opportunity to finish the job himself. Why was he sitting here in his own house with his gun in hand as if waiting—for whom?

"Sorry about the, uh, reception," he explained, laying down the gun. "I'm waiting for unexpected and unwanted callers. Someone took some shots at me this morning, four to be exact. I figure it was one of Delgrin's men the logical choice being Slim Shelley. He could be plotting to take me out now that Delgrin is dead. Since there's no known next of kin left, my guess is Slim as foreman will try to make claim to the ranch. He might figure that I would stand as his greatest threat to getting it by buying it out from under him."

"I see that you're aware that I finished the job."

"Come in and sit down," he offered a big hand toward a chair.

She took the invitation by occupying the offered seat. Pulling Farius's pistol from her gun belt she laid it on the corner of the desk. "Here you go as agreed. When did you find out about Adrian's demise?"

"I found out this morning," he continued. "A couple of my men were in the saloon last night drinking up some of their pay. You must have made a lasting impression on the town with your performance."

"That was a gift to the people of Lamar. Tell me about this bushwhacker who took four shots at you."

"The few hands I still have on the ranch until after the drive went after him. If they catch him I wouldn't want to be in his britches. He had a pretty good head start on them though."

It isn't one of Delgrin's men, she reasoned. All of the ones that had known of Delgrin's death were also soon to be permanent residents of boot hill. The bushwhacker who had shot at Templeton may have been the same one who had wounded her in the shoulder. If he were why was Maxwell Templeton on his hit list? Who was this mysterious sniper? With Max involved this only deepened the mystery.

"I know that your bushwhacker wasn't Slim Shelley," she remarked.

He wrinkled his forehead in wonder. "How do you know that?"

"He and two other of Delgrin's men stopped our wagon on the road to Lamar from Delgrin's ranch. Slim was trying to take Jill and Lilly James back to the ranch. I told him that with Delgrin dead they were going to town with me. Slim and his men tried to argue about it, but I won. By the way, Slim's actual last name was Cramer."

Choosing a cigar from the box on the desk and lighting it he narrowed his eyes in thought. "Slim Cramer, huh. As I recollect he was a killer down in Texas. Nobody has known of his whereabouts for a couple of years. He was reputed to be quicker than a kid caught in a beehive. You beat him to the draw?"

"And his two pals," she finished. "I mentioned Cramer in the saloon last night, but your men must have forgotten to tell you about him. He and his cronies tried to make it tough on me, but I played my cards right. Turned out all right too. Cramer had a price on his head. I was able to pick up the kitty. Speaking of kitty—"

Templeton opened a drawer on his desk and extracted a bundle of bills. He tossed it to Dora who caught it in her lap. While she flipped through the bills he reached over to pick up Farius's revolver and lay it in the open drawer.

"All in hundreds like you wanted," he drawled. Then with a grim smile he added, "With Shelley, or should I say Cramer about ready to be pushing up lilies the number of suspects I have left is now down to zero."

Dora started in surprise. "What? Do you mean that you don't have any other ideas who this bushwhacker could be?"

"None. Oh don't get me wrong," he added in haste. "This old cowpoke is no angel or saint, but he's no devil like Delgrin either. He may have made some hard feelings in his time, but no other mortal enemies like Delgrin was. Now I don't know of anyone who would be out to kill me or have me killed."

"Somebody is."

While rolling the cigar between his fingers out of long habit Templeton gazed in earnest thought at the far wall. Also engrossed was Dora in deducing what little she knew. The bemusement frustrated her reasoning.

"Perhaps this sniper is the same character that tried to take me out," she mused. "To lead Delgrin on I pretended to show interest in him. We rode about an hour from the house before I provoked him to draw against me. Afterward I was just picking up Farius's gun to bring to you as the proof you asked for when someone took a shot at me. Lucky for me the bullet only grazed my left shoulder. I also had some ideas for suspects, but now my list is empty as well."

"You mean you thought I was behind it?"

"The idea had crossed my mind."

"What took me off your list?"

"Three things," she told him. "One, you could have done the job yourself when I walked in here. Two, someone is out to poke holes in your hide too. What's strange is neither of us knows why. Three, I still go by what my father said about you. Of course a man can change, but I've seen no evidence of such in you."

"Good deductions," he lauded her. "If you've got your old man's brains you'll figure out who's behind this."

Dora hoped that he was right, for now more than anything she wanted to discover who was behind the attempted ambushes. She felt certain that the bushwhacker was just a hired gun for someone else wanting Delgrin and Templeton dead. Reason dictated that Max had just forgotten a possible suspect. By stretching Maxwell's brain with key questions Dora figured that she could find the answer.

"Did Delgrin have any other enemies? Any that could pose a serious threat to him?" she queried.

Maxwell shook his head. "That thought had already crossed my mind. There's just no one else left. Adrian took care of them including his father and brother. I was the only enemy left who still posed a threat to his ambitions."

"There's at least one other," she corrected. "He'd have shot Delgrin if I hadn't. He must be your enemy too."

Templeton leaned back in his chair a grim look on his face. "So Delgrin and I had something in common after all the same enemy. What led you to this conclusion? Where's your interest in all this? Got a notion who it is?"

"No notion, but my interest is who the bum is that shot at me from behind and why he did. I'm sure he was planning to pick off Adrian. Maybe I made him mad because I shot Adrian first. I've a hunch that our snipers are one and the same. Anyway I couldn't get a good look at the bushwhacker before he rode away. He was too far out. I did follow his trail a ways. It led out toward open range."

"You think the same person shot at me this morning?"

Dora stood up and walked over to the window. "You own half the territory around here," she pondered as she gazed through the glass. "Adrian owned the other half. Perhaps someone is after both your holdings."

"Could be, but why shoot you? If he were only after Adrian Delgrin you had just saved him the trouble. Trying to kill you seems like a strange way of showing one's gratitude even if he were a little miffed that you did his job."

"I haven't figured that one out yet. That's the one flaw in my theory. All the other puzzle pieces make sense but that one."

The mid afternoon sun drew a sharp line of the shadow of the barn against the ground between it and the house. A deformity in the silhouette caught her eye. A lump in the shadow along the edge was growing larger until it took on the appearance of a man's shape scurrying over the yard. When it had grown complete it broke away from the main body of the shadow to dash toward the house. Shifting direction the lump melted back into the greater shade to vanish. She couldn't quite see the maker of the apparition. The whole scene took less than ten seconds to occur.

"Max," she muttered, "you have company."

15

Bolting from his chair he leaped to the window for a look. No one was in sight. "Our sniper?" he queried.

"Could be. I saw his shadow run around by the side of the house. He's come around to the back."

"The back door!" Max blurted as he grabbed his gun. "Let's go!"

The last two words he flung over his shoulder as he dashed from his office, Dora running to keep up. In three strides he crossed the living room to the kitchen doorway. She was right on his tail.

Opposite where the two had stopped was the back door. Each of them stood on either side of the doorway and peered around the corner.

The latch on the back door was being raised without a sound. The door swung open on well-oiled hinges. Dora and Max jerked back from view to press themselves flat against the wall. Clutched in their fists their pistols were poised for action.

The intruder's footsteps clicked a slow count across the hardwood kitchen floor. Soon the barrel of a forty-four revolver passed through the doorway. Behind it followed a beefy, weathered fist grasping the pistol by the stock. Max brought the barrel of his own gun down with a sharp blow against the intruder's wrist. Dropping his gun the stranger let out a yelp of pain. Retaliating at once he grabbed Templeton's arm with his other hand. With a mighty tug the robust rancher yanked his assailant into the living room.

They collided in the doorway. The ponderous bulk of the stranger had counter-acted the burly rancher's tug. Dora gawked at the two giant men almost equal in size as they battled for control of Max's gun. Soon realizing that she had gawked long enough Dora acted. Finding an opening she smashed the butt of her own revolver against the base of the intruder's skull. In a daze he sagged to his knees.

Max was then able to break the man's grip. With his fingers wrapped around the nape of his neck the stranger shook his head clear and glanced around. Two gun barrels were trained at the young man's head on different sides. He started to get to his feet.

"Stay right there!" Max barked. "Be thankful that Petticoat didn't put a bullet through you just now. Let's have some straight answers quick, or she will. Who are you?"

The man hesitated, but thought better of it when Dora pressed her barrel against his temple. "Botts," he muttered. "George Botts."

"Why did you try to kill me this morning?" Templeton demanded.

"And me yesterday?" Dora added, fire in her eyes.

Botts stared at her in bewilderment. "You? You must be mistaken. I've never seen you before in my life."

"Never seen me before, huh? I can tell if you have or not. You rode in here. Where's your horse?"

"My horse? Why?"

Templeton brandished his gun. "You forget. We're asking the questions here. Answer the little lady."

"Behind the barn," Botts muttered.

Dora marched out the back door still standing ajar since Botts' entrance. "Keep him covered, Max. I'll be back in a moment."

To a corral pole in back of the barn she found his horse tied. The big chestnut mare looked at her and neighed. There in the loose dust of the barnyard where the mare stood Dora could make out her hoof prints. Almost as if she had just asked her to the horse took a side step with her right rear leg. The fresh print that she left behind was unmistakable. The hoof wore no shoe. The other prints revealed the very worn condition the other shoes were in. Dora stormed back into the house to confront Botts.

"So you've never seen me before," she growled through gritted teeth. "I'll freshen your memory. Just yesterday you tried to gun me down right after Adrian Delgrin lost against me in a fair draw.

That bullet you fired struck me across the shoulder. After you rode away I was able to follow you far enough to find the shoe your horse had thrown. My fight with Delgrin was fair and square. You're just a chicken-livered bushwhacker. I don't cotton to caitiffs who sneak up and shoot others in the back. You owe me for that bullet."

Botts stared at her in utter surprise his mouth dropping open. "That was *you* out there with Delgrin? But that couldn't be! That had to be Jill James. The woman I shot was much older than you."

"You thought that I was Jill James? Why would you want to kill Jill James?" Dora pressed, her turn to be astounded.

"Because she would have inherited Delgrin's ranch if anything happened to him. I know she hated Delgrin so much that I wasn't surprised when I saw her gun him down. Or at least I thought you were her. Anyway with Delgrin already dead I only had one shot to make. I just mistook my target."

Dora didn't know whether to feel relief that she had been mistaken for someone else, or offended because of the same reason.

She decided not to let a false sense of pride muddle her emotions. "Jill James was his cook, not his wife. Who gave you the idea that Mrs. James would ever inherit Delgrin's ranch?"

"Yes, who?" Templeton cut in. "I think that's the point here. You're working for someone aren't you, Botts? Who is it? What does he want?"

"I can't tell you any more." He dropped his gaze to the floor.

With a threatening wave of her pistol Dora stepped toward him. "You'd better find more use of your tongue, or I'll collect what you owe me now with a bullet right between your eyes."

She was standing in a direct line between the two men. Seizing the opportunity Botts lunged forward shoving her small frame into Templeton. In attempting to recover she fired a shot that splintered the door frame above Botts' head. Max was unable to get a clear shot with Dora floundering in his arms. Snatching his six-shooter by the barrel from the floor George Botts dived into the kitchen before Dora Kincaid could recover enough to fire again.

Pushing herself out of the hands of the husky rancher Dora leaped into the kitchen her gun readied. Botts had already dashed out the back door. She raced to the door and flung it open. A piece of lead splintered the log siding in the doorway. The shot sent her retreating back into cover. She returned fire at empty space. Botts had already run past the corner of the barn.

By this time Max had reached the back door to peer over her shoulder. Darting past him she raced though the house and out the front door to her horse. Max raced toward the barn from the rear of the house. Within seconds Dora was rounding the corner of the house her steed running for all he was worth. She could hear Botts' horse galloping away. As she passed the corner of the barn two shots rang out from the rear side of the building. A short distance from the barn she could see Botts, gun in hand, riding hard. Grabbing for the calf of his leg Botts lost his balance and went crashing to the ground in a heap.

Dora drew in her mount next to the fallen man. She jumped down and knelt by his side. Rushing through the rear door of the barn to join her Max holstered his still smoking weapon. As he jogged over to her she stood up to face him, a disgusted scowl on her persona.

"No more answers from him," she grunted. "We weren't suppose to play for keeps until he told us everything."

"I wasn't trying to. I was aiming for his leg."

"Oh you shot him in the leg all right," she assured him. "From the way he's lying there I'd say he broke his neck when he hit the ground. That's unfortunate for him and for us. Too bad I was standing too close when he pushed me. He had arms as long as an ape's. George Botts, if that was his real name, was just a hired gun I'm sure. How do we find out for whom he was working and why?"

Maxwell knelt over the man. "Maybe we can find some evidence on him that would help answer those questions." He searched through the dead man's pockets for any clues. All he came up with were a few small bills and coins and an extra kerchief. He put all of it back.

Dora had decided to check George Botts' saddlebags. In them she found some jerky, sourdough, a tin of ground coffee, molasses, a chewing tobacco pouch, matches, a small skillet and cup, and a flask of cheap whiskey. There was enough here to keep a man from getting too hungry for two or three days. None of it provided a hint to the who and why behind George Botts. She doubted that he had a record.

Disappointed she stuffed everything back into the bags and walked back to Templeton's side where he was still kneeling next to the late George Botts. He'd also come up empty handed.

"Nothing?" he inquired.

"Nothing," she returned. "We don't even know where or who his next of kin are. All we know is whoever his boss was he must have an interest in yours and Delgrin's ranches. Question is why?"

Templeton stood up. Grabbing the dead man's arm he hefted him until he had Botts strung over his shoulder. Dora realized then the brute strength in this giant of a man. She knew some tricks on how to heft a dead man onto his horse or into a wagon. Of a truth she knew a man the size of Botts would have proven tricky for her to lift. Max had just hefted him like a sack of potatoes.

"Grab his hat, gun, and horse," he called over his shoulder as he trudged toward the barn. "I'll toss him into a corner until the new sheriff and the undertaker come get him."

Retrieving the dead man's horse Dora led her toward the rear door of the barn. From the dusty ground she snatched up his gun and hat as she passed each one. Within the dark crown a light patch of color caught her eye. Upon closer inspection she discovered a folded piece of paper tucked inside the liner of the hat.

Slipping the paper loose she stuffed it into one of her pockets. After they had disposed of the body in a stall and corralled the horse she and Max returned to the house. She left her horse ground tied.

"I found something that may be what we're looking for," she told him when they were inside. Pulling the folded piece of paper from her pocket she held it under his nose. "This was in his hat."

"Let's take it to my office and have a closer look."

Maxwell seated himself at his desk while Dora looked over his shoulder. With care he spread the sweat stained scrap of paper open in front of them.

"It looks like a simple contract," Dora suggested when she had scanned the writing on the note. "According to this note you, Delgrin, and Jill James were the targets agreed upon here."

"He wasn't getting as much for all three of us as I paid you for just Delgrin," Max snorted.

Dora shrugged her shoulders in insouciance. "I know what I'm worth. Besides I finished my job. Botts didn't."

Templeton pointed at a place on the note. "Some of the words have been washed out by the sweat soaked into the paper. Unfortunate for us so is part of the name of the man behind Botts."

Dora squinted at the blurred scrawl near the bottom of the page. "Looks like the man who hired Botts signed his name 'Red.' The rest of his name is too washed out to read. Who do you know by that name who wants you pushing up lilies?"

Max rubbed his bristled chin with thick fingers. "By gum if I had even an inkling of an idea who it might be, solving this riddle could be much easier. I can't think of anyone who has the name Red."

"Red is possibly a nickname. My guess would be the man has red hair. No old enemies?" she nudged his memory. "No redheaded cowhand you used to have that might be carrying a grudge?"

"None that could afford to hire a gunman like Botts," Max assured her. "By this contract Botts got an advance on his fee to do the job. Most cowhands aren't that rich. Besides I don't know of any ex-hand of mine hating me, and Delgrin, and Jill James enough to hire someone to kill all three of us. Nor are any of my former employees red headed."

In deliberation Dora tapped her chin with a finger as she tried to decipher the last name of Red. Max decided to take the opportunity to make her an offer. "What would you charge me to find this Red and solve this case?"

"I'm no detective," she countered. "You need a Pinkerton man."

"You're a gun fighter," he reasoned. "Right now I need a fast gun more than I need a detective. When this 'Red' finds out about Botts, and I'm sure he will he'll send another hired gun after me or try it himself. That's why I hired you for Delgrin."

"Did," she reminded him. "I finished the job."

"Got another job waiting?"

"Not at the moment."

"Then how can you refuse my offer?"

"What are the terms?"

Max wrinkled his brow. "Well, since you don't have much to go on I'll double your previous fee."

"Make it twenty-five hundred and it's a deal."

"You'll drive me into ruin with those kinds of fees," he retorted, "but it's a deal."

They sealed the deal with a handshake. For Dora she figured that as her reputation spread those she made handshake contracts with wouldn't renege and suffer the possible repercussions.

"Now," Dora went on, "we need to get the U.S. Marshal out here to check up on this George Botts. Even if the town has hired a new sheriff if Botts has a record the marshal is more apt to know. Since none of your hands are back I guess I'll have to ride into town to fetch him."

105

Just then they heard the sound of riders reining in their steeds in front of the barn. Templeton cast a glance over his shoulder. Dora shifted her gaze to the window as well.

"Looks like the boys are back from chasing Botts," Templeton muttered. "He must have doubled back on them."

With Max Templeton in the lead the pair of them made their way to the barn where one of the men made a report on their chase.

"Sorry, Mr. Templeton," the man said, "but he got away. He had too good of a head start. We followed his trail into the rock wash. That's where we lost it. We spread out and searched all the washes that come into it, but he managed to give us the slip."

"And doubled back for a second chance," Max concluded.

The man's jaw dropped pulling his lower eyelids open wider. "What? You mean he came back and tried again?"

"That's right, Johnny. Lucky for us Miss Kincaid spotted his shadow as he tried to sneak up to the house. We got the drop on him, but he made a run for it and lost. You'll find him piled in a corner of the barn. He fell from his horse and broke his neck."

"Who was he?" Johnny asked.

"George Botts or so he said," Dora offered. An idea had just come to her. Maybe one of Templeton's hands would know him. She turned to her renewed employer. "Max, let's all go take a good look at him. One of your men might recognize him."

Max led his four hands into the barn where Botts lay sprawled in the middle of an empty stall. When they had gotten a look at the dead man all of them shook their heads disavowing any recognition of him. Dora frowned her disappointment.

"Don't recall ever seeing him before," Johnny drawled, "but I know someone who might have. She often knows everybody and everything that goes on around here."

Dora perked up. "Who is that?"

"She's an old gal who lives on the outskirts of La Junta. Folks call her Witch Annie. Her real name is Hannah. You can find her real easy. Just ask around. Most everyone in those parts knows her."

"Why do people call her a witch?" Dora pressed.

"Because of her uncanny way of knowing what she knows. I hear that she's told a lot of people when something special was going to happen to them and it does."

"So she has premonitions," Dora mused.

"Premonitions?" Johnny echoed. "What's that?"

"Some people might refer to them as fortune telling," Dora explained. "Hannah may possess the ability to foresee future events before they occur." She turned to the owner of the ranch. "I don't know about witches, but a visit to this old gal might prove to be interesting if not informative. Let's hope this is a break for us. At least we have nothing to lose. I'll go pay her a visit right now. I should be back by dinnertime."

She spun on her heel to jog out of the barn. Leaping onto her horse she rode away toward La Junta.

16

Just as Johnny had said almost anyone in town knew Witch Annie. Dora had asked the first person she had met where the old gal lived. Without hesitation the little girl whom Dora guessed to be about eight pointed at an old rickety looking shack on top of a slight rise just outside the town. As she rode up to the front of the shack Dora figured that the old woman must live the hermetic life of a recluse. She dismounted and walked to the dilapidated door of the ramshackle hut.

Before she had a chance to knock, a high, thin voice from within called, "Come in." In response Dora shoved open the portal. Rusting hinges groaned their protest. Since there was no wooden porch to reveal approaching footsteps Dora reasoned that Hannah had heard her horse ride up. In the middle of the small, almost empty room sat an older woman in an old high-backed rocker. She was sitting with her right side to the door. Her hands were busy sewing a quilt. Without turning to look toward Dora the woman made a strange statement. "I've been expecting you."

Dora figured that Witch Annie was expecting a caller and had mistaken her for someone else. "I'm not the person you're expecting," she told her hostess. "I just now rode into town to talk to you. We've never met before."

"I know, I know," Witch Annie nodded in understanding. She waved a thin, bony hand at Dora. "Come in. Grab yourself a chair and sit close to me. Just leave the door open. The breeze feels good."

Striding across the tidy room Dora grabbed one of the two simple chairs standing against the wall. She carried it to Witch Annie's side to sit by her. Only then did her hostess, whose features were thin and pale, turn to look at her.

"Forgive an old woman's eyesight but I don't see quite as well as I used to," Hannah murmured. "This dark cabin doesn't help any. It has just a few small windows to let in the sunlight. I know you're a pretty, young lady. My mind could see you very well when you left the Templeton ranch to come here."

With raised eyebrows Dora stared at the other woman in stark astonishment. "You knew I was coming to see you? How?"

Witch Annie smiled in response. "If anyone knew why these visions come to me the way they do everyone might call me a wizard instead of a witch. There doesn't seem to be an appropriate name for what happens to me. These visions have been a part of my life since childhood. I can see things happen as they occur. This ability used to frighten me. Now I just accept it as part of my life. God gets all my thanks for this gift with which he has blessed me."

"Do you mean you can foretell the future? That would make you a prophetess."

Wrinkling her brow Witch Annie's eyes took on a distant stare. "I don't know if I can see something happen before it does. There have been times when people have told me that I've informed them of things that happened after they were told about it. These are the rare exceptions. People have called me a fortuneteller as well as a witch. Thank you for calling me a prophetess. If this is so God gets all the credit.

"I do know that I have seen things occur just as they were taking place. I have no control over these visions. They come to me whenever they want."

"Have you seen me in your mind's eye before this morning?"

As if trying hard to remember, Hannah peered at her over wire framed glasses. "There is something familiar about you. Yes, I do recall now. You or your older sister and a man were facing each other. Then the man fell down as if he were dead. Then you or your sister fell. After that I saw a second man, a big man, riding away.

"This morning I saw this second man fall from his horse. You and Mr. Templeton were there, but the vision wasn't very clear."

A tingling chill danced on Dora's spine causing horripilations. Her hostess's eerie account of the past few days fascinated her. Sensing a mystery she pressed on. "Did you recognize the first man whom you saw fall?"

"Oh yes! I've seen him before. About two years ago I saw him kill his brother and his father. He's a horrible man. I know who he is, Adrian Delgrin." She'd just confirmed what everyone knew but couldn't prove. Her "vision" wouldn't stand up in a court of law, but now it didn't matter.

"Do you know who the second man is?" Dora kept the question in the present tense since Hannah's response about Adrian was in the present tense as if he were still alive. She thought that perhaps Hannah had trouble accepting the sight of someone dying in any of her visions. Maybe Hannah didn't want to know.

Hannah shook her head in response to Dora's question. "I don't know him from around these parts. He's a stranger to me."

"Have you ever seen him before?"

The older woman laid her head back and closed her eyes. She sat taciturn for several long minutes before she responded. "I remember now. Several weeks ago he and another man, also a stranger to me, met together right here in town. I don't know what they were talking about. I do know they were up to no good. Their evilness hung like a shroud about them."

"How well do you—'see' these things?"

"They come in flashes to me. Sometimes the pictures aren't very clear. But these two I saw with my two eyes ride into town when I was down at the general store. They went into the saloon. I looked in at them as I walked by the doorway. They were sitting at a table, leaning rather close to each other as if they were saying something they didn't want anyone else to hear."

Hannah sat up in her chair and leaned closer to her visitor in an air of urgency. "Mark my words, young lady. As I said I don't know what they were talking about, but I do know that they were plotting something bad. I know just as I know the sun shines."

For some inexplicable reason Dora felt that she was closer to discovering who George Botts had been. This so-called witch Hannah seemed to have more information than a dictionary. From what she had heard she decided that she would rely on Hannah's "ability" as much as possible to track down the man who met with George Botts.

"The other stranger you saw in the saloon," Dora quizzed. "Did you notice if he had red hair or not?"

Hannah thought for a moment. "Yes, I believe he did. It wasn't quite a carrot color, a bit darker, but not auburn like yours is I'd say."

"Do you know if this stranger is still in town?"

The older woman leaned back in her rocker again. "Well, as I said I stood there by the door for a moment looking at them. But these eyes aren't like they used to be, even with these bifocals. In that dark saloon I couldn't see them very well. I didn't dare stand there very long and have them notice me staring. Unless the images I see in my mind make my vision clearer I sometimes don't recognize people when I pass them on the street. What I'm trying to say is I haven't seen this man since, either with my natural eyes or in my head. He may be around. I don't know."

The day had grown hot. Hannah slumped in her rocker. She patted her wet forehead with an old tattered apron in her lap. "Child, would you fetch me a drink of water from the bucket on the table?"

The word "child" amused Dora Kincaid. Having studied Hannah since sitting with her she felt certain that her unique hostess was not so old. Dora guessed her to be no more than forty. Even in Hannah's wasted condition she was a handsome woman. Dora retrieved the requested liquid in a tin cup and handed it to her hostess.

"Thank you, Miss—uh—mercy, I haven't even learned your name yet," she apologized.

"My name is Dora. Dora Kincaid."

"Dora," Hannah repeated between swallows of water. "That's a nice name. Names don't come to me, just faces. Why is a young woman like you out traipsing around these parts, wearing a gun?"

"It's for protection against rattlers and other dangerous critters." Dora switched the subject. "I might ask why you're out here. Your speech indicates education. You're from the east, aren't you? I'd say New England."

"You have a good ear, Dora. Most folks think I'm a 'foreigner'. Yes, I'm 'educated' as you deduced. My father was a professor of geology at Harvard. He dreamed of coming west to look for oil, but he felt that teaching was his duty to perform.

"Then one of his students went on to fulfill that dream. His name was Hiram Minkle. Hiram told my father he wanted to hunt for oil out here. When he graduated he left Cambridge, Massachusetts with my father's blessings and came west. He helped find oil in Ohio, Indiana, and Illinois. He was working in Kansas when he disappeared. No one has seen him since." Her voice trailed off.

"What does Hiram Minkle have to do with you?"

Hannah peered at Dora with sad eyes. "Hiram Minkle is my husband. I came west with him. After he vanished from Kansas I followed his trail to here before it ended. That was two years ago. I've been here ever since making a meager existence sewing. I don't know if my Hiram is alive or dead."

Hannah's voice trickled to a murmur. She seemed burdened beyond her capacity to endure. Dora hesitated in pressing the subject any farther. Hiram Minkle didn't figure into her search for the man who hired George Botts. She was about to excuse herself to go when Hannah continued in a near normal voice.

"I was almost out of money when I arrived here. In order to buy groceries I took up another talent I have. Sewing doesn't pay much but I get by. People may call me witch but they like my work. This old shack was abandoned so I moved in. It isn't much but it gives me a roof over my head.

"At first I was sure my Hiram was still alive, but I never could see him in my mind. Now I don't know. I can't understand why he didn't take me with him. I know he didn't run away. That wasn't like him."

Something that Hannah had just said perplexed Dora. Since her hostess seemed willing to talk about her missing husband she ventured, "You really love your husband don't you?"

"Without him my life means nothing. All that keeps me alive is the hope that he'll return."

"But you never had visions of anything happening to him?"

"The one time the use of my own peculiarity could help it fails me," she answered, sarcasm tainting her words. "I've tried to make my mind show me Hiram, but I can't. My mind does whatever it does of its own volition. I—"

Hannah broke off her sentence her eyes staring off to nowhere her face twisted with concern. She grasped the arms of her rocking chair in a tight grip. Her knuckles whitened under the strain.

Quite concerned Dora reached out to grab Hannah's wrist. "Mrs. Minkle, what's the matter? Can I get—"

"Wait, Dora! There's a picture coming to me."

Hannah sat back erect in her rocker with her hands over her eyes. Anxious eternities elapsed before she spoke again.

"I see a big man on horseback—riding hard—he seems to be—chasing someone. No—he's being chased. The one chasing isn't coming very clear. I recognize the first man. He's Maxwell Templeton."

Dora leaped to her feet at the mention of his name. "Where is he? Where is he? Can you tell?"

"He's on some kind of—steep ridge—someone is shooting at him—now he's gone. All I can see is his horse running."

"Mrs. Minkle, I'll talk to you again!" Dora shouted over her shoulder as she bolted out of the old shanty and leaped astride her horse. If Annie Minkle had bid her goodbye she hadn't caught it in her rush to leave.

Out on the main road to Templeton's ranch she gave her steed his head. With little urging he spread his powerful legs over the dusty trail. Carrying his light load Spirit covered mile after mile in rapid strides even for the heat. It was as if he sensed her urgency to get back.

Hannah Minkle's nondescript "steep ridge" could fit dozens of washes, draws, or similar deformities in the landscape. Dora could have kicked herself for reacting too fast before getting a better description, but she had no time to turn back. She had to trust on luck and her own female intuition to find the right one.

One place did stick in her mind. The spot had flashed before her own mind when Mrs. Minkle mentioned "steep ridge". She decided to rely on her hunch and head straight for the place.

As she drew close distant shots echoed through the canyon near the ridge she suspected. A rider-less horse bolted from the bushes and crossed the road ahead. Dora recognized it as Max's steed. She spurred her own on with renewed intent.

Just as she turned into the main draw where this steep ridge jutted out of the floor of the wash she saw a man tumble off the edge of it down the rocky slope. Although she had gotten only a quick glimpse she had recognized Maxwell Templeton!

17

Riding headlong toward the direction of the last shot she had heard she drew her rifle from its holster and began firing a volley of shots into the brush. A couple of rifle shots whistled past her ears before she heard the unmistakable clatter of shod hooves retreating up a side draw. All she could see was a faint outline through the dust cloud.

Dora pursued a short distance to make certain that Max's assailant would keep making tracks before she wheeled around and rode back to find her employer. She almost whooped aloud for joy when she saw a bedraggled Templeton crawl out of the underbrush below the ridge. He stood on wobbly legs to dust himself off.

Resisting the urge to throw her arms around his neck in relief Dora slipped off her horse to confront him in mock disgust.

"You're going to make me work for my pay this time aren't you," she snapped, scolding him like his mother. "Either that or you were trying to renege on our deal by getting yourself killed."

He held up his scuffed hands in protest. "Dora, believe me I'm glad to still be able to live up to my end of our deal."

"Who was after you this time? How did you get into this mess?" she queried.

Maxwell dug into his pocket. When he brought his hand out he held up the extra kerchief that they had found on Botts' body. She recognized the pattern printed on it.

"I told my men to take all of Botts' belongings and divide them up among themselves," he explained, "what little there was. One of my men noticed something extra on this kerchief that we overlooked."

He pointed to a corner where two small initials were embroidered near the edge: H. M. Dora rubbed her chin in thought.

"This kerchief didn't belong to Botts according to this monogram," she mused. "Perhaps it belongs to the man who hired him to kill you."

"That thought had crossed my mind unless Botts was an alias. I can't think of anyone of my acquaintance with these initials. The idea came to me that these initials might belong to a known outlaw who's not known from around here. If they do, this could be important enough to ride to town and ask the marshal about them. By the way did you tell him about Botts?"

Dora shook her head. "The marshal is still on my to do list. I was still at Witch Annie's place when she had this premonition about you. She said that she could see you riding with someone shooting while chasing you. Then she saw you fall. There was no time to do anything else but dash out of there to come looking for you."

Templetom's mouth dropped open. "She saw me just now in this fix?"

"She sure did. Hannah has a special talent. Lucky for you her vision and my arrival just in time saved your hide. Do you know who was chasing you?"

"No idea. Never saw him before. There's one thing that's certain. He had sandy red hair."

"Sandy red hair, huh. Do you think that he was the one who signed 'Red' on Botts' contract?"

"That's been my conclusion. He must have been hanging around close to the ranch house maybe waiting for Botts. When he saw me riding out toward town he must have decided that he could do the job Botts couldn't. For a while there the odds were that he was going to. My mistake was not to bring Johnny or one of the others along with me. But they were busy. The idea never occurred to me that someone else would try to do me in so soon after Botts' attempt."

"Why did you roll off the ridge?"

Max looked sheepish. "I was going to jump down off my horse to find cover, but I tripped and fell."

"Well, are you hurt?"

"Just my pride."

Dora swung into her saddle. She offered her hand to her employer. "Hop on. I'll take you to your horse. Then let's see if we can track down your bushwhacker."

Reaching Templeton's horse took just a moment. The animal was grazing a few dozen yards from where it had crossed Dora's path. Once Max had straddled his own mount the pair spurred away up the side draw where the stranger had made his escape. A single set of tracks made a path up the center of the sandy draw. They followed his tracks for a few hundred yards along the wash until they found an easy access up the bank to the rim. From there the tracks led them in a circle back to the main road. The wide spread distance between the hoof prints disclosed that the rider was driving his mount at a fast clip. At the main road the tracks disappeared with a myriad of others on the hard packed surface. Dora and Max reined in and surveyed the horizon in all directions.

"Not even a cloud of dust!" she exclaimed in disgust. "He didn't waste any time getting out of here. Someone sure wants you dead in a big way. I think you'd better stay inside out of sight until we can chase down this pesky varmint."

"The day some jackass keeps me from riding my own range—"

"—is the day he sends you to boot hill. Look, if I'm now going to be your body guard as well you can help out by not being a conspicuous target."

Max tried to fend off her determined expression. "Well, I'll give it some thought," he compromised, "but I'm not making any promises. Johnny or one of the boys can always ride with me."

Dora shook her head in irritation. "Papa sure is right about your mulishness. At least riding with Johnny is better than you riding alone. Tell the rest of your men to keep their heads up. Come on. The hour's grown too late to go back into town today. Let's go on back to the ranch. We'll head for town in the morning."

"I may be a little stubborn," Max countered in self-defense as they headed their horses for home, "but I didn't go riding headlong into the rifle fire of an ambush."

"Element of surprise," she answered as if Max should have known. "The surprise worked didn't it? He wasn't expecting me. His natural reaction was to run first and forget the questions for later."

During the return ride to Templeton's ranch the question as to whom the bearer of the initials on the kerchief could be and also the identity of the red-haired bushwhacker arose. She searched back into the resources of her mind trying to recall from her father's stack of wanted posters and his detailed descriptions some gunman who was red-haired. Alas, she knew that there were plenty of gun-toting cowboys, would-be fast guns, of whom her father didn't know. He

116

was mainly acquainted with those who would face a man in a draw, not sneak up from behind. Since his retirement new blood had come onto the scene of which he had no posters. The identity of Max's assailant remained a mystery at that point.

When she tried sorting through the array of names in her head none of the combinations of which she could recall would fit together to arrive at the initials H. M.

Dora was about to dismiss the subject from her mind, when a name that didn't fit into the group of gunmen popped up into her conscious mind. The name was that of a scientist. She had heard the name just that afternoon from Hannah, her husband, Hiram Minkle.

Could the bandanna belong to him? If so how was he connected to this affair? Was he the redhead? This deduction didn't seem to fit. Dora couldn't imagine that a successful geologist would turn to bushwhacking. He couldn't have been the man who met with Botts at the saloon or no doubt Hannah would have recognized him.

Instead of shedding new light on this strange situation the emerging of this new bit of evidence confounded the issue even more. There was one thing she would have bet on. The mystery of the bandanna's owner would be solved when she showed the kerchief to Hannah Minkle in the morning.

At dinner Dora related her experience with meeting the woman called Witch Annie and the subsequent premonition that had brought her to the aid of her employer just in the nick of time.

Jack, Templeton's cook, remarked, "That's enough proof for me to believe that she's a witch. I hear that she makes people do these things that she predicts so that her predictions will come true."

Max scoffed. "I don't believe that. People do the things they do because they want to. No one can control them like that."

"Agreed," concurred Dora. "Hannah is no witch. The belief that some poor woman living in a shack would have the ability to control other peoples lives by witchcraft is ludicrous. If she could she'd be living in the lap of luxury. She just has a talent that no one, not even she understands. If we did she'd be famous not a freak."

A chorus of general consensus came from the other men.

Finding himself outnumbered Jack acquiesced into silence for the rest of the meal. Later that evening he confided with her that after giving her statement serious reflection, "more thinking," as he said he agreed as well that Hannah was no witch.

That night Dora took a guestroom offered by her host. Although the room sported fine furniture, dust revealed the lack of its use for some time. She lay awake for a long time milling the evidence over and over in her mind. At the same time she remained conscious of the night noises. Max's sniper would try again sometime, somewhere, somehow. Templeton set his few hands at home to rotating a watch. Perhaps for now the mysterious redhead bushwhacker wouldn't be back with another attempt on the rancher, but placing watches should foil any immediate effort if he tried.

At last fatigue triumphed over her thoughts. She awoke to the savory aroma of eggs, sourdough, and side pork. The night had passed without any more incidents.

Max was sitting at his desk with a ledger spread open before him when she discovered his whereabouts. He glanced up from his bookkeeping as Dora took a comfortable position in a nearby chair.

"Morning, Dora."

"Morning, Max. What are you writing?"

"Production records," he replied while he wrote. "I keep good track of the ranch's progress."

"None of that paper record keeping for me. I keep mine in my head."

"No notches on your gun, eh. Haven't you ever considered recording a personal journal for your future children?"

"I keep one, but what makes you think that I'll ever get married and have children?"

Max glanced up from his ledger. "Why not? Your Pa did. You don't think that some man will win your heart instead of your bullet?"

Dora rolled her eyes. "Cute, Max. No, the idea of marriage has entered my future plans. Right now I'm just not looking. There's too much clean up work to be done yet. When there's time for marriage and children I'll put that in my journal. Can't you just see the title? 'Mama, the fast gun'." She held out her hands her fingers forming a square as if beholding some vision.

"Whatever." Dropping his pen into the inkwell Max closed his ledger. "That's enough for now," he said. "When the boys get back from the drive I'll have plenty of book work to do."

"When do you expect them?"

"Within two days."

The call to breakfast interrupted their conversation. After a delicious meal the rancher and his hired gun saddled up. They rode off for La Junta. This time Dora carried the kerchief.

As they rode along Dora recounted to Max the ideas that she'd had about Hiram Minkle being the owner of the kerchief. Keeping a wary eye open for Max's persistent antagonist they reached La Junta without a repeat of the previous day's excitement. Hannah's shack became their immediate destination.

"Who's there?" she called in response to their knock.

"Dora Kincaid, Mrs. Minkle. There's a friend with me."

"Come in! Come in!"

The door swung open to reveal Hannah Minkle standing there a smile of delight on her face. Dora was pleased to see her in much brighter spirits. Her happy countenance took twenty years off her persona.

"This is a pleasant surprise," Hannah greeted. "I don't often have visitors return so soon." She peered over the top of her glasses at Max who followed Dora through the open door.

"Mrs. Minkle, do you know—" Dora began.

"Why, Mr. Templeton, I'm so glad to see you safe from harm," Hannah exclaimed in relief. "After yesterday's vision I didn't know if you were all right."

"Much obliged, Mrs. Minkle. This is a pleasure to meet you. I'm right happy to be walking on two feet still, thanks to Dora."

Dora shook her head. "Mrs. Minkle's the reason I got there in time. Otherwise you might be past tense."

"I meant that thanks to both of you," he amended.

"Oh, my goodness I don't need to be thanked," Hannah replied with a modest nod. "Any thanks to me goes to the good Lord."

"Okay. I thank all three of you, the good Lord for the warning, you for telling Dora, and Dora for hightailing it to come help. This rancher isn't ready to be known as the former Max Templeton."

119

"Mrs. Minkle, yesterday you knew I was coming before I got here," Dora quizzed. "Today though, you didn't know that we were here until we knocked."

"Like I said yesterday, Dora, these visions come to me of their own accord," Hannah reminded her. "I hope you didn't come by just to say thanks."

Dora pulled the bandanna out of her pocket. "No, Mrs. Minkle. We wanted to ask you about this. Do you recognize it?"

Hannah took the kerchief in her hands. With growing concern causing her face to turn ashen she examined the corners until she found the initials. "Where did you get this?" she pleaded almost in tears.

"Is it Hiram's?"

"Yes. He had it on him the day he disappeared. Have you found him? Where is he?"

"We don't know. We found this on the body of the second man, the big man, whom you saw in your visions and in the saloon. His name was George Botts. Do you recognize that name?"

Without looking up from the kerchief Hannah shook her head.

Dora tried a new line of questioning. "Does Hiram have red hair, Mrs. Minkle?"

"Please call me Hannah. I feel old enough without being called Mrs. Minkle."

The question appeared to go unperceived. Dora asked her again. "Hannah, does your husband have red hair?"

Hannah snapped out of her trance. "Red? Of course not! My Hiram has black hair. Why would you think he has red hair? Are you thinking that he was the other man in the saloon with George Botts? Hiram wouldn't be in a saloon, nor would he be doing business with the likes of George Botts."

"Of course he wouldn't. Can you think of any acquaintance, perhaps a business associate that your husband may have had who has red hair?"

Hannah pondered the question for a moment. "Red hair. Red hair. No, I can't think of anyone."

"Maybe this will help you to remember," Max interposed. "His name is Red."

After more mental reflection she shook her head in despair. "I'm sorry. I just can't recall anyone with that name or hair color. What does this man have to do with Hiram?"

"We don't know yet," Dora replied. "Perhaps nothing. We'd like to think though, that there is some connection. If we can find this Red fellow he might be able to lead us to your husband."

"Do you really think so?" Hannah implored radiating a hopeful face. "Do you think the red haired man who was in the saloon knows where he is?"

"That's what we intend to find out. We'd like to keep the kerchief for now. It may help us in finding him."

With reluctance Hannah returned the kerchief. Dora promised to let her know as soon as possible what they discovered about Hiram, when and if they did. They bade her good-bye and left.

Their next stop was the sheriff's office to meet the marshal. After performing the customary procedures of reporting Botts' body Max and Dora covered the incidents of the past few days to the official. Along with an assigned deputy the two then returned to Templeton's ranch. The deputy was being sent to bring in the dead man's mortal remains. The marshal had offered to post a watch on the ranch for a couple of days. Having declined the offer Max reasoned that he still had enough men to do the job until the rest returned.

As they neared the ranch Dora caught a whiff of acrid smoke on the dry air. Raising his hand as a signal Max brought the trio to a halt. He and the deputy had noticed the odor as well.

"That's grass burning!" he exclaimed.

Dora sniffed. "I smell kerosene, too."

Beyond a small bluff to their right near the horizon billows of black smoke began to fill the air. Templeton gasped.

"That's where the boys moved the cows and their calves this morning!" he shouted. "Come on! We've got to get them out of there before that range fire reaches them!"

18

In a flash the three of them were driving hard across open range toward the intensifying smoke. The danger of a range fire had become more imminent due to the drought conditions that had prevailed in the past few weeks. Dora was sure that the odor of kerosene spelled deliberate arson to an already serious situation.

First in her line of arson suspects was the mysterious Red. She had no time for much musing at this time as from the rim of the bluff overlooking the already raging fire they viewed the desperate scene. The wall of flame surrounded the stampeding herd on three sides. They were being driven toward the sheer wall of the bluff. There the advancing flames would panic the cows into trampling the calves to death. Max's four men still on hand were riding hard struggling to turn the leaders.

"I see what they're trying to do!" Max shouted to his two companions. "Come on, we've got to help them!"

Down the narrow cut that scarred the bluff on one side the three rode single file. They egged their horses over the treacherous, rocky slope in reckless abandon until they broke away from the cliff at the bottom out on to the burning steppe.

Pulling their guns and firing into the air the three hopeful rescuers charged the front of the stampede in an effort to turn it from its mindless charge toward the bottom of the cliff wall. They didn't want to turn the cattle around back into the wall of flames. Instead the intent was to drive the cattle pass the edge of the flames, or outside of the circle of fire to safety. With the raging inferno swiftly closing the narrowing gap of escape speed became paramount.

The sudden raucous charge of the newcomers straight at the herd startled the leaders into changing the pattern of the stampede. The herd shifted its direction from the cliff to the dwindling path of escape. Within a few yards the herd resumed its original course once again toward disaster.

When the four hands saw their reinforcements they redoubled their efforts. With the seven riders now shouting and shooting the mass of bovines again diverted toward the vanishing safety zone now just a dozen or so yards wide. This time the herd stayed on course toward survival.

As the front of the stampede plowed through to safety Max and Dora, riding point, drew up against the adjacent cliff wall until most of the herd filed through. They wheeled to the rear of the stampede to help the others drive through the stragglers. When the last of the cattle had dashed through the shrinking passage the riders made their own bid for freedom.

Without warning Johnny's horse balked at the oncoming wall of flames. In a desperate bid for control the young cowhand tried driving his panicky animal through the smoky corridor. His horse refusing to comply, whirled away, only to lose its balance and roll over on top of its rider. Once on its feet again without Johnny astride the horse bolted back into the diminishing circle of unscathed flora.

Acting on instinct Dora plunged through the portal, flames licking out at her and her steed. Johnny had gotten to his feet as She rode up to him. Grabbing her hand he leaped on behind her, but as they whirled around they found that the portal was closed. The inferno had reached the cliff.

"We'll try the other side!" Dora shouted. "Let's go, Spirit!"

She spurred her big stud on. Like an extension of her own body he responded to her command. Driving through the swirling smoke along the face of the jagged cliff they reached the opposite advancing front of the encroaching inferno. There they found sheer rock face being blackened by flames. They were trapped!

"Where's my horse?" Johnny posed.

The circle of blaze had advanced close enough now. Through th smoke they could see all the wall of fire. Johnny's horse could not l seen in the diminishing, unscathed area with them.

"He must have found a way out!" Johnny yelled.

"Or a place to hide!" Dora reasoned aloud.

Searching along the face of the bluff Dora espied the mis horse's hoof prints disappearing behind a large outcrop. ie followed them in. Behind the outcrop they saw a steep-sided ca⁰ⁿ a scant few feet wide. Johnny's steed was fifty feet away in a tile effort to scramble up the precipitous slope.

"He'll never make it! The slope is too steep to climb!" Johnny shouted above the roaring of the threatening flames.

"Neither will we!" Dora shouted back. "This will have to do! We'll just have to wait it out!"

They charged into the deep crevice as the flames bore down on the entrance. Picking his way through the stony rubble Spirit carried his passengers into the relative safety of the inner depths of the narrow break in the bluff wall. The appearance of familiar company helped to settle the other horse. Johnny slid off of Spirit's back to tend to his own animal's welfare. His horse settled down at his soothing voice.

For a quarter of an hour both human and beast suffered the intense heat and heavy smoke that boiled into their tight refuge. Dora tied her kerchief around Spirit's nose in an effort to cut some of the smoke. Kneeling close to the ground she buried her face in her hat. Johnny followed suit. Both horses kept their heads low.

At last the heat began to subside. Dora and Johnny looked up to see that the smoke was almost gone. Visible through the crevice opening were black, smoldering ground and the burnt stubble of bushes and brush against a soot-darkened outcrop.

Since the horses couldn't turn around in the narrow space Dora and Johnny helped them back out. As soon as they had their horses in the clear they heard Templeton's deep bass voice calling, "Dora! Johnny! Where are you?"

Mounting up the two rode out from behind the outcrop to face an astounded Max.

"Hi, Boss!" Dora greeted with a cheery wave. "Looking for us?"

"Either you're the luckiest people this side of Texas, or I'm looking at a bunch of ghosts!" he exclaimed.

"That's right! We just popped out of the rocks," she quipped.

"You can explain that later," Max said. "Right now we'd better et back to the herd. The boys have them rounded up but they're still fidgety as a brand new groom."

As they rode off to return to the others the last remnants of the conflagration flickered here and there along the base of the cliff, dying reminders of the tragic event that might have been.

Keeping silence so as not to spook the restless, lowing cattle the other men waved their hands high in relief at the

124

approaching party. They welcomed the sight of the two missing riders. When the handshaking and backslapping subsided Dora explained their escape. She gave a brief account of how they saved themselves from the fire by finding the crevice in the bluff.

"We're sure glad you did," Max expressed. "Everyone is safe and accounted for." He turned to his acting foreman. "Johnny, what can you tell us about the fire? Do you know what, or who started it?"

"Well," he began, "Jack and I were riding herd while Monty and Claude were checking the fence line and looking for strays. Jack started making lunch around noon. Monty and Claude got back just in time to eat with us. We were sitting around eating lunch when all of a sudden the flames were shooting up all over the place. We just had time to mount up before the herd would have run us down. We were trying to turn them out to safety when you showed up."

"Did you notice anything unusual about the smell of the smoke?" Dora quizzed.

"I sure did! It smelled like kerosene. I smelled it just before we saw the fire coming at us."

"We smelled it, too," the other hands chorused.

"After I take Botts' body into town I'm bringing the sheriff back out here to look around," the deputy announced. "This looks like arson."

"Dora and I are going to go check out the place where the fire started," Max decided, "to make sure it doesn't flare up again. Boys, the cattle seem to be settled down now. Move them to the Cross Wash. Deputy, coming with us?"

The three of them turned back to reconnoiter the area where the fire had first been kindled. In a few places small patches of grass still smoldered at the edge of the burnt, u-shaped fire circle. At each smoldering spot one of the riders dismounted to stomp out the grass or brush.

Following the perimeter of the burned area brought them to the edge of a shallow wash. Its sandy bottom revealed two sets of boot prints, one leading to and the other leaving the spot where the three of them stood. Dora saw a damp spot on the ground near the edge of the wash. She scooped up a handful of the damp earth.

"Kerosene," she sniffed offering it to the other two to take a whiff. They both nodded agreement.

"What do you make of it?" the deputy queried.

"I think that someone with red hair, not successful in his efforts to kill you, is now trying to drive you out, Max," Dora mused. "The question is why? Is it just to try to get your land?"

Templeton shrugged. "I wish I knew."

At that moment an alarming thought popped into her head. Leaping into her saddle she beckoned to the others to follow her.

"Come on!" she yelled. "We've got to get back to the ranch house quick!"

Not understanding yet sensing the urgency in Dora's command the two men scrambled into their saddles. Spurring their mounts they galloped after her already several yards ahead.

"What's the hurry?" Max shouted when they had caught up to her.

"The house is unguarded!" Dora threw back with the wind. "This fire bug may be planning to burn it down!"

The impact of Dora's statement furrowed Max's brow with grave concern. Envisioning the possible destruction of his home he spurred his horse on faster.

When the ranch house loomed into sight the three riders reined in their huffing steeds. They surveyed the situation for several moments. The building revealed no signs of activity. Was this just the quiet before the conflagration?

"We'll separate and approach the house from three sides," Max directed. "I'll follow the draw that goes around behind the back of the barn and pass through it before sneaking up to the house."

"I'll sneak up on the front," volunteered the deputy.

"Max, I'll follow you up the draw and come up on the back door," Dora offered.

"Good," the burly man approved. "Let's go."

The three split up. While the deputy headed for the front of the house Dora and Max circled down to the draw. The dry wash meandered its way across the rear of the barnyard then off through the bulk of the Templeton spread. About twenty yards from the barn Max rode out of the draw to approach his vantage point behind the barn. Dora rode a few yards farther on before she ascended out of the draw in the direction of the rear of the house. She watched Max leave his horse behind the barn while he slipped through the back door.

More cautious than a cat climbing a cactus she approached the house. No trees or shrubs to use as camouflage or cover occupied the grounds. She kept a wary eye open for the slightest movement at any of the windows.

At the front corner of the barn she dismounted to leave her faithful steed standing just out of sight of the house. Alone she stole toward the rear door. Although the distance between the back door and the corner of the barn was only about one hundred feet Dora felt like a sitting duck. Were there alien eyes peering at her from one of the windows? With her weapon drawn she dashed across the open ground.

Having reached the back door without incident Dora glanced back to the front doors of the barn. Max would be coming out as soon as he had determined that no one was in the barn. She reasoned that the deputy should be positioned by the front door by now or soon. Gritting her teeth she lifted the latch, gave the door a slight shove, and waited for several seconds while listening.

Not a squeak sounded from inside. Peering around the doorjamb she stepped across the threshold. Her gun was poised for business.

The kitchen reeked with the pungent odor of kerosene. Littering the floor were the fragments of shattered lamps, their flammable contents soaking into the hardwood.

Remembering how she and Max had surprised Botts in the kitchen doorway Dora scrutinized the portal up close. No one was there. She tiptoed into the living room.

The scene in the living room mimicked that of the kitchen. One difference was that the hoop rug had sponged up most of the spilled kerosene. Dora's surmise that the house might be next to be set aflame was right.

Just then the front door latch lifted. Dora stepped away from the kitchen doorway with her weapon trained on the far door. Creaking on its hinges the heavy door swung open part way. The barrel of a pistol preceded the deputy's face through the opening.

Dora motioned to him to come in. Surveying the mess in the room he gave her an understanding nod. Pointing to the hallway in the opposite wall she met him there. Together they searched each room for signs of the intruder. Each room they checked was a repeat of what they had seen throughout the house. Kerosene lamps were smashed on the floor with their contents strewn about. For an unknown reason the last two rooms had escaped the vandal's mark. By the time they were checking the last room Max caught up to them. The vandal was gone.

"Maybe he saw or heard us coming and hightailed it out of here before he could finish the job," the deputy mused. "We got here just in time."

"Don't anyone light a match in here," Max ordered. "Let's open some windows to air the place out. The boys can help me clean up this mess tonight."

Dispersing through the house the three of them accomplished Max's order in a short time. They met back in the kitchen.

"Deputy, we'd better get you loaded up with Botts' body and get you back to town," Max decided.

"Okay, Mr. Templeton. I'll have the sheriff come out here to investigate first hand what's been going on."

They started for the barn when the sudden sound of pounding hoof beats reached their ears. Rushing to the corner of the barn they got there in time to see a red-haired man, riding fast, disappear down into the draw.

"My horse!" Dora shouted. "He stole my horse!"

19

"Come on, Deputy!" Max barked. "After him!"

The men ran off to fetch their own tethered mounts. While the deputy ran around to the front of the house Max barreled around the barn to his. Moments later they galloped around the far end of the barn in speedy pursuit of the horse thief. In the meantime Dora had run into the barn to saddle up another horse. Finding the tack room door locked she shot off the lock. If Max was concerned he could deduct it from her bill.

Scant minutes later she raced from the barn to follow the trail of the desperado. Only a settling cloud of dust on a distant rise revealed the direction the others had taken. Undaunted she tore off in hot pursuit. She now had her own score to settle with this thieving outlaw.

Dora had just topped the rise where she had seen the cloud of dust when she saw two riders coming toward her. A third horse was trotting along after Max and the deputy. Without a rider here came Spirit.

"Did you get that louse?" she quizzed as they met up.

"No, he got away," Max answered, chagrined "He got over into those badlands," he waved his hand at the rocky countryside, "and we lost his trail."

"How did you get Spirit back?"

"Red, if that's his name, must have left his horse farther up the draw from where we climbed out to sneak up on the barn and house. He must have hopped on Spirit just to get to his own horse quicker. Spirit was just standing in the draw when we got there. I guess he decided to tag along with us for the chase. He's been following us ever since."

Dora dismounted, trading the horse she had borrowed for Spirit. "I'm going after Red," she said. "I'll try to pick up his trail again. Which way was he headed?"

"West when we lost the trail."

"Let's hope he keeps going that way. See you before dark unless I catch him."

She spurred away, a strategy developing in her brain. First she'd ride to the high ridge points to see if she could spot any sign of Red riding in the distance. If she couldn't she'd look for his tracks.

From the half dozen or so vantage points that she topped she could see no sign of the fugitive. Once she had ridden across the stretch of badlands she followed the perimeter in search of Red's tracks. She found them heading at first north and then east. The depth and space of the hoof prints showed her that he was driving his horse hard and fast. In a flash she was urging Spirit just as fast in an effort to overtake her quarry.

Mile after mile rolled under hoof. Nary a sign of a dust cloud nor another rider was visible between her and the horizon. The terrain was rolling enough to help obscure a lone rider. He had doubled back once. He could change directions again. The ground she was covering was rocky. In the soft sandy spots an occasional hoof print or two might appear now and again. If he were to change course any more she could ride several hundred yards or so before realizing that he had. Much time could be taken to pick up a trail again. This would put her even farther behind. Reining Spirit in Dora decided that further pursuit was fruitless at this time. Dusk would soon fall hampering her search. In disgust she headed back to the ranch house. Red had managed to elude his pursuers again.

"That's enough for you, Spirit," she consoled proffering him an affectionate pat on his neck. "Red may ride his horse into the ground in this heat, but I won't. Next time don't let anyone else ride you unless I give the okay."

With a neigh Spirit tossed his head in agreement.

By the time Dora arrived back at the ranch house the deputy had long since left with his cargo for the undertaker. She left Spirit in Marty's care and went in to a late supper. Her mood matched the moonless night, dark.

"I can see by your expression that you didn't catch our friendly neighborhood bushwhacker," Max greeted her as she trudged in.

"If that guy's horse doesn't fall over dead it won't be due to any favors he gives it," she snorted. "Red's more elusive than a snowflake in the Sahara. He left just enough of a trail to follow

130

though. Tomorrow I'll start out early with some rations to last me a few days. With luck that trail will lead me to the end of this mystery."

"If it doesn't rain," Max added.

"Although we need the moisture there's not a cloud in the sky," she countered. "We may have a whole summer of drought ahead of us."

"I hope not. A couple of days more for your sake will be long enough. My range grass needs the moisture."

* * *

That evening the rains came. Throughout the night the rain fell in a steady shower. The rainfall quenched the thirst of the parched ground, filled the washes with swirling torrents, and erased all traces of tracks with soupy quagmire. Several times during the night Dora stirred to the incessant drumming of the rain. Above the patter she could hear the new river rushing along the draw behind the barn. The last time she awoke before sunrise she justified to herself that the rain was needed much more than the trail of Max's antagonist. Red would be back. Rolling over she went to sleep again.

By morning the rain had subsided to a drizzle. The new dawn was not yet an hour old when the skies began to clear. Within the hour the river in the draw reduced to little more than a trickle leaving a muddy wake in its path.

Recipient of the draw's discharge along with many more such washes the Arkansas River rode high in its banks. The surrounding farms relished the revitalizing moisture. Even with all the overnight shower the ground had soaked it up like a sponge.

Dora was already up before the first rays of light. She was giving Jack a hand in the kitchen. After bolting a quick breakfast she threw a few provisions into her saddlebags. Max sauntered in at that moment.

"Still going to follow that trail?" he asked. "Even after all this rain? All the tracks will be gone."

"I've got a hunch where Red was going," she replied. "Going east like he was the next stop would be Kansas a good week's ride from here. I think he changed course and headed for Las Animas."

131

"Las Animas? That's only a stage stop between Lamar and La Junta. What makes you think he'd go there?"

"To hole up. Las Animas is the closest settlement to your ranch. Even though the stop is not much more than a spot in the road Red might be staying in one of the few rooms available. The owner has a small store as well. Red could be getting a lot of his provisions and supplies there."

"Hmm, maybe you've hit on a good clue," Max agreed. "Good luck."

Dora shouldered her bulging saddlebags. "If my hunch doesn't pay off I'll be back tonight. If it does—well, don't wait up for me." She tromped out of the kitchen door toward the barn.

The previous night's rain had done little to alleviate the daytime heat which was already dancing in steamy mirages in the distance. Driven inside by the rain the flies swarmed worse than normal around the horses in the barn.

Spirit pawed the earthen floor. With impatience he neighed his desire to vacate the fly-infested building. Empathizing with him Dora hastened to saddle up and ride away.

In hot weather the trip to Las Animas took almost half a day. When she rode up to the singular structure a gray-headed sexagenarian was sitting in the shade of the veranda. Hanging between his smoke stained teeth was a well-used corncob pipe. He offered a passive nod behind horn-rimmed glasses as she stepped off her horse.

"Howdy," he greeted, his scratchy voice accenting his age. "Help ya?"

"Maybe. I'm looking for a redheaded fellow. He calls himself Red. Has he been this way?"

"Yup. Until this mornin' the feller was stayin' here. Packed up 'n' left first thing."

"He did? Did he say where he was going?" She hid her chagrin.

"Nope. Headed toward Lamar though."

"Thanks for the information. What's for lunch?"

"Stew. Made it fresh this mornin'. Stage will be here in an hour." He glanced at his pocket watch as if to confirm his report.

"Sounds good. Dish some up."

The old man sauntered into the station to dish up her order. While she waited Dora reflected on why Red was heading for Lamar. She came in on the road from Lamar, yet she hadn't met him along the way. Perhaps he had already passed before she had reached it. He could also have crossed the river to ride along the opposite shore.

Although no road ran on the other side she could see someone like Red wanting to avoid the main road. Plenty of trees along its banks offered cover. As she ate she quizzed the stage stop owner about her quarry.

"How long was Red here?"

"Off 'n' on, 'bout two weeks."

"Did he say why he was here?"

"Nope."

"Did he say anything about himself?"

"Nope. He didn't say. I didn't ask. Quiet type."

Who? You, or him? Discretion kept her from uttering those questions aloud. "Did anyone ever meet him here?"

"Nope."

Finishing her meal Dora paid the tab. "Good stew. Thanks for the information," she said, trying not to sound facetious.

"Yup," he grunted. "Any time."

Departing from the stage stop after such a scintillating conversation she rode toward Lamar. The sky had become overcast again allowing the afternoon to cool down. She and Spirit were able to make better time. By early evening she had reached town. She rode straight to Peter Hyatt's house where she received a hearty welcome at the doctor's back door.

"Come in, Dora," Pete greeted. "What brings you back to Lamar so soon?"

"In search of a fugitive," she answered. "I have a favor to ask of you. Before I do will you check this shoulder out to see how it's doing?"

"Be happy to. Let's go into the kitchen."

She sat on the edge of the table while he examined the injury.

"This is the same bandage I put on," he scolded in mock sternness. "You should change this more often."

"You're the only doctor I know, Pete. Make this new bandage just as good. It'll probably be on there until the wound is healed."

"You're Amos' kin all right. He said the same thing when I patched up his leg years ago."

"You did a good job, Pete. He walked on it to the end."

133

"You win," he relinquished. "What's the favor you wanted?"

"Can you do some inquiring for me? This man I'm chasing was coming this way. He may be here in town. The saloon would be my first guess. He's not to discover that I'm following him. Can you find out for me?"

"Of course, Dora. For whom do I look?"

Dora recounted a brief description of Red along with his attempts on Templeton's life and property over the past couple of days. Then she changed the subject. "How's the town doing?" she inquired.

"With Adrian gone Bill Oates as you know the president of the bank has been working on getting his estate cleared up. Seems there aren't any known relatives with which to leave it. In any case the folks are a whole lot happier. I don't think they'll let someone like Delgrin ride herd on them again."

"What about the James?"

"Rebuilding their farm. Lots of folks are helping them. He's got most of his crops planted. This rain we just had should have filled up his irrigation ponds. They've got a good chance of succeeding this time."

"Good. I think I'll pay them a visit. One of Jill James's dinners would suit me just fine. I'll be back tonight to see what you've found out."

The bell on the office door tinkled. A voice called out, "Hey, Doc, you here? I came to pick up that medicine."

"Be right there," he said, his voice so loud it echoed. In a quieter tone he said to Dora, "That bandage should do it for you. You can take it off in a few days."

She shoved some money into his hand. "Thanks, Pete. This should cover the bill. I'll let myself out the way I came in."

The thirty-minute ride along the river to the James' farm invigorated Dora. Farius Delgrin had sold Arnold one of the best pieces of ground off of his ranch. As she rode in she found fresh furrowed fields and a new house well under construction. Their good neighbors had put a lot of effort in to get them re-established.

Around the corner of the house came Jill toting a bucket of water. Upon seeing Dora approaching, a grin of delight spread across her pretty face.

"Arnold! Lilly!" she exclaimed. "Look who's here!"

When brief greetings had been exchanged Jill invited their guest to supper. In mock modesty Dora accepted. "I thought you'd never ask," she kidded.

"You make the best meal out of the simplest fixings," Dora complimented her hostess at the end of the meal.

After a brief visit which included a tour of the developing farm and several of Arnold's inventions in progress Dora bid her friends farewell. She thanked them again for their hospitality.

"Do you have to go so soon?" Lilly implored.

"I'm afraid so, Lilly. There's some business in Lamar for me to tend to. The next time through I'll plan to stay longer."

"Come any time, Dora," Jill offered. "You're always welcome."

Dora waved good-bye as she rode away. With the evening bringing in cool breezes Dora spurred Spirit into an easy loping gait. Within minutes she was back at Pete Hyatt's back door which stood open to the welcome air. Pete was sitting at his kitchen table.

"Come in," he invited. "I just got back myself."

Dora pulled up a chair. "What did you find out?"

"Your man was in town all right. A red head is easy to spot when there's only one in the crowd. He was sitting in the saloon with three other strangers. They talked for a while after which they all left together. I saw them riding west out of town."

"Back toward La Junta," Dora pondered. "He must have hired him some more gunmen. Looks like the time has come again to ride. I've got a job to finish."

Pete objected. "The hour's late. Dusk has fallen. There's no moon out tonight. Why don't you stay and sleep in my extra room or on my couch? Those men couldn't be camped more than half an hour's ride from here. You could get an early start in the morning. Chances are you'll catch up to them before they break camp."

"Yes, I guess you're right. Spirit will need to be tended to first. Do you have a place to keep him for the night?"

"There's an extra stall in the barn with plenty of feed."

"Thanks. Once Spirit is put away I'm going to sack out then. See you in the morning if you're up when I am."

20

The first streaks of dawn found Dora on the trail of Red and his three new henchmen. Figuring that the four men would camp close to the river she rode the riverbank. About half an hour's ride from town her search was rewarded. Remains of a campfire lay on the rim of the bank. No warmth remained in the embers. The occupants had dowsed it well. The evidence of flattened grass around the bed of coals proved that several people had bedded down there the previous night.

Not knowing how far ahead they were Dora hastened her pursuit.

She picked up their tracks nearby. They led her back to the main road where they continued west toward La Junta. In an effort to shorten the lead the four men had Dora spurred her horse into a demanding gallop. With luck she might catch them before the heat of the day set in.

During the next hour she noticed the skies growing cloudy once more. With the sun's heat diverted for the time being she kept up the pace. While she was able to let Spirit continue to make better time the fact was clear that the four men had the same advantage. Were they in as big a rush? Did they have reason to be?

By mid morning the stage stop of Las Animas loomed ahead. Spirit's endurance was praiseworthy, yet Dora knew that he needed a break. She let him walk the last quarter of a mile to the station. As she rode up she found the old man sitting in the same seat where he had sat the day before. Hanging from his mouth was the same dilapidated pipe. If she hadn't seen him move last time when she ordered his stew she would have sworn that he was glued to his chair. Reining in at the water trough she let Spirit quench his thirst.

"Morning," she greeted. "Did you see Red ride through here with three other men this morning?"

"Yup," he responded between puffs of acrid smoke.

"How long ago?"

"Fifteen minutes mebbe." He tapped the bowl of his pipe on the arm of his chair to loosen the tobacco.

"Did they stop?"

"Yup. Watered their horses."

"Good! Maybe I can catch up."

"Dunno. They went outta here a-runnin' faster'n they came in."

This bit of news proved alarming. "Did you say anything to Red?"

"Told 'im you was asking about 'im yestiday."

Dora wasn't happy to hear this report. For once he could have been quiet. Hiding her dismay she queried, "Did he say anything to you?"

"Nope. Seemed surprised, that's all. After watering their horses they took off like blazes. Mebbe they saw yuh comin'. Don't know why he'd run from a purdy little gal like you. You sure he's worth chasin'?"

Pulling Spirit's head up from the trough Dora muttered, "I'm not after him for him, I'm after him for what he owes me. Thanks for your concern." She charged off in hot pursuit of the four men.

"Any time," he hollered after her.

Now that the men knew of her interest in Red they might have grown more determined to reach their destination. Maybe they were even now aware of her pursuit. If they were only about fifteen minutes ahead they may have spotted her dust cloud on the road behind them. As a precaution the men might assume that she were the one trailing them. Dora felt positive about their destination and the purpose for going. She gave Spirit's neck an affectionate pat.

"Sorry for the workout, old boy," she consoled, "but this is all in the line of duty. I'll give you a break when we're done."

Showing renewed vigor Spirit responded in step to her commands. If he could keep up the pace they would reach the Templeton Ranch and Dora hoped the four gunmen before noon.

She was riding through a deep gorge on a road to Max's spread when without warning Spirit came to an abrupt halt. Pawing the ground he snorted at the trail ahead of them. Something was disturbing him. Dora could sense it now. Danger to the tune of death awaited them somewhere ahead.

Were the four gunmen waiting in ambush for her? Retracing the road from where she had just come she found a wash that Spirit could ascend to the rim of the gorge. She left him tied at the top.

From there Dora stole ahead on foot along the rocky rim. About two hundred yards up the gorge she spotted one of the men. He was sprawled on his stomach on a shelf of rock some twenty feet below her. Gun drawn he was watching the road where she should appear. On her hands and knees she crept closer to the edge, crouching right above the would-be sniper. The brim of his hat shielded his eyes from spotting her on the rim. Red was written all over this attempted ambush.

Just the one man was visible. Heavy brush and scrub oak lined the rocky ravine bottom affording ample concealment for an army of bushwhackers. While she could have disposed of this one with ease the others could escape through the undergrowth. As this scenario suggested she reckoned that Red and his henchmen were waiting to see who was following them. Taking this one man out would betray her presence to the other three. They would then know of her intent and whereabouts for certain. Although they lay below her their concealment could turn the advantage to their side. She needed a stratagem to trick them into revealing their hiding places before they grew impatient and suspicious. She needed something that would—

Brrrrrrrrrt!

Before she had even looked around to find the source of the buzz she had recognized the disconcerting rattle on the tail of its owner. A scant six feet away coiled into its striking stance a western diamondback rattlesnake reared its solemn warning to unwary, careless trespassers in its immediate realm. With great caution Dora backed away from the menace. As she did she glanced behind her to keep an eye out for the possible mate to this one. Putting a safe distance from one would be fruitless if she were to step on or over another one.

The presence of the snake only complicated the problem at hand, unless—. Brainstorming an idea she checked the ground around the rim of the gorge. Several yards from the edge an occasional scraggy piñon stood. On the ground near one of these she found a stout limb that had the semblance of a fork at one end. She approached the snake once again with stick in hand.

The snake had slithered a few feet from its original spot, but coiled again as Dora closed in. Brandishing her stick in front of the snake Dora coaxed it to strike at her. This it did striking a counter attack at the stick. She tried to pin its head but missed. On its second lunge she managed to pin the snake's head with the forked end. Keeping a steady pressure on the stick she grabbed the reptile with a firm grip behind its triangular head. Dropping the stick Dora held the writhing, lethal viper with both hands. She stole to the rim of the gorge positioned above the waiting gunman. With a heave she tossed the reptile over the side and ducked from sight. A couple of seconds passed before she heard the reaction.

"Hey! Yeow!" the man screamed. "Rattlesnake! I've been bit!"

The man's incessant screams brought his comrades out from their concealment. Three heads popped up at various places in the bushes. Dora spotted the man she wanted most, Red. She knew that if she took him out the others might just abandon their original intents. As she drew a bead on him he espied her.

"Look out above!" he shouted, diving back into the bushes just before she fired. The bullet missed its intended target. She cursed her luck. Before the other two had registered Red's warning shout or the sound of her shot Dora had put a bullet between the eyes of one of them. The second man dived for cover. Neither had found the chance to return fire. She pumped several more shots into the bushes where the men had been hiding. Then she pulled back to reload.

The snake victim returned a volley of shots which ricocheted away off the rock rim. Scurrying back along the edge she sought a vantage point where she could see the man below without becoming a target for the other two. Soon she found a good spot just as she heard the man scream again. The snake had struck once more.

Peering over the edge Dora saw the man cursing and stomping on the snake's body. Before he crushed its head with the heel of his boot the serpent managed to make a third strike. The snake continued to twist and wriggle in death. As the man glared down at the crushed, writhing reptile Dora pumped a bullet through the top of his head. He crumpled into a heap without a whimper.

"I just saved you the agony of a painful death," she muttered to the corpse. "That was more than you deserved."

Once again she crept along the rim for a new vantage point. As she neared a spot on the rim right above where Red had been hiding she heard two sets of pounding hoof beats. The last two miscreants had abandoned their foiled ambush. They were heading out of the gorge. Dora sprinted back to her waiting steed. As quick as she dared she urged Spirit down the wash to the road through the gorge.

By the time she reached open range the evidence of the other two riders was a distant cloud of dust. The cloud billowed in the direction of Templeton's ranch.

That Red, whoever he is, is an obstinate cuss! she thought in disgust. *Even now, with me after him he's going for Max.*

All of a sudden hot lead was flying all around her. She glanced back over her shoulder to see Red's last henchman charging full bore after her. In each of his hands blazed a revolver spitting its lethal charges straight at Dora!

21

No close cover lay ahead of her. Their trick had worked well. Thinking that two riders created the dust cloud Dora had followed them into open country allowing her pursuer the advantage. Somewhere near the gorge he had hidden until she had passed. Her only choice was to try to outrun him. Shooting from the back of a galloping horse made accuracy a fleeting skill even for her.

Dora realized that the pursuer's shots would be the cue for Red to turn around and head back. If she didn't come up with a plan quick she would be caught in their crossfire. In this situation two against one didn't balance the odds to her liking.

Searing pain ripped across her right thigh. Acting on a flash of inspiration Dora shifted her weight to the left side while at the same time yanking Spirit's head in and around to the right. Spirit slammed on the brakes. Her maneuver threw him off balance causing him to have to roll to his left as he stopped. She stuck her left leg out to roll out of the saddle onto the ground. Sprawling on her stomach while facing the direction of her antagonist she whipped her gun into readiness.

To the onrushing gunman Dora appeared to have been shot out of the saddle. Since Spirit lay between the two of them as he rode up he couldn't see her lying ready. He would conclude that she was dead or badly injured and relax his guard. Risky as it was at least this was the deception Dora was hoping for.

Spirit scrambled to his feet and bolted to one side enabling Dora to see that the outlaw had holstered his left weapon and held his right one by his side. She took instant aim and fired.

Realizing Dora's successful decoy the outlaw jerked on the reins to turn his horse in its speed causing the bullet intended for him to strike the animal in the neck. With a whinny of pain the horse lurched and fell throwing its passenger to the ground. The free gun went flying from his hand as he attempted to catch his fall.

In the flick of a cat's whisker Dora had gained the advantage. Scrambling to her feet she leveled her gun at him before he had even quit rolling. He tried to jump to his feet as he stopped.

"Hold it, buster," she barked, "or the next bullet won't miss!"

The gunman seeing that she had the drop on him sagged in defeat. Dora moved to the other side of him where she could look beyond the man to keep track of the dust cloud that Red was raising. If Red were to return to his henchman's aid Dora would be able to see him coming.

"I want some answers and fast!" she ordered. "Why is Red out to kill Maxwell Templeton?"

The gunman hesitated, then decided better to answer when Dora cocked the hammer of her gun. "He wants Templeton's ranch."

"Why?"

A murmur rolled off his tongue. "Oil."

The startling answer was the last one she had expected. When she had passed herself off as an oil-drilling company representative to Adrian Delgrin she had fabricated her story as part of the ruse. Dora had no idea whether there was any oil under Delgrin's or Templeton's properties. She had done enough research on the topic just to be convincing to Delgrin. Had Red somehow overheard her conversation in the hotel room with Delgrin and from there decided to try seizing the pretended oil? How ironic for him if this were the case. Or was there another reason that had convinced him that oil was present?

"What makes him think that Templeton's ranch has oil under it?" she quizzed, quite curious as to what the answer would be.

"Unknown to Templeton he took a geologist all over the ranch. The geologist told him that oil could be found in several places."

"What geologist?"

"I don't know. Red didn't tell me."

"Is he in cahoots with this geologist?"

"I don't know. All I know is he's supposed to be staying in the mountains somewhere until Red needs him again. That won't be until Red gets rid of Templeton so that he can get the ranch."

"Does the Delgrin ranch figure into this oil find?"

The outlaw nodded. "It's supposed to have oil under it as well."

"What do you get out of this?" Dora queried.

"A fourth of the oil profits. That was when Charley and Ralph were still alive before you shot them. Now I'd get half."

"Charley and Ralph? The two corpses still back in the gorge?"

"Yeah," the outlaw muttered dropping his gaze to the ground.

The puzzle made more sense now. Red had hired George Botts to kill Delgrin, Templeton, and Jill James. Botts may even have been a partner as this man claimed to be. When Botts got himself killed Red had decided to get rid of Templeton on his own and keep all the oil. Failing at this he had made an agreement with these three he had met with in Lamar. The motive for murder was enticing. Oil could make a man rich almost overnight.

Two puzzle pieces were still missing. One, was Hiram Minkle the geologist in question? The outlaw hadn't known, but he should know the answer to the second piece.

"How does Red plan on gaining possession of both the ranches?"

"He had some phony documents made up that says he's a cousin of Adrian Delgrin," the man replied. "As for the Templeton ranch Charley and Ralph were brothers and nephews of Templeton. They were going to step in and claim his place as the closest next of kin once we got rid of him."

"Nephews? This is a strange way to show their uncle their love."

Since she had circled her assailant Dora had been keeping an eye on Red's dust trail. The cloud had continued to move away from them and had almost dwindled from view. Red must have reckoned that his partner would succeed in gunning her down without his help.

"Why did Red ride on alone instead of coming back to help?" she quizzed.

"He figured I'd circle behind you and pick you off before you'd realize the trick. Then I was supposed to meet him near the ranch to help him finish off Templeton."

"You're still going to meet him," Dora informed him. "The only difference is I'm going to be right behind you. Come on, get up."

With feigned effort as if bruised from his tumble the outlaw stumbled to his feet. Without warning he went for his holstered gun. CRACK! His weapon had just cleared the holster before Dora's shot sent it sailing. Holding his stinging hand with his other the outlaw stared in disbelief at the female gunslinger.

"You're asking to be left like Charley and Ralph, aren't you?" she growled, brandishing her pistol at his chest. "No more tricks. I've got use for you walking around by yourself."

He shook his sore hand. "I've never seen such fast or straight shooting before, ma'am." Respect and humility rang in his words. "I reckon Red's lucky to be alive. May I ask you one question?"

"Make it snappy. You've got a meeting to keep."

"I've heard of a young woman who's as fast as lightning with a gun. Folks say she gunned down Slim Cramer of Texas *after* shooting two of his men. Just bang, bang, bang; one, two, three. Are you the one folks call Petticoat?"

Dora fought back the urge for a gratifying smile. "I am," she answered in a gruff tone, then changed the subject. "We'll have to ride double on my horse. You take the front. Get on."

Offering no more resistance the beaten gun fighter swung into Spirit's saddle. Dora swung on behind him. Gazing down at the moribund horse lying quiescent on the ground, she fired a shot that struck the animal just below the ear. It died without a quiver.

"Such a shame to have to destroy a good animal like that," she commented with condolences, "but you won't have any use for a horse for some time where you'll be going."

Of slender build the man that she had apprehended was just a couple of inches taller than she. A quick, mental calculation told her that Spirit would have to pack a little over double his accustomed load. She wouldn't push him too hard with the extra weight.

Since the outlaw controlled the reins Dora ordered him to continue to follow Red's trail to the ranch.

Once they were riding Dora gave some attention to the stinging wound on her leg. She felt fortunate that the graze was no worse than a bad rope burn. The blood had already dried to a scab. What was more upsetting to her was that a good pair of pants had been damaged. The first chance she'd get she would take them to Hannah Minkle and have her mend the tear.

As they neared the ranch buildings Dora scanned the terrain in case Red came popping up out of a ravine or from behind a stand of juniper. Such was not the case. When she did spot Red he was astride his horse standing in a small clump of evergreens right ahead of them. His attention was focused toward the ranch house a thousand yards away. The sound of their approaching hoof beats caught his attention. He twisted his neck in their direction.

Red called out, "Bill, why are you riding that dame's horse—"

His question was cut short when Dora's face appeared over Bill's shoulder. She leveled her weapon at Red.

"Real slow and easy, Red," she commanded. "Take your holster off and drop it to the ground."

As instructed Red moved to comply. He reached down as if to untie his holster strap. Instead, he dove off the far side of his horse and dashed into the trees. Dora couldn't draw a good bead on Red. His horse was blocking her aim. Her first shot was too late.

The bullet splintered the tree that Red had ducked behind.

"Quick! Take cover!" she barked to Bill.

They spurred Spirit for the nearest trees. While they did Red returned several shots, one of which struck his partner. As Bill toppled backward off of Spirit's back Dora knocked off balance slid off with him. Almost on instinct she flattened into as inconspicuous a target as possible. Thus positioned she fired a couple of shots to keep Red behind cover. Her opponent was no longer interested in the battle. Running and leaping upon his steed that had followed him into the trees he dashed away through the junipers. Dora couldn't get a clean shot. The miscreant had eluded her again.

Spirit was standing a number of yards away. Dora whistled to him as she knelt down by Bill who was sitting on the ground with his hand pressed against his opposite shoulder. She took a good look at the bullet hole. It had passed through the edge of the muscle below the socket and out the other side.

"The bleeding is bad, but you'll live to stand trial," she diagnosed as she took her bandanna and pressed it against the wound. "Hold this in place. It'll help the bleeding to stop."

Spirit trotted up to them. "Come on," she ordered, helping Bill to his feet. "I'll get you to the ranch where they can see to your shoulder. I've just one more question. What's Red's last name?"

Bill shook his head. "With him having shot me I'd like to tell you but I can't. All of us that ever worked for him knew him only as Red. He wouldn't tell us his last name. He said it was best not to know too much."

Dora had to let Red get away again for the sake of Bill's wounded shoulder as she walked Spirit to the ranch house. He had surrendered. She felt obligated to tend to his need. Templeton with a number of his men came riding out to meet them.

"We heard some shooting," Max declared as he drew alongside. "We got here as quick as we could." He eyed Bill and his wounded shoulder. "Looks like you got yourself a lucky one, Petticoat."

"I didn't put that hole in him," Dora informed her lumbering employer. "Red did. If Bill here hadn't caught a bullet I'd be hauling in that red-haired varmint right now dead or alive. As it is he got away again."

"Which way was he heading?"

Dora pointed to the northwest. "That way when I last saw him. He was running so fast his shadow couldn't keep up."

Max turned to his foreman. "Art, take a few men and see if you can catch him. Bring him in any way you can."

"Right, Boss," Art acknowledged. He called out to three men who galloped off with him in hot pursuit of Red. They raced off in the direction Dora had shown.

Max turned to Dora's prisoner. "I remember you. You're Bill Reilly, a wanna be fast gun. You hang around with my no-good nephews, Charley and Ralph Slade. I had to fire you because you loafed too much and tried to steal some of my hands' belongings. Dora, how does Bill Reilly fit into this mess?"

"He's Red's cohort in a plot to get rid of you," Dora related. "So were your nephews, Charley and Ralph."

In a few words she adumbrated the events of the last two days up to the present moment. Max shook his head as he heard how his two nephews had met their fate in the gorge and where their bodies would be found. He turned to two more of his men.

"Johnny, Marty, go fetch their worthless carcasses from the gorge. The least I can do is to give my late sister's scalawags a decent burial. I'll only do it because she'd want it done."

"On your way you'll pass Bill's horse," Dora told them. "I had to shoot it. You might as well get the saddle and tack off of it. Bill's two guns should be lying close by."

The two men rode off in the direction of the gorge.

"Sorry about your nephews, but it was either you or them," Dora rationalized. "Besides they were waiting in the gorge to do the same to me. I managed to turn the tables on them."

"There was no love lost," Max snorted. "You did what you had to do. They were just like their no-good father who was shot down in an attempted bank robbery five years ago. After they ran their poor mother into an early grave they came here trying to hoodwink me into supporting them. I knew them too well. I sent them packing and told them not to darken my door again. If it weren't for my sister's memory they could lay in that gorge, and be buzzard bait."

Following Max the rest of the group headed back to the house. As they approached the buildings Dora noticed half a dozen or so extra men milling around the bunkhouse and barn. They were storing saddles and brushing down their mounts.

"Looks like your men are back from the cattle drive," she said.

"They got back about an hour ago," Max replied. "Jack is fixing lunch for them now. We might as well go eat."

"Bill will need to be taken to town after lunch. Can you have a couple of your men get him there? I'll want to follow after Art and the others as soon as we eat. Right now I've got a little of my own doctoring to do plus change into some fresh clothes."

Max noticed the bloody trace across her leg. "So I see. Is it serious?"

"Just a scratch. My jeans took it worse than I did."

"We'll take care of Bill. Most of the boys will be going into town tonight to drink up some of their wages and wash down the trail dust. This hombre will have the privilege of a full escort," Max assured her.

"Bill, you should have been a fast gun for the good guys like me," she said.

Dora made quick work of tending to her own injury and changing her clothes. She joined the others in the kitchen for roast beef and beans with corn bread. After polishing off a plateful she restocked her provisions for a long ride before mounting up.

"Success and be careful," Max counseled with a father's gleam in his eye. "This Red seems to be as slippery as a fish and a dangerous cuss."

She recognized his expression. Her father had used the same one on the day she rode off on her own. In a lot of ways she found Maxwell Templeton and her father similar. They had kicked around together a lot in their younger years. Being good friends they must have swapped many traits in those earlier days.

"I intend to return," she smiled a grim smile. "This Red has been eluding me long enough. If Art and the others don't run him down I'm going to follow after him until I do. With the trouble he's been he's going to be another cipher in my memos. Adios."

Reining away she spurred Spirit into rapid pursuit of the desperado. The trail left by Art and the other hands led from the stand of junipers in the general direction of west toward the distant mountains. Before she rode after them she espied Johnny and Marty returning leading two other horses with their dead owners tied on.

As the tracks led her farther from the ranch house they turned and proceeded in a northern direction. Dora figured that they went in the general direction of La Junta. The road to La Junta was now very close. When she reached it the tracks continued on toward the town.

Dora hadn't followed it very far when she saw a group of riders heading her way. Art was leading them. Red was not among them.

22

Art spoke as soon as they had met in the middle of the road. "We went all the way to La Junta, Miss Kincaid. We checked around and asked if anyone had seen a red-haired man ride into town just before we did. No one saw him. Either he sneaked in the back way, or he took the route around. I'm sorry we didn't catch him."

"That's okay, Art," she replied. "I'll try to pick up his trail again. The odds should be in my favor by now. Oh by the way Dora or Petticoat works for me. No need to be formal."

Dora headed on for La Junta while Templeton's men continued for the ranch. Since Hannah Minkle was the only person in La Junta that she knew she decided to stop by her shack first. The older woman received her with delight when she arrived.

"Goodness sake, Dora," she exclaimed. "You're the first person that I've seen so much of so soon in the last two years. That's on or off my mind stage. What can I do for you today?"

"I haven't much time, Hannah," Dora confessed. "I just stopped by to ask you a question or two. First, can you mend my jeans? Second, have you been having any visions of late?"

Hannah held the hollows of her hands against her head. "Mercy! I'll say! If all the things I've seen have been happening to you, young lady, you certainly lead a dangerous life. You've been the star performer on my mind stage for the past few days."

"I hope I've turned in a sterling performance. How have I done?"

Hannah took Dora's pants. "Looks like you've done all right. You're standing here now. I couldn't always see much of what was happening to you. In fact I often don't 'see' things happening. They're more like indelible ideas that become etched into my thoughts. Then I create the pictures in my mind. Well, this is what I think is happening. Do I sound like a crazy old woman to you?"

While she spoke the older woman fetched a needle, a patch, and some thread and sat down to mend the tear.

"Not at all," Dora averred. "You have a unique talent that no one understands. Perhaps someday, maybe tomorrow, maybe years from now we will."

"Until then people will continue to call me a witch."

Dora swayed the conversation back to her questioning. "I don't. I'm glad you have such a talent. You don't appear to be an old woman either. Tell me, do you know if the red head has shown up any more?"

"He's a bad one isn't he?" Hannah frowned her eyes narrowing. "He keeps flashing into the pictures always causing trouble. I know he's the one responsible for all your problems."

"I think I've followed him to La Junta. Have you seen him in town, I mean in the flesh in the last hour or so?"

"No. I haven't been out all day. Except for the few flashes of him in my mind I haven't seen him since that time in the saloon."

Sewing up the hole in quick fashion Hannah returned the jeans to their owner who handed her a payment for her work.

Thankful for the repaired pants Dora was about to take her leave when Hannah held up her hand to suggest as an afterthought, "But I know someone who might have seen the red haired man. If old Mushy is sitting outside the saloon he may have seen him. For the price of a drink he'll tell you."

"Who's Mushy?"

"The town drunk. I don't think that anyone knows his real name. Believe me you'll know him when you see him." She bobbed her head in emphasis. "He begs a drink from anyone going into the bar."

Dora patted her on the arm. "Thanks, Hannah. As a return for your help I'm going to tell you this, but don't take it as real fact yet. I have to verify it."

Hannah's brow furrowed. "What is it?"

Dora answered her question in slow deliberation. "I think the red head has something to do with Hiram's disappearance."

A gasp issued from the lips of her listener. "Do you—think he's still alive? Do you know where he is?"

"Yes and no. My belief is that he's still alive. My thought is that Red can lead me to him. Remember this is just conjecture. It comes from some information given me. Try not to get your hopes up too much. I could be wrong."

"Oh! I hope not!" Hannah exclaimed. Fretful she wrung her hands together. "Why hasn't he come home? Do you think he could be hurt, or—or—"

"Or he's turned to a life of crime?" Dora uttered the question that she knew Hannah couldn't. She wanted to see how Mrs. Minkle would respond.

The older woman rejected the notion. "No, no, not my Hiram. He wouldn't ever do that. There's some other reason why he hasn't come home. My Hiram is too intelligent to resort to being a criminal."

"I believe you. There are so many unanswered questions," Dora consoled. "I just hope I can find the right answers for you."

Departing on that note Dora Kincaid rode on into town. As she thought about Hannah's unique talent she realized that Mrs. Minkle seemed to get these images just during dangerous moments with those she "saw," such as when Dora shot Delgrin, Red chased Max, and others. This reasoning would conclude that Hiram had not yet been faced with a life-threatening situation. The thought renewed Dora's cause to believe that Hiram Minkle was still alive.

Dora kept a sharp eye open for signs of Red or his horse. As she reached the saloon she found Hannah's brief description of Mushy accurate enough. Slouched against the wall close to the saloon doors was a scraggy-headed, unshaven tatterdemalion dressed in clothes that had long since lost their usefulness. Whenever a fresh candidate started into the saloon the ragamuffin would beg him for a drink. Getting denied his request the bum would slump back into a placid stupor. After watching him importune a couple of customers without success Dora sauntered over.

"Hey, fella, woncha buy a drink for—" he slurred his plea, cutting his soliloquy short when he gazed bleary eyed at Dora's face. "Oh, 'xcuse me, pretty lady. Guess you're not goin' in the s'loon."

"You the one called Mushy?"

He tipped his battered hat in a clumsy motion. "That's my favorite name."

"If you have the information I'm looking for I'll buy you a whole bottle that you can sop up."

Mushy's face brightened in anticipation. "Well now. I do hope I can be of service to you, ma'am. I'm gettin' mighty dry."

151

Grabbing his arm she pulled him to his feet. "Let's go in and sit down. We can talk easier in there than out here."

Dora led the way into the saloon with a smiling Mushy stumbling behind. The several customers that inhabited the establishment at that time of day stared at the odd pair. Ignoring their gawks Dora sauntered up to the bar. Mushy staggered up. The bartender glared askance at them.

"You old enough to be in here?" he quizzed to Dora.

She glared right back at him. "I'm old enough." She thumbed at Mushy. "Give this man a glass and a bottle of whatever he wants."

The bartender nodded his head. "As long as it's paid for. What do you want, Mushy?"

Mushy made his choice. Dora threw an appropriate silver piece upon the counter. "Keep the change."

"Thanks," the bartender muttered, sounding friendlier. "Anything for you?"

"Not me," she declined. "Fouls up my shooting hand. Besides, I don't have to try to prove that I'm a man."

The bartender cocked an eyebrow, a quizzical expression on his round face. *A little slow, are we?* Ignoring the bartender's facial gesture Dora dragged Mushy to a table in a far corner. She shoved him into a chair.

"Have you been outside the saloon very long today?" she queried before he had even set the bottle on the table.

"Since the s'loon's been open." He popped off the cork lid. She seized the bottle by the neck.

"Did you see a red-haired man ride into town in the past hour? He was wearing faded jeans and a plain blue shirt."

"About medium height? Kinda skinny? Wear's a brown hat?" Mushy filled in some more details.

"The same."

Dora released her grip on the bottle. With a deft motion of much obvious practice he filled the shot glass and swallowed the liquid in one continuous sweep spilling nary a drop. Even in his inebriated condition he controlled a steady enough hand to accomplish such a feat.

"Where did you see him?" she pressed.

"He walked into the s'loon. I tried to talk 'im into buying me a drink, but he said some real rude things to me. I could tell he wush havin' a bad day. That 'n' his red hair make 'im easy to remember. He comes in sometimes. Once he bought me a drink. Guess he was havin' a better day then. Goes by Red."

Mushy downed a second drink. This time he allowed the fluid to swish its way down his throat in satisfying gurgles.

"Did you overhear him talking in here today by chance?"

"Yeah. The bartender was ashking 'im where 'e was coming from, 'n' where 'e was going. You know, jus' some chitchat."

"Did he say where he was going?"

"Pueblo."

"Pueblo, huh. Did he say anything else?"

"Nope. I could tell 'e wushn't very cordial today. Jus' said 'e had bushness there 'n' tol' the barkeep to go bother someone elsh."

While Dora pondered her next question Mushy bolted down yet a third swig of liquor. His blurry eyes and slurred speech divulged the imminent insidious effects immanent of alcoholic beverages. She knew soon that he would be too inebriated to answer any more questions.

She decided on one last query.

"How long was he in here?"

"Well, leshsee." Mushy rolled his eyes back in lethargic thought. "Ten minutes is all. Yep. 'M sure. 'Bout ten. He had jus' one drink. Don't know how a man can survive with jus' one."

"Thanks, Mushy. The bottle is yours, compliments of Petticoat."

Dora left the drunk at the table to ingest this statement while she strode over to the bar to put the same questions to the bartender. He confirmed every one, including Red's curt reply.

"Must be in a bad mood today," the barkeep concluded.

Hurrying from the saloon Dora leaped into her saddle and headed west out of town. If the clouds held she could make Pueblo before dark with good fortune. Right now she wanted better than just good fortune. She hoped that she could catch up to Red before Pueblo. This would take some serious riding. Once Red had reached Pueblo, a small city of several thousand people nestled on the Arkansas River, he could be tough to track down. If he ever suspected that he was being tailed he wouldn't be the needle, he'd be a piece of hay.

One of Bill Reilly's statements popped into her mind. He'd mentioned that the mystery geologist connected with Red was staying in the mountains. Pueblo lay on the eastern fringe of the mountain foothills. Perhaps Red was passing through Pueblo on his way to meet the geologist. Or perhaps they were going to meet in Pueblo. The more she weighed the evidence the more she was certain that Hiram Minkle had to be the scientist in question. Geologists of his caliber were rare in the west. Red's trail was sure to lead her to Hiram, she deduced.

Several small settlements and stage stops lay between La Junta and Pueblo. Dora rode on through, trusting on the information from Mushy and the bartender that Red was heading straight for Pueblo. She did keep her eyes peeled for his horse as she passed each site.

Dusk was settling in as she rode into Pueblo. If Red were stopping for the night here she had a hunch that he wouldn't stay in one of the hotels on the main street. Just in case She kept a wary eye in case his horse was tied outside one of the hotels or saloons.

By the time she'd reached the last hotel on the west edge of town twilight had taken over. Not a sign of Red had shown itself. Boarding Spirit at a nearby stable she paid for a room in the hotel and went for a late dinner in its lounge.

During her dinner Dora cogitated the aspects of Red's sudden departure from his diabolic attempts on Templeton's life and property. He had abandoned at least for the present this objective with his westward flight. What was he scheming now? Was he suspicious of being pursued? Where was he at that moment?

This last question plagued Dora like a migraine. Where was he? She didn't have time to chase around Pueblo to see if he was, or had been, in any of the several hotels or saloons. If Red were still heading west from Pueblo she needed every waking moment to overtake his trail and follow him to his destination. If he had already managed to elude her again—no, this was an option she wouldn't entertain at least for now. Red could have no idea that he sported a persistent shadow.

Dora decided to concentrate on the theory that he was still heading west to rendezvous with the geologist, but that he would stay the night in Pueblo. After the day's ride both she and Spirit were in need of a good night's rest. As a last idea before she went to her room she decided to bring the desk clerk into her "confidence."

"Someone was to meet me here," she informed him, "a red-haired man. He may have come in before I did. Has he been here?"

"No, miss. I haven't seen a red head this evening. Shall I send him up if he calls?"

"Not now," she huffed in mocked annoyance. "He was supposed to meet me here for dinner. If he can't show up on time, then he doesn't need to know that I'm here. Please say nothing to him if he comes in. Would you let me know though? I'll decide then whether he's worth my time to give him a piece of my mind. This isn't the first time that he's stood me up. It just may be his last."

"I understand, Miss Kinley," he nodded in agreement. "I'll let you know if he shows."

"I'm going to bed now. Would you please leave a call for me for five in the morning?"

"Yes, ma'am. A call for five." He made an appropriate note.

The possibility that Red had entered this particular hotel was rather slim Dora knew. Yet a baited hook could attract nibbles from strange places. She'd cast it in as good a place as any.

At around five o'clock the next morning a soft rap sounded on her door. A male voice called out, "This is your five o'clock call, Miss Kinley."

"Thank you," Dora acknowledged. She was already up and dressed. Before five more minutes had passed she was turning in her room key at the lobby desk and leaving.

"Oh, Miss Kinley," the morning clerk called after her. "There's a note left here for you." He grabbed the note from the key slot.

Dora retraced her steps to retrieve it. "Thanks," she expressed, puzzled at who knew she was here. She crossed the lobby to read the note in private. It read:

Dear Miss Kinley,

Your caller never arrived. However, my son who is a messenger boy for the telegraph office just a few doors from here mentioned that a man with red hair sent a telegram to Lamar yesterday evening. This happened about an hour before you checked into the hotel. My son remembered him because they bumped into each other at the entrance. He said that the man was very rude about it. I trust that this is not your friend, but thought I would mention it.

The note was signed "the night clerk."

Not her friend was right. The man in question just had to be Red. This news brightened her expectations that she was still on his trail. To find out what the contents of the telegram he sent, and to whom he sent it, would be no easy task. The telegraph office wouldn't open for several hours yet in all likelihood plus the operator would not be at liberty to divulge the contents of a private 'gram. She would have to resort to subtle tactics to find out. Borrowing a pen at the desk Dora jotted a quick thank you note to the night clerk and left it for him.

The first glimmer of dawn greeted the sleepy town. Dora found the street deserted. With resolve she sought out the telegraph office from the directions she received from the morning clerk. The sign on the door gave the hours that it was open for business from eight to eight.

This meant that Red had sent his telegram a little before closing the previous night. Since the Lamar station would have been closed by then the telegram wouldn't be sent until that morning. With luck she should be able to find the message waiting to be sent lying on the operator's table.

Slipping along the alley to the back door Dora pulled from her pocket the bundle of skeleton keys she had utilized at the Delgrin ranch. She found the right make and shoved it into the keyhole.

Once inside she headed straight for the telegraph key. On the corner of the desk lay a stack of papers each appearing to have a message to be sent that morning. The top slip had a Colorado Springs destination. The second message was going to Dodge City, Kansas. Number three carried a message to Lamar. A quick glance told her that Red had written this third message. This was one 'gram that wasn't getting sent. Stuffing the paper into her pocket with the keys she beat a hasty departure through the rear door. Locking it behind her Dora retraced her steps to the street. She jogged the few blocks to the stables without seeing another soul. There she found the morning keeper busy feeding and watering all of the animals.

"Howdy," he nodded. "You must be an early riser."

"Best time of the day," she returned in a cheerful voice. She went to Spirit's stall. "Looks like he's had his breakfast as I requested."

"Yes, ma'am," the keeper agreed. "He's ready to go."

He took Spirit out of the stall. Upon paying the board Dora saddled him up. Mounting up she prodded the big stud into a swift gait west out of town. Not until she was out of Pueblo did she take the note that Red had left to send from her pocket to read its entire message. It was addressed to Bill Oates of the Lamar bank.

> Am heir to Delgrin ranch stop
> Hold settlement until I arrive two weeks stop

Red had signed it with what Dora reckoned was an alias. Now she knew that Red was still intending on mulcting the town of Lamar from any claim to the Delgrin ranch. The telegram fit the pattern of the plot that Bill Reilly had confessed to her.

Without reception of the telegram Bill Oates could continue settling the estate without a fraudulent interruption. She could only wonder if Red had given up on disposing of Templeton at least for the time being. As it was she was now faced with a choice to make among three roads to take, each branching out toward the mountains. Dora decided to stick with the main road that followed the Arkansas River. Keeping close to the river Dora spurred Spirit into an easy loping gait that covered the miles at a rapid pace. As she rounded a bend in the river a column of smoke floated aloft from a small stand of cottonwoods on the bank. She reined Spirit to an abrupt halt. He pawed the ground in eagerness bobbing his head in rhythm.

"Easy there, big fellow," she consoled stroking his mane. "I think I'd better sneak up on foot from here."

Tying Spirit to a tree Dora crept through the little grove of silver willow trees and sand cherry bushes toward the rising smoke. The dead debris strewn over the ground like jackstraws forced her to creep catlike to avoid snapping a twig. Through the trees she could discern a clearing where the remains of a fire smoldered. Wary she stole in on the spot. The clearing was devoid of another human.

Except for the visual sign of crushed grass that one person had slept the night there the occupant and all of his provisions were now missing.

A muffled voice turned Dora's attention toward the river. Whoever had bedded down in the clearing had not yet left the area. She scurried across the clearing toward a thick clump of hackberry bushes near the riverbank. Peering through them she caught a glimpse of a man on horseback just riding away. The shock of red hair below his brown hat line revealed his identity. At last she had caught up to Red.

23

Before tailing him Dora filled her hat with water from the river to douse his hot coals. Pueblo and the eastern plains didn't need a devastating grass fire due to his carelessness. With his tendency to want to burn things she figured he was a confirmed habitual arsonist. By crushing the wet coals under foot she was satisfied that the fire was out. The sizzle, the smoke, and the steam had subsided.

Smiling to herself she dashed back to where Spirit stood waiting for her. While she was grateful that she had deduced all of the right trails in order to track him down, the task of tailing Red without being discovered would be at least double the risk.

Dora could just catch up to him, call his hand, outdraw him, and be done with her job. Then she could return to Templeton with the body of this killer and collect her fee. Another consideration compelled her to continue to follow him and bide her time. She hoped that Red would lead her to the mystery geologist. Her intuition told her that she needed to locate this earth scientist.

Dora rode to the edge of the grove. Hiding in the cover of the trees she watched Red lope down the trail until his cloud of dust obscured him from sight. He never looked back. When she felt confident that she had allowed him a good lead Dora urged Spirit into the same loping gallop. By doing so she maintained a comfortable distance without having to eat Red's dust while still tracking him.

By mid-morning both of the riders had entered the foothills. Cottonwoods, willows, and Russian olives lined the riverbanks, while junipers, piñon pines, cactus, and yucca dominated the arid uplands. The roadway continued to parallel the river for a number of miles until the narrowing, deepening canyon forced the road to follow the easier route along the rim. At this point was an intersecting road heading north.

Before leaving the river behind Red allowed his animal a long drink. Waiting behind a stand of piñon pines Dora watched until Red had finished and had ridden on. Before following she let Spirit have the same privilege of drinking his fill. While he did she topped off her canteen just upstream from Spirit.

Red had headed north on this junction road ascending into the front range mountains. The steep incline didn't compromise the effort needed for their horses to gain altitude in the thinner, cooler, mountain air. As they ascended higher into wooded canyons both riders kept their horses at a fast walk.

The conical juniper and compact piñon forests began to give ground to the larger, imposing spruce and ponderosa pine, dotted with stands of quaking aspen. Rugged, rocky canyons mellowed into more rounded, forested peaks as they penetrated into the high country. Even the slope of the trail tended to run more level as they climbed.

Still many miles west of their location stood the loftier peaks that pierced the sky, some reaching beyond fourteen thousand feet above sea level.

Up to twenty-five hundred feet of their ragged tops jutted above the timberline, the elevation where trees couldn't grow in the harsh weather conditions. Small patches of the previous winter's snow glistened like diamonds in the morning sun upon those distant peaks. Some of this snow would linger as perennial patches until the next winter season.

Under hoof the sagebrush, salt bush, rabbit brush, and yucca abandoned their influx to the more altitude adapted scarlet Indian Paintbrush, the purple Loco, and the lavender Columbine. Bright hues of every color of wildflowers flowed and billowed with the cool breeze through the nearby meadows.

Dora continued to keep her distance even though Red appeared oblivious to being followed. While he pressed on at a quick pace to his destination he wasn't making a race out of getting there. Tailing him turned out to be easier than she would have had reason to expect at first. She just had to stay back far enough.

As she stood waiting at the edge of a clearing until Red had crossed it into the forest again a lone rider entered the clearing from the other side. Exiting the trail Dora pulled back into a thick grove of aspens to conceal her reconnaissance.

The approaching rider drew closer to Red. Was Red riding to meet this man? Were they going to rendezvous here? Or was he just a passerby? Dora waited and watched.

The two men passed in meeting, each exchanging a courteous nod. A twinge of disappointment betrayed Dora's face. Although the chance was remote she had found herself hoping that this would have been the mysterious geologist. Patience was imperative she knew. Coaxing Spirit into heavier brush she waited for the stranger to pass on by her. He moseyed on by, giving no indication of detecting her presence. She watched him until he had disappeared on down the trail.

On the main road out of Pueblo they'd met a few fellow travelers as the morning progressed. This was the first that had come their way on this less-traveled route. Dora realized that she just wanted Red to meet the geologist along here a quieter trail so that she could at last solve the mystery of this adventure. Patience was not her motto but she needed it now.

By the time the stranger had ridden beyond view Red had also passed from sight. Dora was weaving Spirit back out of the dense cover of bushes back to the trail when distant thunder rippled the air. She glanced up at the foreboding sky. A large, dark gray cloud obscured the sun. So engrossed in trailing Red she hadn't noticed the rain clouds that had rolled in so fast. Swift summer squalls that could catch a rider unaware were common in the mountains. The nearness of the next peal of thunder announced the threatening storm moving over. Picking up to a brisk blow the wind kicked up the dust of the dry road into small dust devils.

The threat became reality. Dora had barely reached the far side of the clearing when a shower commenced. Spirit didn't seem to mind so Dora kept on. Before he got too far away she wanted to catch sight of Red again to pace her distance.

Without warning the whole sky broke loose like a full bucket flipped over. Within seconds the deluge had drenched the young woman and her faithful steed. Dora pressed on with dogged determination hoping that Red was still on the trail. When pea-sized hail boosted to a blasting sting by the blustery wind began to batter them she reined Spirit off the trail to the shelter of some large trees. Although her hat nullified most of the effects of the hail on her head

Spirit had no protection for his. She slipped off his back to lower her height. To be a lightning rod wasn't her interest. They stood close to the trunks of the trees to weather out the storm. The branches above them helped to alleviate much of the pelting downpour.

Ten eternal minutes later as sudden as the storm hit it stopped. Dora wasted no time in getting back on the trail again. The clouds disappeared over the nearest peaks, allowing the warm, drying sunshine to show through once more.

The fast working squall had churned the dry road into a muddy sludge obscuring all recent tracks. Another ten minutes of riding changed all that. The mud gave way to just damp surface, then back to dry, dusty surface once more. In the dust were the fresh tracks of Red's horse. Dora had passed the edge of the squall's cover of rain. Alarmed at this fact she knew that Red could have escaped the storm altogether, or at least the main brunt of it. If this were so, that meant that while she had to sit out the hail he had gained ten more minutes lead on her.

The next little town ahead of her was the ghost town of Oroville. How far to town she had to go, or the circumstances of the roads branching off from there she had no idea. Once there Red might switch to a different route. She knew that she needed to catch up to him if at all possible before Oroville.

The problem was to push Spirit too hard at this altitude could deplete his energy before they caught Red. A second choice would be to increase Spirit's pace a little from what he had been keeping. With this approach she could hope that she would catch up to Red before he reached town. If not she could always keep track of his horse's prints in the dust as long as they were visible.

For some fifteen minutes Dora was in the attitude of coaxing Spirit to keep a little quicker pace. Ahead of her around the next bend she could hear a team and coach approaching. In a moment she met an eastbound coach heading for Pueblo. After it went by she examined the dusty trail. Sure enough as she'd expected the coach and team had obliterated Red's tracks. She cursed her luck.

If Red got away from her now all this tailing would have been in vain. Dora had no wish to return to Lamar to wait for his arrival in two weeks. Wanting to find this geologist and the story behind him doubled her desire to continue. Still concerned that she'd wear Spirit down Dora spurred him into a gallop. As she rode a new idea came to her. Instead of trying to overtake her quarry all at once she would keep Spirit at a good gallop for five minutes then slow him back to the easier lope for the same amount of time. In this way she hoped to catch up to Red again without doing Spirit in.

After five minutes she slowed Spirit to a lope. The road had remained somewhat level since she had lost Red back at the meadow. Spirit was able to keep his stride although the effect of the higher altitude showed by his heavier breathing. After another five minutes she increased his speed again to a gallop. If he could keep this up she might yet catch up to Red.

Minute after minute and mile after mile rolled by giving no sign of Red. Dora kept a sharp eye for a dust cloud, any visible prints still on the road, or any other helpful sign of a rider ahead. Spirit's laborious respiration warned her to slow him down again. Until he became acclimated she could overwork his endurance before she overtook her objective. Breaking his namesake wasn't her wish.

The choice of Spirit's gait was soon chosen for both of them. Dora had to slow him to a walk as they ascended a steep hill. Once they had reached the top the road curved to follow the opposite slope down to the town of Oroville. The road was visible the rest of the way to the ghost town. Red was not on it.

She quickened her pace again until she had reached the edge of Oroville. The town was not much more than the ghost remains of a gold mining camp that had sprung up overnight when gold was discovered nearby. When the gold ran out so did most of the residents. Many of the buildings had already fallen in from disrepair. Only the last old house at the far end of town showed any signs of habitation.

As she reached the last house Dora could see that a short distance out of town the road branched into two trails. The left fork was about twice as wide and revealed handling more traffic. She reasoned that the left road went to Poverty Gulch, but she didn't know now where Red was or which way he could be heading. A stop at the old house was in order. If anyone was living there perhaps he might have seen or heard Red pass through town. A quick knock on the door produced a grizzled old man with spectacles and a toothy grin. Short on time she dispensed with introductions.

"Did you see anyone pass by here in the last few minutes?"

He shook his head. "Nope. Heard somebody though."

"Then you don't know which fork he took?"

"Don't matta," the old man smiled. "They both go to Poverty Gulch. Wagons and stagecoaches gotta take the left one. Horseback riders will use the right one if they know about it. It's shorter but steeper. Gets kinda scary in a couple of places for some folks."

"Is there a way to tell which way a rider has gone?" she questioned.

"Yep. I'll show ya." Waddling along ahead of her the stooped old man led her out onto the road and pointed a crooked finger to a distant rugged crest to the north. Dora could see the faint line of a trail climbing to the top. "The trail goes 'round the side of that peak. It takes a rider 'bout ten minutes or so to go over the top there. If your friend went that way you might see him soon."

As the man spoke a lone rider appeared along the trail where she was observing. Because of the distance Dora wasn't sure if she imagined it or not, but she thought that she descried a shock of red hair showing from under the rider's hat.

"There he goes now," the old man acknowledged, "like I said."

"Thanks!" she yelled, bolting to her horse to go tearing off up the north road. In a couple of minutes she had reached the foot of the peak that boasted of the rugged trail.

The trail was not steep as she had interpreted the old man's description to mean. It wound along the precipitous mountain in a series of rocky, treacherous switchbacks that narrowed as the trail ascended. The climb itself wasn't too steep just the mountain slope.

Goading her steed as fast as she dared she gritted her teeth as he scrambled over the loose rubble that the trail cut through. Twice he lost his footing almost to the point of hurling the two of them over the brink of the trail to disaster. Both times she swallowed her heart and pressed on not slackening her pace.

At last she passed the point where she had seen Red from below. The trail widened to a more passable road. Checking her pocket watch she found that she had made the top in just six minutes. Dora had trimmed four minutes off of Red's time. Would she be able to make up the other six?

The road wound in and out of large, craggy boulders, hiding any sighting of the man that she was pursuing. She pressed on at a good gait, trying to regain ground and spot him again. The rocky surrounds amplified the clatter of Spirit's shoes on the rocky trail. His clip clops echoed between the walls. Dora had to wonder how far the racket he was making would carry. She couldn't hear Red's horse. She hoped her's wouldn't carry to Red's ears and persuade him to quicken his pace. A softer path would have been welcome. At last the pavement of rock reverted back to packed dirt.

If she could chop a minute off Red's lead for every five minutes she rode she would catch up to him in half an hour. Regardless of that plan she had no way of knowing whether she was gaining on him.

She checked her watch again. The hour was almost noon. She hoped that Red would stop for lunch. Then again if he were near his destination he might keep on going until he reached it. That would be her choice. Since she didn't know she would just have to press on, hoping that he would stay on the road.

"Stop where you are!"

24

Startled from her concentration Dora reined Spirit to a sharp halt at the command. Like shadows taking on life two armed masked men stepped from behind the boulders. They stood in the center of the road, their guns drawn.

"Reach for the sky!" one of them barked as Dora halted.

She obeyed with reluctance. Sizing up the scene quick she figured that these two would be no match for her. The one on the right was so far off on his aim that if he were to fire, the bullet would miss her by a good three feet to her right. Her only problem of blowing this road trash away right then was that the shots might warn Red and put him on his guard. Shooting them would be a last resort. She wondered if he had run into these two highwaymen. The obvious leader, the one who gave the halt command, was toting an extra firearm tucked within his gun belt.

While she was sizing up the situation the two highway men were glancing at each other in amazement. Their gawks soon became lecherous leers.

"Woo wee!" the one on the right chortled. "Have we got us a prize, huh, Jake! Boy, are we going to have some fun with this one!"

"Shut up, you fool!" Jake snapped at his partner. "I told you, no names!" He turned back to Dora. "All right, pretty little gal, swing down off of your horse."

Dora hankered to give them both third eyes right at that moment. Before she finished off these reprobates she wanted some information. She feigned the motions of preparing to make a slow dismount. In a quivering voice she stammered, "What—what did you do to my brother?"

"Your brother?"

"Yes, the red head. I've been trying to catch up to him."

"Oh, him. Ha! We took his money and his gun and sent him packing," Jake boasted in satisfied tones. "Now get down."

Again Dora feigned slow obedience. "What are you going to do to me? If you let me go I'll give you money."

"Oh, we'll get your money anyway," Jake sneered. "But from pretty little gals we take something else, too. Your virginity."

"Yeah!" Jake's cohort chortled. "If you still have it!"

"Har! Har! Har!" the two men guffawed at their own foul remarks as Dora, whimpering, started from her saddle. An instant later the two miscreants lay quiescent and supine, their voices forever silenced. Each man sported a blood red third "eye" in the middle of his forehead. Dora's legerdemain had thrown them off guard. They hadn't felt a thing. Two shots had been fired, but two were noisy enough.

"Tough luck, boys," she muttered. "You weren't my type."

Instant death wasn't what she had first intended for these two lecherous barbarians. She'd rather have made them suffer. Jake's statement about Red had changed her designs. If she figured right Red wouldn't have gone far before circling back to recoup his losses. She was sure he would vindicate himself as soon as he could.

Leaping from her horse she searched the two corpses in quick time. Jake had a roll of bills and a pocket watch and chain in his pockets, along with the extra gun, perhaps Red's, in his belt. Dora felt certain that Red would be carrying a spare. She confiscated all of this, plus the dead thieves' own weapons, and stuffed them into her own pockets or gun belt. On his covert return Red would recover nothing.

Red's ruthless cunning made these two late roadside robbers look like rank neophytes. Knowing that Red would be slinking back at most any moment she leaped into her saddle and charged back along the road. There she found a hiding place close by among the boulders and trees in which she secreted herself to watch the scene of the foiled robbery. She was none too soon. Her hasty retreat left a fine layer of dust hanging in the quiet air.

A moment later Red appeared from cover near the dead men. He surveyed the scene in a glance, stopping to prod the bodies with the barrel of his second gun. Peering around as if looking for their executioner he made a quick search of them. Finding nothing, with a growl he jammed his weapon into his holster and stalked off into the rocks from where he had appeared.

Dora waited until she heard the sound of distant hoof beats riding away. Without hesitation she took up the pursuit again before he got too far ahead and she lost him again. If Red had no suspicion of being tailed before, he had two reasons to believe that he could be now. First, he found the two highway robbers lying dead in the road with no sign of their assailant. Second, he hadn't met anyone else on the road. That left the conclusion that someone had been following behind him, someone who didn't want him to know who she was.

Dora figured that Red would reason this out in no time if he had any sense at all. Her hope now was that he wouldn't figure out who, and that this sudden discovery of a shadow for how long he could only guess would be disconcerting enough to keep him running to his destination instead of trying another bushwhack. That was her main objective for now. She wanted to find the geologist.

Red continued to lead her along the winding trail at a fast clip. From the intermittent glimpses she caught of him he never looked back. He seemed to be bent on where he was going without concern for who might be behind him.

As she galloped around a bend through a thick, forested area she reined Spirit to an abrupt halt. The trail stretched straight ahead for another half a mile. Red had not been that far ahead, and yet he was nowhere to be seen. Like water in a hot desert he had vaporized from sight.

Was he now lying in wait for her in the trees? If this were so why hadn't he picked a spot where his sudden disappearance wouldn't have been so noticeable? But then she already knew of Red's odd, subversive ways. In this cat and mouse chase the pursuit became dangerous when the mouse discovered he had a stalker. This mouse that could be hiding had big teeth. With gun drawn Dora moved circumspect through the forest. Were there eyes below red hair looking back?

About fifty yards from the last bend in the road she espied the tracks of Red's horse veer onto a faint path into the trees. Patches of grass betrayed its infrequent use. Dora started upon it with caution.

An occasional fresh hoof print revealed that the path was the way that Red had taken. Whether he was near the end of his journey or was trying to shake off his tracker she didn't know. With this path almost invisible he appeared to know where he was going. She didn't. She would have to keep following his trail to find out.

The path continued deeper into the forest. Sporadic breaks in the dense growth showed her that the path was climbing into a wide canyon. The grade grew steeper in ascent until the trail came to an abrupt end. Red's horse stood tied in the trees a few yards away.

Near where Red had left his horse Dora found a faint foot trail winding through the trees toward the south side of the canyon. With increased circumspection she left Spirit ground tied to follow the foot trail. Before doing so she put the spoils from the roadside robbers into her saddlebags. Then she led Spirit farther into the forest to hide him before starting along the footpath.

Every rustling leaf, every popping twig caught her attention. About a hundred yards up the trail against the base of the south mountain stood a small, ramshackle cabin. While its construction suggested that an adept carpenter had placed the logs together, time and neglect were causing the chinking to fall out.

Flitting from tree to tree Dora crept closer to the structure which was set back into the side of the slope. From her angle of advance she could make out a small window in the front and one on the side. The door she guessed was on the opposite wall from where she approached. The last side pressed up against the mountain appeared to lack a window. In this country glassed windows were luxuries. Many cabins had no glass just having hinged shutters to close out inclement weather.

Dora decided to sneak up as close to the front window as she could to see if she could determine whether the cabin was occupied. She hoped to find Red sitting alongside his mystery geologist. Encouraged by this thought she stole up to the window to listen and look. With great caution she peeked over the sill. To see into the room she had to rub the heavy dust from the glass with her hand.

The singular room that comprised the whole of the cabin boasted of only a few rough furnishings, a table, two rickety chairs, and an old cot in the corner. No human occupied the room.

All right! If he didn't come to the cabin he must be somewhere near at hand, she reasoned to herself. Searching around the general area of the cabin she found that the trail more pronounced here went by the door to continue on up the mountain beyond it. Dora continued to follow it.

About a hundred yards above the cabin Dora encountered a huge heap of rocky rubble. Once while traveling through the mountains several years previous her father had pointed out to her similar rubble heaps. She knew at the top of this heap of "tailings" as her father had called them would be an adit, an entrance to a mine. Recalling from memory some history of this area she knew that Poverty Gulch was famous for the myriad of gold and silver mines in its surrounding mountains. Gold fever, a gold mine, and Red all fit together in this strange set of circumstances. While he was out to get oil he must have been looking for gold or silver as well.

Dora was sure that this was the end of her search. Red could have gone into the mine. Perhaps he was waiting for her. Circling around the mine tailings she climbed the mountainside until the adit a little more than a man-sized hole in the rock became visible. She stopped to listen.

The place was as quiet as a graveyard. The heavy oppression of foreboding hung like a foggy shroud over the area. Dora debated her next move. To go charging into a mine she knew nothing about would be reckless and foolhardy. Red would blast her away in an instant. She could call out to him, but he could choose to remain silent and not betray his presence. A stick or two of dynamite would have been handy right then to rouse her opponent from the mine.

Dynamite! Maybe there was something there. If Red knew anything about mining he kept his explosives in a safe magazine a short distance from the tunnel. He might even keep some in the cabin. Finding the dynamite cache might be in her best interest. She turned in her tracks to survey the forested mountainside.

CRACK! Bark flew from the big pine tree right behind her as the rifle shot rang in the air, echoing through the narrow gorge. More from reaction than reason Dora dived down the slope out of sight from the adit. Several more shots whistled by her ears to ricochet off the rocks around her until she managed to gain some safety behind a small boulder a few yards away. The trail she came up was too open to use as a retreat.

Peering with caution from her hiding place Dora scrutinized the rocky slope above the mine entrance. Those close shots had been fired after she was out of the line of sight from the adit. Red must have been hiding in the rocks above the opening. At the moment he had the advantage on her. Her location was known while his wasn't, and he was above her with a longer-range weapon.

Scowling Dora mentally booted her behind for not having grabbed her own rifle from its saddle holster. She'd left it on Spirit, reckoning that she'd force a confrontation with Red face to face. She should have remembered that Red's murderous sniping made Nero look like a hero. Now she was pinned down in a precarious position. Staying here for very long would give her adversary time to improve his advantage.

Somewhere in the rocks and trees above Red watched and waited. He wasn't doing a song and dance to expose his whereabouts to her either. Coupled with her eyes her feverish brain searched for some place of action to reverse, or at least improve her situation. At the moment the advantage was his being familiar with the area. Red may have already been maneuvering to bring her into his sights again.

What she needed was a better refuge while at the same time closing in on Red. Surveying the adjacent terrain Dora saw how she could get to it. Typical of a mountainside mine the tailings, or waste rock from digging, were dumped down slope just outside the entrance. The more waste rock extracted in the pursuit of precious gold ore the further the tailings extended from the entrance.

Dora was hiding a few yards from the base of the present tailing pile. Crouching with her knees almost in her face she darted across open ground to press up against the pile. Red hadn't fired. Either he hadn't seen her, or he couldn't react in time. She hoped he hadn't seen her maneuvering closer.

The grade of the pile was steep, a good forty percent, and high enough to obscure her from view from the mountainside above the adit. Pressing closer to the loose rubble she slithered on her stomach around one side. Soon she was just below the mine level. Sprinting to the nearby trees and rocks for cover she clawed her way up slope to gain the original excavation of the adit. Again the precipitous angle of the rock right around the mine's entrance obstructed the view of it from above. Like a long lost love Dora hugged the face of the mountain until she reached the opening. With pistol aimed ahead of her she slipped inside.

As her eyes grew accustomed to the gloom she espied an ore car parked several yards in from the entrance. The tracks that it ran on extended from the edge of the tailings outside into the black recesses of the mine. Propelled by man or beast a full ore car would be pushed to the end of the rails where it would be rocked forward on a center pivot to dump its contents down slope on the tailings pile.

Her plan was simple. Hiding in the dark mine she'd wait for him. The ore car could provide a good place to conceal herself. If Red came calling his silhouette would stand out at the entrance. She knelt behind the car—and bumped into something softer than the surrounding stone.

Quicker than a cat on a canary she leaped to the side of the ore car her gun poised on the dark figure crouched on the ground nearby.

"Please! Don't shoot!" a voice, strained with emotion, begged. "I didn't mean to startle you!"

"Who are you?" Dora demanded, keeping her own voice subdued.

"My name is Minkle. Hiram Minkle."

Minkle! The geologist husband that Hannah had been missing for two years had just been found. As she'd figured Hiram's disappearance *was* connected to this man called Red. Like a light lending its rays to dispel the dark Dora realized that a lot of answers to her queries lay here before her in the form of a man named Minkle.

"Why are you hiding behind the ore car?"

"When I heard the shooting I ducked behind here for cover."

Hiram Minkle rose from his crouched position. With him standing just a couple of inches taller than Dora she could discern a matted, disheveled beard and hair in the dim light. Sporting broad shoulders and muscular arms he reminded her of more like a side show strong man attraction than a geologist.

"Hannah has almost gone crazy since you left her," Dora decided to throw at him to get his unrehearsed response.

The man gasped. "You know my Hannah? Oh, how is she? How is she?" he implored. Grasping the edge of the ore car he struggled to walk closer to the adit.

"Lonely," was Dora's terse reply. "She thinks you're dead."

"Dead? Heavens, I'm alive, though I'm not sure how. Didn't she send you to find me? I would think by now someone would find a clue to my whereabouts from the wire I sent."

"Wire? What wire?" Dora pressed, his rambling statement a total puzzle.

"The telegram I had Red send when—" Hiram cut his sentence short. "I should have guessed. That scoundrel has lied to me ever since—"

"Wait a minute!" Dora cut him off. "You've lost me. Quit talking in circles, and start from the beginning. How did you come to disappear from Kansas two years ago? Does Red figure into your story at that time?"

"You know about Kansas. Then I was right. Hannah did send you after me. Whatever your fees are we'll pay. Just get me out of this!"

For a moment Dora was almost convinced that she was conversing with a raving lunatic until he bent over and, with notable effort, hefted the ball and chain attached around his ankle. Now a few more pieces tumbled into place. Here was a man who, having been a prisoner for two years, was too overjoyed at being found to be anywhere near coherent. She'd have to get him away from there before she'd get his full story without the rambling.

"I came of my own accord. We'll have to find a way to get that shackle off of your ankle so that we can ride," she determined. "Are you strong enough to ride?"

"Just get me to a horse!" he exclaimed. "I'll ride to Kansas without stopping." He stared down at his shackled ankle. "Why don't you just shoot the lock off?" he posed.

Dora shook her head. "I would, but I don't think Red saw me make it into the mine. A shot would give away my presence. I don't want that. I came in here hoping to surprise him if he shows up. In doing so I got the surprise from you. We'll need to find another means of removing that ball and chain."

"Well," Hiram Minkle said with feeling, "Red has the only key."

"Key or not I'll get you out of that shackle. First, I want to get rid of that murderer Red. Then we'll work on that lock. Once you're free you won't have to ride to Kansas. Hannah is here in Colorado. Come on."

Leading the way Dora took two steps toward the mouth of the tunnel. All at once a thunderous blast shook the earth beneath their feet. They struggled to keep their balance. Within scant seconds the mine opening disappeared as tons of dislodged rock and debris rained in. Dora whirled with a shout, "Behind the ore car, quick!"

Hiram who had not yet stepped from behind the car dropped the iron ball and flung himself to the ground. Dora huddled beside him. Both of them covered their heads with their arms.

After several seconds the deafening din died down to dead, sickening silence. Thick dust hung like a cloud in the black air, causing the two of them to gasp and cough.

"Come—on!" Hiram managed between coughs. "Follow—the tracks!"

Dora caught his meaning. On hands and knees she began tracing the tracks deeper into the mine. Somewhere just ahead she could hear the clanking of the ball and chain being dragged over the ties.

At last the air became clear again. From across her mouth Dora jerked off the bandanna that she had wrapped around her face. "Is there another way out?" she gasped.

"No," came the grim reply. "The single exit is now sealed."

Dora shook a wave of panic away as reality struck home. They were trapped and doomed to die!

25

Blackness thicker than a moonless, misty night enveloped them. Succumbing from slow suffocation didn't set with her plans for a long, successful career. This time her dogged determination to catch and defeat Red had doomed Dora to destruction. At least she had company.

"The front door is locked from the outside," she quipped in an effort to keep a positive mind. "Where's the back door?"

A pause. Then, "There isn't any—yet."

"What? Explain yourself, Hiram Minkle."

"Back in this tunnel there's a drift that curves around almost one hundred eighty degrees to the left. I'm not sure just how much rock is left before breakthrough to the hillside, but maybe we can blow our way out at that point."

"Is that the only way out?"

"We could start digging out the entrance. But our air might run out before our rock pile would. We won't have the air to try both. There's always the chance that the ground overhead might cave in on us while we're trying to dig our way out."

"Moving all this rock would take a long time," Dora considered. "If the rock caved in on us there would go any chance of digging our way out of here. We'd just bury ourselves. Let's try your back door. Got enough dynamite to blow it open?"

"Yes. I've been hiding it away from Red a stick at a time for just such an opportunity to create a possible escape path. However, I expected something other than this to try opening another portal."

"Why can't we just blow out the cave-in?"

"The ground is too bad. We would just seal ourselves in worse."

"Okay," she agreed. "You're the expert. Can you find your way in this dark? Don't you have some sort of cap lamp?"

"It's in the cabin," he replied. "Stand up and give me your hand. We'll get there faster by walking."

Dora stood up and groped in the direction of Hiram's voice until her hand found his shoulder. Following down his arm which felt hard and muscular, confirming her initial observation she perceived a strong, callused hand grasp hers. The condition of the geologist's arm at first amazed her. She hadn't expected that a man of science would develop the physical strength of a manual laborer. Red had been forcing slave labor upon the poor man for quite some time.

Through the inky mine the two of them groped. Lacking sight she tested each step before placing her foot. Her guide's pace revealed that Hiram was also being just as cautious. She felt the sole of her boot skim the top of the track rail.

"Watch your step over the track," He cautioned. "I'm leading us over to the side. We'll follow the rib, or wall of the tunnel, to the corner."

In response Dora reached out her free hand for the invisible, but impending, vertical rock surface. Soon her fingers brushed the rough face of the jagged wall. "Okay," she acknowledged. "I've reached the wall, or rib, as you called it."

Hiram quickened his pace from a snail's creep to a snake's crawl. "I keep the floor picked up of loose rock," his voice broke the black silence. "I was concerned that we might trip over the ties if we continued to follow the tracks. We won't trip here."

Dora had to admire this geologist for his bravery. Maybe inside he was scared—no, apprehensive—like she felt, but his equanimity in their critical situation gave her a calming assurance. His thinking had become coherent now.

"Here's the corner," he announced after several moments.

They scuffled into the offshoot drift for several dozen steps before the scientist called a halt.

"We're at the face," he told her. "That's the end of the drift. Wait here. I'll bring back the dynamite and a torch."

The face, Dora reasoned, must have been the blank wall at the end of the drift. Drift would be another name for a tunnel. Obedient to his command she stayed put. The time seemed to creep by. Was the air getting stuffy? Not knowing just how big the mine was she didn't know how far Hiram would have to go to get the materials he needed. Neither did she have any idea how long the air in the mine would hold out. Perhaps the air would last hours, perhaps days, but not be indefinite. She'd heard about what miners called bad air. It killed.

After what could have been ten minutes or ten hours, she wouldn't judge, Hiram returned. His steps echoed heavier and slower as if he were packing extra weight besides the ball and chain still affixed to his ankle. She could hear him setting something down then scuffling a few steps away.

"I'm going to light this torch, then we'd better hurry with the dynamite," he instructed. "The fire will be burning up part of our oxygen."

The flickering light of a torch soon began to illuminate the interior of the mine. She squinted as the welcomed light dispelled the darkness around them. After Hiram had stuck it in a niche in the wall about twenty feet away he trudged back to Dora. In one hand he was carrying the ball by a short section of chain.

"That's got to go first," she declared. "Now that I can see what I'm doing I'll shoot off the lock."

She pulled her gun and blew the lock into pieces. For a moment the roar of her shot was deafening, echoing within the close confines. Hiram jerked away the shackle and rubbed his ankle in gratitude.

"Thanks," he offered. "I'm not going to miss that thing."

"Okay, what next?" she pressed on, knowing time was a luxury.

"See the holes here in the face?" he indicated with a pointed finger. She peered at some dozen drilled holes where he pointed. "I'll fix the fuses while you shove the dynamite into the holes." He snatched up a long pole he'd carried back and handed it to her. "Use this tamping rod to push the sticks to the end of each hole. Don't be shy. They won't blow up while you're tamping."

Under Hiram's instructions Dora filled all of the holes until there was just enough room for one more stick of dynamite in each. Meanwhile Hiram had been fusing the last sticks to go in together. Once they had been placed he bound all of the fuses together with a single, longer length. Dora figured that the whole operation took them less than half an hour.

The air was growing warmer and stagnant. Sweat trickled down their brows and off the tips of their noses. Dora noticed that they were both breathing deeper in an effort to maintain the necessary oxygen levels in their bodies. Although the dilemma went unspoken she knew that this was the only chance they had for freedom.

Hiram held up the loose end of the fuse. "We have about a minute's worth of fuse here. That will give us enough time to get back to the ore car. We'll be safe from the blast there. Would you get me the torch, please?"

Dora snatched the torch from the rock niche and scurried back to his side. Using it to light the fuse they dashed from the drift to the main tunnel. With their hands over their ears they crouched behind the heavy ore car for protection.

And waited.

Slow Seconds ticked by.

BAROOOM! Once, twice, thrice, in lightning repetition the blasts shook the mine. Dora lost count after that. Each instant the air compressed, decompressed, countless times as the rapid explosive charges went off in immediate succession. The settled dust kicked up again, filling the adjoining drift with a gritty fog. Even with Dora's ears covered by her hands the fluctuating air pressure caused her ears to pop and plug numerous times. Just as the last shot quit resounding off the walls of the mine the air pressure ceased its fluctuations. Hiram looked up over the ore car toward the dust-choked drift.

"All of the charges went off," he announced. "I counted them. We don't have time to let the air clear. Let's go!"

The thickening dust hampered visibility with the wavering flame from the torch. Dauntless the two of them hastened back into the offshoot drift. Big chunks of shattered rock caused them to slow their pace in order to step around them. The choking dust made them pull their kerchiefs around their noses and mouths once again. When they could see through the dust to the end the sight was enervating. A new face of solid rock appeared beyond where the old one had been. Hiram slumped in despair. Dora leaned against the rib with her head drooped.

"I thought the rock was thin enough to blow away," he muttered in exasperation through his kerchief. "Now the oxygen is even thinner, used up in the blast. We might as well put the torch out and save what air is left."

"Not yet," she gasped, the lack of oxygen telling on her speech. "There are a couple of sticks of dynamite left. Can't we do something with them to try to blast our way out of here?"

"Not enough," he panted, leaning against the opposite rib. "Most of the shot would just go down the drift. Nothing to hold it in the rock. No time to drill a hole. I'm afraid this is the end of the line."

The rock dust was settling fast. Although their bodies felt weak and heavy they remained standing to keep their heads above it. Dora let the torch fall to the floor where it died to a glowing ember. She stood with her head bowed for several moments fighting the lethargy that was spreading over her. At last she cast her eyes toward the face. In the dark it had a strange appearance. Little threads of white crisscrossed the rock. Dora's dulled senses tried to make sense of it. She thought her imagination was playing games with her eyes. With effort she gasped, "Look! What's that light?"

Hiram looked over to the face. His eyes narrowed as he, too, tried to make sense of what he saw. When reality caught hold he blurted out, "That's daylight! We cracked the wall to the outside. There's still a chance!"

The geologist staggered around until he found his ball and chain. These he took to the face and with all the energy he still possessed he flung it at the rock. The wall quivered. Again he threw the iron ball. The rock shook. Again. The rock shifted. Again. Some of the higher face crumbled away. Light and fresh air seeped in. Dora brought Hiram the last sticks of dynamite.

"Now will these do?" she breathed, both of them sucking in the small but welcomed flow of new air.

"Yes. Bring the torch."

She grabbed up the once dying torch which was also being revitalized by the air. Hiram had placed the explosive. He lit the fuse to the set charge before they staggered away to safety as fast as they could. They just made the main tunnel when the dynamite blew. After the blast settled as they peered around the corner they saw a dazzling sight. In the corner of the face was exhilarating sunlight!

As brisk as they could they picked their way through the rock rubble scattered around the floor. The welcomed light beckoned them to come. At the new opening big enough for them to squeeze through the freed captives drank in great gulps of fresh air. In a few moments their minds cleared and their strength returned.

"Hiram, you'd better wait here while I see if our adversary is still around," she instructed. With her revolver drawn for business she stepped away onto the open mountainside.

All nature lay as still as a graveyard. Nary a bird call was heard. The last blast had alarmed all forest fauna into unequivocal silence.

Dora wound her way around the rocky mountainside toward the original but now buried entrance. From there she could view the near side of the cabin below. Finding a suitable boulder to conceal herself behind she watched and listened for signs of any human habitation.

Several minutes passed. No signs of life emanated from the building. Their assailant no longer appeared to be at the mine site. Forest sounds once again became prevalent as the startled reaction to the explosive noises was forgotten. Dora scrambled back to the mine's new opening where Hiram lie waiting.

"Red must have cleared out right after he caved in the entrance," she informed him. "Otherwise he'd have come running if he had heard the blast."

"I hope I never see that scoundrel again!" Hiram exclaimed. He crawled out into the open sunshine and fresh air and took another deep breath. "Free at last! How can I repay you?"

"By rustling up some grub," she answered with a relieved grin. "Is there any food in the cabin?"

"Yes, ma'am, there is. And right now I feel mighty hungry myself for a change."

The two ex-captives marched down the mountain trail toward the cabin. At the door before going in Dora took the extra precaution of giving the singular room a sweeping glance. Finding the room vacant they went in.

Hiram headed for the cook stove. "I'll see what I can whip up."

"Wait! Don't light the stove," Dora directed. "Just in case Red shows up again we don't want any telltale smoke. I'd want to catch that scoundrel by surprise."

"A good point," he concurred. "That hadn't occurred to me. I'll see what I can find that doesn't need cooking."

"I'm going out to look around."

Leaving Hiram to his own devices Dora went back outside. She picked up the trail that led down the mountain to where she had left Spirit tethered. He was still standing, looking patient but bored, where she had tied him. She stroked his neck and mane with long, affectionate pats. He whinnied his delight.

"I thought for a moment there, old boy, that you'd be an orphan. You're no doubt hungry as well, huh, Spirit. Let's see what we can find for you."

The absence of Red's horse plus fresh tracks leaving from where he had been tied assured Dora of Red's departure. He had gotten away again. Would he be back? Blowing shut the tunnel was a manifestation that Red had no more use for Hiram or the mine. She doubted that Red would ever be returning.

Dora led Spirit over to the cabin site where there were some clumps of grass growing that he could eat. Flowing near the cabin was a small brook. An old, battered bucket lay on the bank. She scooped up a drink for her horse. Letting him drink it dry she fetched him a second draft then returned to the cabin. Hiram poked his head out through the doorway.

"It's nothing fancy but at least it'll fill up the cavity between the ribs."

"Right now the Waldorf Astoria couldn't offer better."

He shoved a plate into her hands as she entered the room. She took it with a nod of thanks. As for Dora she couldn't have eaten a finer meal. They both devoured their platefuls.

"You got a horse?" she queried between bites.

"No. Red took away the one that brought me here. He wanted to be sure I didn't try to escape."

"You never tried?"

"Once. I stole off one night but Red caught up. He left me hanging on the rafters in this place by my wrists for three days. He threatened to kill me the next time only after I would have hung there for a week. The first time wasn't a very pleasant experience."

"Were you up in the mine when you tried your escape?"

"The only time I was working up there was when Red was around. When he was gone he left me chained to that eye in the wall." He nodded at the iron eye bolt. "So how do we get out of here?"

"We'll have to ride double on my horse until we get down to Florence," she decided. "I'll get you a horse there. What were you mining here? Gold?"

"Yes. There was a small but rich vein up there. It played out a month ago. Red got most of it, but I managed to hide some." He stepped over to a small floorboard in the corner near his eye bolt and lifted it. In the cavity beneath was a small sack of gold nuggets. "Not much, but a little to help recoup my losses," he said, stuffing the bag into his shirt.

"If the mine had played out why was Red still keeping you here?"

"Being greedy he was easy to convince that there was still another vein to find. Once the mine was through Red would have just disposed of me. I was trying to buy some time. My hope was that someone would still find me. You came along just in time."

"I thought Red was interested in oil as well. Wouldn't he keep you around to help him find it?"

"We had already gone to mark the best areas on what, I thought, was his property," Hiram explained. "That was before he brought me up here to make me a prisoner. I've been working here for close to two years."

"What happened when he showed up today?" she questioned.

"He ran into the cabin, unlocked me from the shackles secured to the wall over there, then we ran up to the mine where he had me clamp the ball on. Then he ran out. Never said a word except stay put."

"Then I stumbled in, and he saw a chance to seal us both up," Dora concluded. "Good thing you were planning another way out."

Tossing her empty tin aside she stood and stepped to the door. Pausing she turned to Hiram. "If you have anything you want grab it and let's go."

Following her lead he threw his dish aside and rose to his feet. "Besides the nuggets there's nothing for me here worth taking."

Dora had noticed that the clothes he was wearing were past their life expectancy. If he had nothing else he would need more than a horse with which to return to Hannah. She vowed to herself to get him some new clothes in Florence.

As they started out the door Dora came to an abrupt stop, her hand raised. "The sun is low," she said. "We're going to have to make camp somewhere along the road tonight. I don't want to stay here in case Red should come back. Better grab a bedroll and a few provisions for breakfast."

Hiram gathered the suggested items while Dora fetched Spirit up to the cabin door. They strapped the supplies to his saddle. Swinging on first Dora helped Hiram climb up behind her.

With the cabin behind them Dora kept Spirit at a brisk pace, but not fast enough to tire him from his extra load. When they reached the main trail she stopped to examine it for fresh signs of Red's tracks.

The side path's surface lacked signs of frequent use. With ease she spotted the distinctive marks of a fast-ridden mount. They came off of the cabin's trail to head north. Somewhere in that direction lay the town of Poverty Gulch.

Dora turned Spirit south. She resolved to herself to return to chase down Red as soon as she could. In the meantime Hiram Minkle needed to be outfitted and sent home. As they approached the spot where she had shot the robbers she saw that their bodies had been removed. This was a welcome discovery. Hiram wouldn't have to be exposed to the sudden appearance of two corpses in the middle of the road.

When they arrived back at the ghost town of Oroville Dora once again questioned the old man for directions. This time she wanted to know how to find the road to Florence. As per his instructions they took the left fork for Poverty Gulch for about a thousand yards to another left fork that would take them into Florence.

Just before dark Dora left the road to find a suitable camp for the night. Their earlier ordeal left them craving for a good night's rest. Moments after they had crawled into their bedrolls they drifted into dreamless sleep.

26

An early dawn found them finishing a cold breakfast of jerky, sourdough, and beans. Before the sun appeared over the eastern mountains they were on the trail again. After they had been riding along for a short time Dora ventured a question.

"Why do you think Hannah never—'saw' your run-in with Red? Or do you believe that she really 'sees' these 'visions' she claims?"

"My natural skepticism held sway for a long time after we first met when she told me about her unusual ability," he admitted. "She never tried to exploit it, though. Furthermore, as a scientist I've learned to expect the unexpected. My thought is she did sense my dilemma, but I believe that her mind utterly refused to accept it."

"Why do you believe that?" Dora queried, a little amazed at his answer. "She told me that she wished she could have known what had happened to you. Yet you're saying that she didn't want to know?"

"The mind is a wondrous thing that we know little about," Hiram explained. "Hannah practically always 'saw' the dangerous situations and dilemmas that would occur to various individuals. Sometimes these were fatal occurrences for those that these visions were about. She never liked that part at all. She'd be distraught for days."

"I noticed that pattern in most of her visions," Dora concurred.

"Hannah once told me that she could never bear to see anything terrible happen to me. She was merely stating a self-fulfilling prediction. Because of her love for me she had already programmed her own mind to reject any such messages. She couldn't see what she refused to see."

"That's plausible. I understand what you mean," she mused. "As a child I was plagued with this terrible nightmare that recurred a number of times. It was so frightening that it scared me awake. Ma would find me crying but the memory of what the nightmare was would be gone. It still is. My mind blocked the nightmare out."

"Yes, that's what our minds can do," he affirmed.

Dora kept her passenger busy ambling on about his past which he was most willing to do. She reckoned that he needed someone to whom he could talk again. He spoke about Hannah, and Harvard, and himself. This kept up until they reached the town of Florence. Dora rode straight to the stables where she bought Hiram a horse and saddle of his own. Then she took him to the general store and outfitted him in some new clothes.

From the store proprietor she got directions to a barber for Hiram and a place to clean up for both of them. Within half an hour Hiram looked like a new man. With his square jaw and cleft chin, a clean shave and a good haircut, he was handsome. Dora could see why Hannah was attracted to his rugged good looks.

"All I have to repay you are some of these gold nuggets," he confessed. "I don't know how many nuggets the horse, saddle, and other things equate to."

"Get them assayed in Pueblo and convert them to cash. We'll settle up later. Right now I have one more item of business with which to attend. Follow me to the sheriff's office."

As they rode to the sheriff's office Hiram's face reflected shock. "Why, I've never even learned your name yet! All this talk we've had has been about me. I know nothing about you except that you've saved my life!"

"That's enough for now," she replied. "If you think about it we saved each other. My name is Dora. More about me you'll learn soon enough."

"Dora," Hiram mulled over her name aloud. "Your name is Greek based. Useful to a geologist Greek was one of my minors in college. Your name means 'gift' as I remember. How appropriate! You gave me the gift of freedom. Did you know what your name meant?"

"Yes," Dora acknowledged. "My mother is a big fan of ancient Greek culture. That's how she chose my name. Being her only daughter I was often told how she considered me her special gift from heaven. She wasn't very happy when I chose to follow after Pa."

"If your life's vocation is what brought you to rescue me I'm glad you did," Hiram declared, showing wonder in his eyes as to what her career might be.

They slipped from their saddles to tie their horses to the hitching post just outside the sheriff's office. A dark-bearded man of medium build glanced up from his desk as they entered. He wore the appropriate star upon his vest.

"Can I help you?' he said, greeting with an expectant lift of his eyebrows.

Dora stepped up to his desk. "Sheriff, have you been having trouble with a couple of highwaymen, one named Jake, on the short road to Poverty Gulch?"

His eyebrows raised a notch. "We sure have. Not only there but all over the roads up there, at least until yesterday. A couple of travelers coming from Poverty Gulch on that road came upon their bodies in the middle of the roadway. Since they had no wagon they found those outlaws' horses tied in the trees nearby. By strapping their bodies across their horses the two men were able to haul those varmints in here. The bodies are at the undertaker's now. Do you know something about them?"

"Just that they stopped me on the road yesterday and threatened my very life and then some. So I shot them both in self-defense."

The sheriff rose to his feet while leaning over his desk. Hiram looked as much surprised about his new friend as did the law officer. "*You* shot them?" the sheriff exclaimed wonder echoing in his query.

"I didn't stutter," she stated with an easy smile.

A look of doubt crossed his face. He glanced at Hiram who just shrugged his shoulders in response. "I find that story a little—strange to believe," he mused. "Just where to be exact did you shoot them?"

"Right between the eyes. Both of them," she answered as a matter of fact.

"That's true," he agreed. "What other proof do you have?"

Dora picked up a wanted poster she had noticed laying on the corner of the desk and read: "'Wanted dead or alive. Jake Barnes and Clyde Upston for attempted murder, horse thieving, numerous highway robberies, bank robbery, rustling, etc.' Are these the two I put down?"

"Those are the two that were brought in," the sheriff answered instead. "Can you give me any more proof?"

"I see there's a two hundred, fifty dollar reward on each of them," Dora went on. "For that I'll give you proof. Would you like to step outside with me for a moment? I'd like to give you a little demonstration."

The sheriff obliged following Dora and Hiram into the street. Hiram, perplexity written all over his face, looked on in wonder.

Dora handed the sheriff two silver dollars from her pocket.

"Toss these high into the air," she instructed. "Together."

The sheriff stepped a few paces away and flipped the coins straight up into the air. In a flash Dora's weapon was in her hand.

Two rapid reports resounded off the surrounding buildings. Both coins responded by arching up and away from the trio below them.

Faces appeared at doorways and windows. A crowd began to gather around as the sheriff marched over to the places where the two coins had landed. Scooping them up he held each up between the forefinger and thumb of each hand. Both sported windows in their centers.

"Shot clean through the middle!" he whistled in amazement.

"Need more proof?" she asked.

A buzz filtered through the crowd. The sheriff kept staring at the coins. He shook his head in disbelief. "I haven't seen shooting like this since Amos Kincaid—." He let his statement hang. "No, I think you've proven your point. Come back into the office. I'll take care of that reward. If it's all right with you I'll trade you two fresh coins for these. I'd like to keep these for souvenirs."

She nodded consent. "Be my guest."

He turned to the crowd that had materialized. "Folks, the demonstration is over, so you can go back to your business now."

Back in his office the sheriff opened a strongbox and withdrew five crisp one hundred-dollar bills and two replacement silver coins. He handed them to Dora along with a voucher for her to sign. She did so post haste. Turning the paper back and forth the sheriff squinted to read her signature which was indecipherable.

"Just who are you?" he queried.

"Some folks call me Petticoat," she called over her shoulder as she waltzed out the door. Hiram was right on her heels. Dora left the sheriff standing there reflecting upon her response.

Outside the office Hiram found his tongue. "You're a sharp-shooter."

"That's the first time I've been called that, but the title fits. That reference to Amos Kincaid the fast gun that the sheriff made? He's my father."

As they remounted their horses Dora asked Hiram, "Do you think you can find your way home? I'm going after Red."

"Good luck to you. Just show me the road to La Junta."

She pointed down the street to the east. "Keep your horse at a good clip and you should be in La Junta before dark. Hannah's place is on a slight rise just outside of town." She leaned toward him and pressed two of the new bills she had just received into his hand.

"What's this for?" he asked in surprise. "I owe you already."

"I figure you deserve at least half of this reward money. You're at least part of the reason that I met up with those two characters. Since the horse, saddle, and clothes cost me fifty dollars this makes us even. The rest is on me. So long, Hiram. Give my regards to Hannah. I may see you again. Safe journey. Oh, and don't talk to red haired strangers. When you see Max Templeton about oil tell him I sent you."

She whirled away leaving Hiram Minkle staring after her in wonder as she headed Spirit back along the road to Poverty Gulch.

27

Spirit's great stamina carried Dora to the struggling town of Poverty Gulch by nightfall. En route she had detoured just long enough to check out the cabin again at the now abandoned mine. No changes had taken place in the twenty-four hours since Hiram and she had left it. The cabin was as constant as a photograph.

As she reined in Spirit to an easy walk down the main street of Poverty Gulch she tried to match the present scene of this declining gold mining town with the tales her father had told her about it in its hey day. At first the town had exploded into life the same as Oroville had. Strike-it-rich hopefuls flocked into the area after the discovery of the precious metal. The town had started out as Placer Gulch. When poverty replaced the placer gold the new name stuck.

Gold mines big and small dotted the surrounding hillsides as mute witnesses. Most were now abandoned, played out or never productive.

Time proved to be the winner. Over the ensuing years the less valiant to their cause had abandoned their dreams of instant, easy wealth. They had moved on to other delusions of greener pastures. Only the most tenacious miners who knew the real toil of wrestling the precious metals from the stubborn ground stayed on. Some of these were fortunate enough to make a comfortable living even to amass a small fortune from their labors. Others eked out the best they could. The real money earners were the merchants who provided tools, machinery, and supplies to the miners. While the town wasn't thriving it was still somewhat surviving.

The dwindling town also attracted blackguards like vultures circling a moribund animal. The difference was vultures were useful for cleaning up carcasses. This influx of desperadoes caused some of the more civil folks to leave. Many of those who remained had to do so because every asset they owned was wrapped up in the town. They couldn't afford to leave.

Dora could see the visible results of such a change in the status of the town. Parts of the town including the part that rested upon the higher surrounding slopes were fine, well-kept homes. Other houses showed neglect due to vacancy. Many of the once thriving businesses now struggling from the weakened economy were in need of non-affordable face lifting. Others such as the saloon were neglected out of disinterest. Saloons always seemed to prosper whether well kept or not. That type of setting would attract men like Red.

Most of the establishments including the sheriff's office were already closed for the night. She wondered what sort of "law" this town still had. The lifeless streets sustained almost no traffic, equestrian or pedestrian. Were the local citizens afraid to walk their streets even in the cool twilight of a summer evening?

The few signs of life that Dora witnessed this night clinked, clicked and clattered in the saloon. Lights glowed as well in the building directly across the street, the quiet hotel. She turned Spirit's head in the direction of the hotel.

As she approached the deteriorating structure a familiar figure caught her eye and brought a satisfied smile to her face. Tied to the saloon's hitching post stood Red's horse. Leaving her own trusty steed hitched outside the hotel Dora sauntered into the building. Behind the counter the night clerk, or so she supposed since no one else was around, was slouched down in light slumber in a chair. She cleared her throat to stir him.

"Ahem!"

The clerk grunted and jerked his head erect. When his senses came to him his face brightened at the sight of the pretty, young, pony-tailed woman smiling down at him.

"Good evening. May I help you?" he inquired in his best manners, leaping to his feet. His clothes appeared fresher than the hotel décor.

"I think I should like a room for the night," she said in honey tones. "A quiet one, please. I've come a long way and am very tired. The insides of my eyelids need extensive examination too."

"As you wish, ma'am," he drawled, revealing no reaction to her repartee. He reached for a key hanging on the key rack and handed it to her. "This here room is upstairs on the back side. That should be plenty quiet for ya."

"Thank you. How much?"

"Four bits."

Dora paid the fee, took the key, and started for the front entry.

"Uh, ma'am," the clerk called after her. "You got some luggage with which I can help you?"

"Oh, no, thank you," she declined with a gracious smile. "I just have a small pack. I'm traveling light as I would like to reach my destination as soon as possible." On a hunch she decided to add, "Right now I'm going across the street to the saloon."

An expression of stark surprise betrayed his face. "The saloon? Why, ma'am, you wouldn't want to go to the saloon."

She cast him a questioning stare. "Just why wouldn't I?" she asked, her query searching.

The clerk groped for the right words. "Well, uh, because a pretty, young lady shouldn't be in such a place. Why, those old booze hounds would give mean looks at you and expect something in return, uh, if you know what I mean," he finished, his plea sounding lame.

"Well, thank you for your compliment and for your concern," she tried to assure him, "but I'm not going there to offer any 'favors'. Besides, I don't drink. I'm going over there on business."

"Business? Who do you have business with, uh, if you don't mind me asking."

She walked back to the desk. "Well, since you did ask," she mused, "perhaps you can be of help. Do you know the owner of the big gray gelding tied up outside the saloon? He has sandy colored hair and goes by the name of Red."

Alarm flashed through his eyes at the name. "You mean Red Flannigan? What do you want with him?"

"Ah, you *do* know him," she smiled in acknowledgment pleased with her luck while avoiding a direct answer to his question. "He's the one. What can you tell me about Red Flannigan?"

"Ma'am, I can tell you a lot about him. He's a no-good thief, swindler, murderer, you name it, and you should stay away from him."

"Well, that hasn't told me too much yet. Those occupations should have him behind bars. You say you can tell me a lot. Why should I stay away from him?"

The clerk lowered his voice as if speaking some dark secret that he didn't want the walls to hear. "Because he's dangerous. He's a fugitive from Kansas. I understand he's wanted for everything you can imagine down there. And I imagine soon enough he'll be wanted for the same things in Colorado if he isn't already."

"If that's so why hasn't your sheriff done something about the man?" Dora quizzed. "He could get Red Flannigan extradited back to Kansas."

"Because the sheriff is scared to death. But I don't blame him. I would be too. I wouldn't want his job. The last three sheriffs come up missing kind of strange like. Not that the sheriff is a coward he's just careful. Red doesn't have many friends, but the ones he has are all in this town. They're probably in the saloon with Red right now. When he came here a couple of years ago he just sort of took over. All the other trouble makers kind of took to him."

"Do you mean Red runs this town?"

"Well, not all of it. The richer part of the townspeople got together and hired themselves some armed guards. Red and his bunch have left them alone so far. It's the poorer side of town that Red pretty much controls. When he's not around his gang is keeping tabs on everyone. Most folks are scared half to death of them. Everyone figures that he and his pals are the reasons that our former sheriffs are missing. Nothing's been found out about them. That's why our present sheriff treads a ticklish trail."

"I see," she nodded as if ingesting his warning. Red sounded like another Delgrin. Dora started for the entry once more. "I'll remember what you told me," she tossed back over her shoulder as she marched out the door.

"Well, ma'am, don't say I didn't warn you," he called after her. She was gone before he could finish his statement.

Striding across the street Dora stepped up to the saloon doors and, remaining in the evening's shadows, peered over them. The tables in the center of the big room were easy to survey, but the tables in the corners against the front outside wall were out of her view. Closed shutters prevented her from looking through the front windows to see these outside tables. The saloon sported plenty of patronage, but Red was not sitting anywhere in her line of sight.

Dora retreated into the shadows of the night to ponder her next move. Walking right in would be foolhardy. Her very presence would attract ubiquitous attention which she didn't want. Plus, if Red were sitting in one of the forward corners where he might see her first he just might recognize her and start shooting. Shoot first and forget the questions marked his style. All of his cronies would follow his lead. She'd be caught right in the middle. Coming out looking like a sieve wasn't her idea of fun at all. The enemy had to be located and identified before she faced them. No sense giving Red any advantage. He'd had too many of them already.

She headed around to the rear of the building. From the swinging saloon doors she'd espied a flight of enclosed stairs that emptied into one far corner of the barroom. Those might be her best bet to offer her an unobstructed view of the invisible corners. She needed to reach the upper landing of these stairs from the second floor. At the back of the building Dora found a small balcony jutting from the upper level. Below it was situated the rear entry to the saloon. Using the door frame she managed to climb up to the balcony and hoist herself over the railing. A small window and a door occupied the otherwise solid slab wall before her.

Through the window she could see a fair sized chamber that appeared to be a dressing room. Standing in front of a large mirror a barmaid was touching up her makeup and hair. With a final check of her dress she sashayed out of the room to descend the stairs.

Dora tried the doorknob. It was unlocked. Mimicking a mouse she eased the door shut behind her and slipped to the room's inner door to check the stairway. By the time she reached the landing the footsteps of the barmaid had faded. The path was clear. She retreated to a makeup table close by.

Picking up a brush from off the counter she brushed her ponytail out with rapid, adept strokes. Then she grabbed a washcloth from next to the hand basin and wiped the dust of the trail from her face and arms. When she crossed the room to the wardrobe rack she peered out the open door to the landing again. Still clear.

I wish I had my own costume, she thought while she made quick work of sorting through the line of dresses hanging on the rack. Much to her dislike all of them were sleeveless, having only shoulder straps. She had to be content with what she could find. At last she located a dress that looked her size. She pulled it off the rack and— just then voices from the stairway startled her.

"...that creep does it again, so help me, I'll—" the voice, a female's, was low but full of anger and coming closer up the stairs.

"Now, dear, you've got to expect his kind in this line of work," another female answered. "They come along once in a while."

No time to run! The balcony door was too far. Dora slipped between the dress racks and stooped to hide.

The first female was speaking again. "Well, I still can't stand the big baboon!" she snorted as she stomped into the room. "He gets a little drunk and he gets too fresh and rough. Look at the bruises on my shoulders. I'm afraid to see the places under my dress that he's pinched. Good customer or not I'm tempted to have him bounced."

The second woman had followed the first into the room by this time. Dora had just managed to conceal herself in time. She held her breath. Her boots were exposed below the hemlines of the other skirts still hanging on the rack. She hoped they wouldn't notice.

"Okay, I'll try to save you from him," the second woman consoled her companion. "I know how the big galoot is with his wandering hands. You wouldn't believe where he's bruised *me* before!"

"Thanks, Margel. I don't want to abandon you to him, but I just can't take any more of his rough fondling. I'll pay you back later."

The voices, for Dora didn't dare peek out and chance on exposing her position, came from near the large mirror. She reasoned that this luxury was acquired during the town's former heyday.

"Don't worry, kid," answered the second voice. "If I need a favor later, I'll remember. In the meantime I'll handle the big oaf. With a few more drinks in him he won't have the strength to pinch a daisy off its stem. Give me a few minutes to make him forget where he is before you come back down. You go ahead and spruce up a bit."

"I will. Look at the mess my hair is in."

Dora heard the soft scuff of shoe leather across the hardwood floor leave the room and descend the stairs. Then her ears caught the faint sssst, sssst, of a brush being pulled through tangled hair. Being extra cautious she peered over the tops of the dresses on the rack. Standing in front of the mirror a dishwater blonde was brushing her hair. This was not the same woman that Dora had seen upon her initial entry.

From where Dora was hiding she could see the barmaid's profile. Taller and heavier set than Dora, but not fat, she was fair looking although no raving beauty. Her thick, gaudy makeup made her facial features appear more angular than they were. It was applied as an actor would do to bring out the eyes and mouth at a distance such as on a stage. Not an attractive sight at close range, but suitable for an audience.

Dora always reckoned that barmaids wore their makeup this way so that they would look better to the saloon's customers when the more inebriated the patrons became. With bleary eyes the customers might still recognize the female attendants.

The barmaid put down her brush on a nearby table. She brushed down her skirt, gave a last sweeping look at her person, and left the room. Dora waited until her footsteps on the stairs faded away.

Breathing a sigh of relief at not being discovered which could have foiled her impromptu plan she stepped from behind the dress rack with the dress she had picked out. Since the shoulders of the dress were bare Dora had to remove her shirt. The injury that she had received on her left shoulder was thus exposed. By then it had healed enough that she hoped it wouldn't be noticeable in the dim lights of the bar.

Slipping on the standard barmaid's apparel she rolled up her pant legs so that they wouldn't show. With her pocketknife she split the seam of the dress over the slight bulge of her gun. She cut open enough line of stitching to make the gun accessible yet still hidden until she wanted it. A few tries showed her the opening was enough.

Posing in front of the mirror Dora could see that her boots did not match the outfit. She had noticed that the woman who had just left was wearing black, high-laced shoes. Her boots were black. Dusting them off she was counting on the general drunken condition of the men and the dim lighting in the saloon to prevent any one from noticing the trivial difference. Besides they should be content just looking at her face.

The last part of her ruse came to play with the application of makeup. This she did with the skill of an expert highlighting her pretty features. When she was finished Dora felt certain that she could rival any barmaid on the premises or in town for that matter.

Now all she had to do was to pull off her masquerade. With caution she checked the stairway again. There was a small landing just beyond the door at the top. The shadowy staircase itself being encased in solid walls down to the bottom provided ample shaded protection from immediate detection. The combination of talking, laughing, and the clinking of glasses from below covered any noise she might make going down.

Before descending Dora stepped onto the balcony where she dropped her shirt to the ground. She would retrieve it later after she'd finished her business. Returning to the landing she reached the bottom of the steps without anyone's notice. Dora remained in the darkness of the staircase.

From her vantage point she could see the near corner through the mirror above the end of the bar opposite where the stairs entered the main barroom. Red wasn't at that table. That left the far corner to see. Dora realized that she would have to step into the room beyond the end of the counter to see that corner. If Red wasn't there either, then she might have to do some furtive maneuvers to exit the premises and remain undiscovered by the personnel. She was relying on Red Flannigan being in the adjoining room.

The closest table boasted of a couple of cowboys slumped across from each other. They were sharing a bottle of cheap whiskey and were betraying prominent signs of succumbing to its contents. The conversation they carried on when they talked came out slow and slurred.

Now's my chance! She thought. Dora strolled on over to sit in the chair between them. Upon realizing her presence both the men rolled their blurred eyes toward her. She smiled a pretty smile while fluttering her eyelashes.

"Hello, boys," she murmured in honey tones. "Your table looks lonely."

"Well, yeah, ma'am!" the one on her right muttered with what little volume he still had. His eyes went wide, or as wide as a drunk's eyes could go. The other cowboy just gawked in pleasure a cockeyed grin on his mouth.

"Mind if I join your little party?" she cooed as sweet as sugar.

"You're here, aincha?" the right one slurred. "Sit right there. I'll gitcha a glass."

His head swaying on his shoulders he tried to turn toward the bar. Dora reached over with a gentle hand to pull his stubbly face back toward her before he could call the bartender over. He smiled at the touch of her hand.

"That's all right, Sweetie," she purred. "I don't need a glass. Here's a better idea. I'll just use yours."

She picked up his glass, put her delicate lips to the rim, and feigned a drink. Making sure that the now noticeable lipstick smears faced the man she offered him the glass. He gazed with droopy eyes at her action his mouth hanging open.

"See if I didn't sweeten it up for you, Honey. That's the best kiss I can give you right now. Go ahead and drink it all."

Like a hungry bear in a beehive the man did her bidding lapping at the liquor and the lipstick while she performed the same feat for the other man who almost drooled while awaiting his treated glass.

"You're new here, aincha?" the left man managed to burble as she kissed the rim of his glass next. He took it with eager and hungry anticipation licking the edge where her lips had touched.

"I sure am, Sugar, and I aim to keep my customers *very* happy. Now, don't you think this makes your drink taste lots better?"

While the left man gulped his down the right one propositioned her while she refilled his glass and returned it to him once again "sweetened" for his satisfaction.

"Shey, purdy lady. How 'bout you 'n' me—findin'—a nishe, quiet plashe—"

She pinched his cheek with affectionate fingers. "You devil, you!" she scolded him with a mischievous smile. "Tempting me like that! You know the rules. Not during working hours. Maybe we'll talk about it later when I'm not working."

"Yeah, me (hiccup) too," the second man mumbled.

She poured the left man another drink complete with a kissed rim. While they were both draining their glasses again she took the opportunity to get her first look into the far corner. There—was Red!

28

Red Flannigan, notorious outlaw from Kansas, was indeed the Red she hunted. He was seated at the farthest table, his back to the wall, along with four other men all seated to face the rest of the barroom.

She scrutinized her adversary from across the room. At last she had caught up to this murderous marauder. Although she had been farther from Red on the day she was riding behind Bill Reilly Dora recognized him at once. His chiseled features gave his long face a gaunt expression. Even without his red hair his sinister look made him stand out from the crowd. A perpetual sneer curled the corners of his crooked mouth. He had no drink. A dark alley was not a place to meet this man.

Two on either side, the four men seated with him, Dora reasoned, were his henchmen. None of them had glasses in front of them. Oblivious to the rest of the saloon's clientele Red appeared to be giving instructions to his gang. They would have to be reckoned with as well. She didn't recognize any of them either from wanted posters, or her father's descriptions. Satisfied with her find she surveyed the rest of the barroom to check the layout.

At another nearby table stood the blonde from upstairs with another woman. They were on either side of a fat, burly man who was sprawled all over the tabletop. The second woman was, Dora deduced, the one named Margel who had been upstairs with the blonde. Margel, an older, plump brunette with passable looks was without a doubt accomplishing her promise to disable the man's roaming hands.

A third and last barmaid, the youngest and best looking of the three, was a short, slender brunette. This was the woman Dora had spied from the balcony. She stood at the bar with another patron. From the smiles on their faces they were enjoying each other's company more than the other two women. A couple of beer steins sat on the counter in front of them.

At a table near the center of the room close to the pot-bellied stove was a card game going on between four men. The game appeared to be hotter than the stove which was out for the summer. A few other tables had some sundry customers in various stages of drunken stupor or conversation. Only a couple of tables were without clientele.

The nearest corner to her table weighed in with another card game while a passed out drunk occupied one of the two tables between them. The bartender was busy chatting at the far end of the counter.

No one else but the two men she was sitting with had noticed her unscheduled entry. Dora continued to fill their glasses and "sweeten" their drinks as they emptied them until they too became placid table decorations. Again she patted the whiskered cheek of the right hand man who had passed out last.

"Sorry, Sugar," she murmured. "Looks like I'll just have to take a rain check on your offer. When you wake up you'll think this was all a dream except for the nightmare of a hangover you'll have."

The next step was to get rid of her "competition". This was bound to be a little trickier for she knew that she needed to gain the attention of only the other women. No one else in particular the bartender was to notice her just yet.

From her reconnaissance position Dora felt relative safety from discovery for the moment. The table where she was seated occupied a darker corner. The two drunks laid out cold across the table gave her some screen from the other patrons who were already engrossed in their own activities. If necessary should she need to exit in a hurry the back stairway was just a couple of steps away.

The bartender was busy gabbing to a patron at the far end of the bar. His back was turned to her end of the room. By sliding her chair back against the wall just behind her she was even more in the shadows while keeping an eye on the three barmaids. She concentrated her attention on the two at the big man's table.

Judging from his prostrate position Dora could see that the fat, burly man who bruised shoulders and other places had surpassed his limit of alcoholic intake. The table strained under his ponderous bulk spread out upon it. With disdainful expressions his two female companions stepped away from his table. Since he was the sole habitant they left him passed out on his own.

The woman named Margel had already relocated at an adjacent table to the burly man's. There she took up what looked to be a continuing conversation with its two other occupants. With a beer glass already sitting on the table in front of her Dora could guess that she was returning to a former engagement before the blonde sought her help.

The blonde barmaid now standing alone was glancing around the room at the various tables as if searching for another more appealing patron with which to fraternize. When her gaze fell across each occupied table her facial expressions gave away her thoughts about the aspects of taking up residency there. Her gaze then fell upon the two unconscious cowboys on the table where Dora sat. No company there.

The blonde at first looked on beyond this table before she realized that sitting in the shadows was a fourth barmaid one that she did not recognize. In a double take her gaze flashed back to Dora. This was the notice Dora hoped to attract. Sporting a smug smile the impostor just shrugged her shoulders to the puzzled look on the blonde's face.

In short order the barmaid's astonished stare turned into a glare of suspicion. Dora, mellowing her face into a sheepish grin stood up and backed over to the stairs. Just as she started back up the steps she saw the blonde motioning to Margel. She was heading up the stairs in rapid strides before Margel saw her. In just a moment the two, with luck all three of the other women, would be coming up the stairs after her without the bartender tagging along. She hoped the three could handle this without him.

Like a fleeting shadow Dora returned to the dressing room to "hide." In reality she stood where she could be seen from the doorway when someone entered the room. There she waited. Before long she heard many muffled footsteps of several people scraping the stairway. Once they reached the landing the three barmaids soon appeared in the doorway. No one else was with them.

They all espied Dora almost at once when they entered the room. The last one in pushed the door shut behind her. *So far, so good.* As if fearful of having been discovered Dora backed up against the wall.

"Okay, sister," the older, more buxom brunette named Margel, and obvious leader of the trio, snarled. "What's your game? Who are you?"

With minatory expressions they advanced toward her. Being three against one the trio figured they had the upper hand.

"Please!" Dora implored in a pleading voice pretending for her safety. "No harm done. I just needed the work."

"We've got enough help," the third barmaid showing no pity threw back at her. "There's no room for any more."

Margel mellowed a little at Dora's feigned fear. "Look, once upon a time we could have used you when Poverty Gulch was a booming town. We didn't have enough girls then. But times have changed. There's just enough work for the three of us."

"That's okay," Dora responded with a mysterious reply in a commanding voice. "You've already done your share. Now it's time for you to take a break."

The three women glanced puzzled looks around among them. Barmaid number three raised the next questions. "How did you get in here, anyway? Where did you get that dress?"

"That's one of ours," the blonde accused. "Give it back!"

By now the trio had advanced in slow motion to the center of the room. They were about to continue their progression toward Dora when she stepped away from the wall. The trio stopped, their eyes riveted upon the lethal steel that had appeared from nowhere to occupy Dora's hand. Within two flicks of an eyelash the odds of three to one no longer had any meaning. She proffered a grim smile at the three women who stood with jaws dropped while eyeing her revolver.

"I took the liberty of making some alterations," Dora stated, now exhibiting the voice of authority. "Now I'm making some more. The three of you are relieved of your duties for a short time." She waved her gun barrel at the blonde. "Grab a couple of sashes and tie your friends' hands behind them. Tie them just the way I tell you and be prompt about it. Start with Margel."

As the dishwater blonde, although reluctant, obeyed Dora's directions, Margel, her hands now behind her, repeated her original questions, except in reverse order. "Who are you? What's your game?"

"I regret to have to tie you ladies up," Dora replied, "but right now I don't know who's friend or foe. There's no time to find out. Does the name Petticoat mean anything to you?"

The three women exchanged wary glances. Margel spoke for the group. "We've heard of a female gunslinger who goes by that name. We thought the stories were just that, stories. Is that you?"

"At your service," she said giving them a nod. "Right now I have a date with a man downstairs. Things could get messy. For your safety I'm disposed to leave you up here with some minor restraints."

Having followed Dora's directions the blonde finished binding her two companions. Dora grabbed a third sash and ordered the blonde to turn around. Without warning the blonde being somewhat taller and heavier than Dora, and thinking that she could overpower her made a lunge for the gun. Sidestepping the foolish attempt with ease Dora brought up a smashing left fist that sent the woman reeling. Stunned by the blow the barmaid sank to her knees.

"That was not a smart move," Dora reproved holstering her weapon. "You'll wind up with a bruised and swollen jaw, not a pretty sight for a barmaid." With a few deft motions she finished the job the blonde started including gags and bound ankles. "This will be a little uncomfortable, but it can't be helped. Make no attempt to attract attention from below or otherwise mess up my game plan. My fight is not with you, but will be if you interfere. Now be good girls."

Leaving the three women lying on their sides in the middle of the dressing room floor Dora headed back downstairs for the bar.

At the bottom of the stairs Dora once again paused to peer around the corner this time looking straight at Red's table. Her jaw dropped. Red was not there! Astonished She swept her wide-eyed gaze around the entire saloon. Red Flannigan was no longer in the bar!

29

Had he given her the slip again even without knowing that she was there? Perhaps he *had* seen her just as she had left the room a few minutes earlier ahead of the three barmaids. Even if he had noticed her he couldn't have recognized her dressed and made up as she was, she was certain. To Red Flannigan he should be convinced that she was just a corpse buried in a caved-in mine of his own making.

His departure must have occurred for another reason besides her presence, she mused. What was she to do now? Undecided she resisted the temptation to just march across the barroom floor and out the swinging doors. There was nothing that said that Red could just be outside somewhere. As well Dora wasn't ready to reveal her hand just then and let the bartender see her. She was hoping to play a few more cards yet. Perhaps he would return soon. His four stooges were still seated at the table.

A motion behind the bar caught her attention. The bartender had stepped away from his patron to also survey the room. *He must be looking for his barmaids,* she deduced. In a snap Dora whirled around. With her back to him she bent over to fuss with her dress. Peering from under her arm she saw him pivot until he spied her by the stairs. With a slight nod to himself showing that he was satisfied with his find he turned back to continue his chat with his patron.

That was close! she thought in relief. If she had been discovered with Red no longer in the room her whole strategy would have evaporated. Standing up straight again she took her former place at the adjacent table to rethink her plan.

Following her intuition Dora resigned herself to waiting for a time in hopes that Red would soon return. Her location here was safe enough for now. Plus where would she go? After a moment a movement beyond the far end of the counter caught her eye. Someone was coming through a door that had escaped her attention before. It was Red!

She now understood his disappearance through the back door. The outhouse was out there. Relieved that her wait was short and also thankful that she hadn't decided to leave Dora watched him return to his table to resume his seat before she made her move.

Now! At a slow pace she strolled along the counter front until she came alongside the third barmaid's customer. He was standing at about the center of the counter leaning on his elbows all the while waiting for the woman's return. Red was paying no attention to her re-entry. He was too busy talking to his cronies.

"Mind if I join you?" she cooed close to the man's ear.

A weathered, middle-aged face of nice features looked over into hers. At first expectant his eyes reflected momentary widened surprise.

"Well, hello there," the face spoke a quiet greeting. The man brightened into a delighted smile. Resting his beer mug on the counter he offered, "Be my guest. What happened to Maude?"

"Oh, she's tied up right now," Dora purred. "Something came up. Since she couldn't come back to join you for a while I told her that I'd look after you. I'm Dora."

Considering that she could have gone elsewhere he said, "Thanks. That's very considerate. I'm Jim. Care for a drink?" He started to turn to the bartender who was still at the far end gabbing with the same patron he'd been talking to since Dora arrived.

"Not right now," she replied in haste touching his hand to shift his intent. "I've had my limit for tonight. You live around here?"

"Just outside of town. I've got a working gold mine near here. No boast but it's the biggest one in the area. You must be new in town."

"I arrived in town today. Just started working here." She glanced around the room. "Do you know everyone in here?"

Her companion also glanced around the room. "Most of them."

Without looking at Flannigan she asked, "The red head at the corner table. I've seen him somewhere before. Who is he?"

"I'll wager that you've seen his mug on wanted posters," Jim answered her fourth question without looking at Red either. "He's wanted for killing, cattle rustling, horse thieving, bank robbing, you name it. I've had to increase my guard at the mine because of him and his lackeys."

"My, my!" Dora breathed. "If he's so bad why isn't he in jail?"

"Maybe because he's wanted for all those things in Kansas," her companion replied. "His name's Red Flannigan. Besides he's got the sheriff in this town cowed. There's enough evil faction here that the town is at a stalemate. So far he hasn't done anything here that I know about, but I've heard rumors that he's eyeballing my mine."

"That's not very nice of him," she observed. "What of the other men with him? Are they as notorious?"

"His gang if you will." The man downed the rest of his beer. "None of them big names. All of them with local records. Nothing too serious, just trouble making."

"I see," Dora nodded making mental notes. Keeping up her pretense she posed, "What about the rest of the customers?"

"Local residents and hired hands. There are a couple of cowboys from the Double J spread not far from here. For some, cattle have been more profitable than gold. I'll admit I've been lucky." He examined his stein. "I think I'll have another. Care to join me?"

She laid her hand on his arm. "No thanks. Remember my limit? I don't think you should either. There's going to be fireworks in here very soon. For your sake I recommend that you go on home tonight for your own safety."

He gave her a concerned although confused expression. "What? Fireworks? What are you talking about?"

Dora's mind was cranking out an idea. In subdued tones she rolled out her thoughts. "There's a trap being set to catch Red Flannigan and his gang tonight. We have it on good authority that they're planning on trying to take over your mine this very evening. I've been sent to warn you. For security reasons I can't say any more. For your safety you should leave here pronto."

He stared at her in wonder, but Dora left the mystery of what she had said hanging in the air. He nodded his head in resignation. "So the rumors are true," he considered. "I didn't know he would move on it so soon. I don't know who you are, who you're with, or how you know this, but I wish you luck." He started to get up; stopped. "I was just getting to enjoy your company. I don't suppose you'll be here tomorrow?" A wistful glint filled his blue eyes.

She shook her head. "I'm sorry. My job will soon be done. I was enjoying your company too." This time she spoke the truth. Jim was handsome, pleasant, and a good man with a natural rapport. Yet she wasn't in the saloon to make social visits. As a testimony to her words she offered him a demure smile to his disappointed stare.

Jim nodded his understanding. He set his empty glass on the counter. Turning he headed for the doors. Her eyes followed his departure. Just as he reached the exit a voice called out to him.

"Jim Foley." The call came from Red. Jim stopped at the saloon doors. He took a deliberate look at Red who continued, "Leaving a little early tonight?"

"I've got some business to tend to," Jim threw back as he took another step, reaching out his hand to push open the doors.

"Jim, don't be so hasty," Red called after him again. Foley halted again. "Me and the boys have been talking. We got a little deal we want to make with you."

Foley cast a furtive glance in Dora's direction as if wondering if this were part of the trap. "What kind of a deal?"

A hush had fallen over the place. The bartender and the man to whom he was talking turned to view the scenario taking place. At this point the bartender noticed Dora still standing at the bar. He wore a puzzled expression but kept quiet in light of the conversation that was now taking place between Red Flannigan and Jim Foley. Keeping a keen eye on Red Dora ignored the bartender.

"Why don't we go over to your place and talk about it?" Red slid his chair back in preparation to stand. Foley dropped his outreached arm.

Dora stepped away from the bar. The story that she had just concocted to Jim Foley appeared to be coming true. She took command of the situation. Red wasn't going to leave the bar under his own power. "Why don't you make your offer right now?" she interjected with a growl. "Everyone in here would love to hear it."

Surprised by her remark Red switched his gaze to Dora. His brow wrinkled in question. "Who are you?" he snapped.

Dora smiled in satisfaction. "You've forgotten so soon? Let me refresh your memory. First I chased you off from trying to gun down a man named Maxwell Templeton. That was after George Botts tried and failed. Then I helped to save his cattle from a grass fire you started and almost got caught in it myself. Next you stole my horse after you were foiled in your plot to torch Templeton's house."

Red's forehead furrowed deeper. He studied her made-up face in an effort to determine who she was.

"After that you and your gang tried to ambush me in a canyon," she went on. "You even shot your own partner, Bill Reilly, in that affair. Just yesterday you tried to bury Hiram Minkle and me in a mine. You've been lucky up till now eluding me on every turn. Now your luck's run out, Red Flannigan. I'm here to collect your dues."

Dora's weapon was hanging in plain sight on her hip now. All eyes that could still focus stared in disbelief at a gun-toting barmaid challenging a notorious killer from Kansas to a showdown. If not for the deadly nature of a shootout the scene would have been comical. Even Jim Foley's expression wore perplexed confusion. A look of recognition betrayed Red's face. He tried to hide it behind a lie.

"What do you mean? I've never seen you before in my life."

Dora scoffed. "Not only are you a bad apple, Red Flannigan, you're a rotten liar. Your murdering days are over."

"Look, little girl, whoever you are," Red retorted. "There are five of us and only one of you. We don't want to hurt you. Go home and play with your dolls."

Dora's poker expression was set in stone. "Never had time for dolls. Too busy learning how to rid the earth of scum like you. All five of you if necessary. That would be a good night's work."

A sneer began to curl on the corner of Red's mouth as he slowly rose to his feet. "That's pretty big talk from a punk kid. You're a fool to take on five of us in a gunfight by yourself."

Dora remained unruffled. "Who says I'm alone? I've got Jim, here, to help." She flicked a nod in Foley's direction. Tensing Foley gave her a quick glance but said nothing. "Between the two of us the odds are in our favor. No brag. Just fact."

Jim Foley stepped back a pace to face the sinister group at the corner table. One of Flannigan's gang started to get to his feet.

"Sit!" Dora snapped with such authority that the man almost fell back into his chair. The others froze to their seats. She went on, "We know your plans, Flannigan, you and your goons. That's why Jim's working with me. Together we're blowing your scheme off the map. So, you big blowhard, make your move. Find out if I'm just a punk kid or the angel of death."

Red's finger twitched. He shifted his stare back and forth from Jim Foley to Dora. Foley poised his hand near his side. The rest of the patrons who were still conscious took refuge wherever they could.

Now!" he barked to his men as his hand went for his gun. In an instant hands were reaching for side arms. Four other men were rising out of their chairs. Hot lead was flying. In less than a heartbeat the battle was declared, fought, and finished. As the smoke cleared five people lay dead on the floor. Two still stood, guns still in hand, regarding the fresh corpses in front of them. The rest of the sober eyes in the room peered from their hiding places.

The fat, burly man who pinched barmaids stirred in his seat. Lifting his head from the table he slurred at no one in particular, "Hey, quit makin' sho much noise. You're givin' me a headache. Margel, tell 'em to go away." His head thumped back on the table in a drunken stupor.

Jim Foley shifted his astonished gaze from a dead Red and his cronies to Dora. After a moment his tongue found words to fit his frame of mind. "You did this town a huge favor tonight, ma'am," he muttered with reverence. "I can't say I've ever seen anyone who can shoot like you. You made me more than a little nervous though when you included me in this fight."

Dora nodded in gratitude to him. "Thank you for your help. You were never in any real danger. As Red pointed out though there were five of them. I dare say I couldn't have done this alone."

"Alone?" he scoffed. "Ma'am, you were done with the fight before I even got started. I never fired a shot!"

She smiled a wry smile at him. "You were great moral support," she replied being candid. "You kept them guessing at whom to draw against, you or me. I just took advantage of their indecision."

"I suppose that they guessed too long. I counted only five rapid shots," Foley observed. "They must have all been yours."

"That's right," one of the other more sober patrons agreed. "I counted only five. If Jim didn't fire they must have been all yours, miss."

Finding his voice the bartender broke in. "I don't know what's going on here. Who are you, miss? Where are my girls?"

Dora motioned upstairs with a nod. "You'd better go see them. There was no time to explain so they had to be detained." She reached into a pocket and extracted a bill. "I had to use one of your girls' dresses and make some minor alterations. This should cover its cost." She tossed the bill on the counter.

"Thanks," the bartender acknowledged with a terse nod. He swooped up the bill as he hastened past the end of the bar for the stairs. Taking them two at a time he was soon out of sight.

A new face appeared over the top of the saloon doors. He stepped into the saloon with circumspection, his revolver in hand. "What's all the shooting about?" the tall, slender man quizzed.

The newcomer wore the familiar star. Jim Foley nodded at the five dead men. When the sheriff saw the body of Red Flannigan lying in the corner his mouth dropped open. Dora offered her statement.

"Sheriff, we have plenty of sober enough witnesses here to supply sworn statements about what just happened to these characters. Shall we sit down at this table and get on with it?" She took a seat at the closest table. Jim Foley and the sheriff joined her while many of the other patrons pulled up their chairs to offer their unanimous account.

That evening Dora Kincaid slept in serene satisfaction in the hotel across the street.

30

Maxwell Templeton sat at his desk as he counted out the agreed upon payment for Dora's services. From a roll of bills in his hand he procured the money. Handing Dora her share he returned the balance to his safe in the corner. "Well, Dora, with this and all the reward money you've collected you can retire and take life easy for quite some time."

"What? And die of boredom at a young age?" she quipped as she fanned through the cash. "No time to rest, Max. There's another engagement waiting for me to tend to. Before coming here I swung by to see the Minkles. They're doing great. Hiram told me to let you know that he'll be along at the end of the week to make arrangements for a drilling team. Once they strike oil you'll be even better well off than you are. You could even get out of cattle ranching if you wanted to. Maybe I should have charged you for saving Hiram's life."

"If you keep in touch with me by wire," Max returned, "I'll give you a piece of the oil profits. I owe that to you.

"Also, in case you didn't know Adrian *did* will the Delgrin ranch to Jill James. The James have moved into the main house. Arnold is learning how to run a full-fledged cattle ranch. He's told his hands that with Delgrin gone he'd forget any past wrongs they may have done if they prove to be loyal employees to him and his family. That's about as bighearted as a man can get. I'm sure the James will make as good neighbors as Farius and his wife were."

"In the meantime I'll be sending Hiram over to see them once he has things squared away here. If Hiram is right the oil we bring in should take care of both of us for the rest of our lives."

"Well, I'm glad to hear that. Jill James must have had a change of heart about going back to the ranch. She once told me that she never wanted to see it again. Concerning your statement about the oil taking care of the both of us is this some kind of proposal?"

"A score of years ago it would have been. I'm twenty years too late. Besides your profession would have me worried into an early grave. Just stay in touch. I'll let you in on the royalties. Deal?" He extended a hand.

She took it. "Deal." She spun on her heel to go. "Time for me to ride. The Minkles have invited me to dinner. Hannah has taken on a whole new appearance since she got Hiram back. She looks a good twenty years younger.

"Pete Hyatt wants me to stop in again before my next job."

"Where are you going for this one?"

"Buena Vista. There's a highwayman up there who's been stealing from the locals while wearing a flour sack for a mask. He's known as the Flour Sack Bandit. I thought I'd check into it and lend a hand to catch him."

"I've been meaning to ask you. Why do you go by Petticoat?"

"It sets me apart in my chosen career. Men don't wear them."

"This may sound redundant, but I'm saying it anyway. Take care of yourself," he counseled that fatherly gleam in his eye. "You seem to do a good job of that. I'm going to miss you."

"Thanks. Me, too." She led the way outside to Spirit. Once on his back she waved as she rode off. "Adios, Max."

He raised his hand in response. "Adios, Petticoat."